Dancing With Audacity
Sourcing Inner Strength

Geoffrey K. Leigh

Noussentric Press

Second Printing, July, 2023

Library of Congress Control Number: 2022923008

ISBN: 978-0-9985966-2-4

Cover Design: Geoffrey K. Leigh, PhD

Formatting: Geoffrey K. Leigh, PhD

Acknowledgements

I begin with gratitude for my daughter, Kati Leigh, who suggested the idea for this book and the name of the protagonist. Because of her birthplace, the setting for this book was easy.

I am grateful for my oldest granddaughter, Ellie Leigh, who gave me ideas for situations as well as language or styles of conversations and texting. I hope her suggestions helped create a more realistic atmosphere for the dialogue and interactions between characters.

There are other situations or references to events that come from my other three children; Jen Long, Greg Leigh, and David Leigh. These three and Kati have been an inspiration for the work and commitment to creating this book. Thanks to you all. And I hope none of you are embarrassed by what is included herein.

I am grateful for useful feedback by my dear friend and ally, Marianne Murray. Her encouragement in writing and suggestions have been welcomed and are greatly appreciated.

I also appreciate feedback and suggestions from my local writing group partners: Marianne Lyon, Jim McDonald, Lenore Hirsch, and John Petraglia. Most of all, I am grateful for their encouragement.

Finally, thank you to Peter Ho Davies, a faculty member and mentor at the Napa Valley Writers Conference. His feedback and suggestions improved my writing, along with the other 11 members of our group. Your comments were timely and helpful.

Chapter 1

The Fatal Photo

S he may "tweet" like a goldfinch, but she devours like a vulture.

Cheryl, the self appointed class 'Queen' and Audri's nemesis, has done it again. This time she posted a pic of Tanika, Audri's best friend, and Audri on Twitter that could jeopardize them both, with the school and, more importantly, with her parents.

Cheryl innocently flutters around student interplay, then zeros in on her cuisine. What is left of Audri's recent cadaverous adventure will surely end in the consumption of misery. And soon, if she doesn't do something with that damn pic!

Audri can hardly hold her phone still. She falls back on her bed, rumpling the white comforter that was so neatly spread. Her bedroom seems compacted now, even with the new shelves her dad put in last week to organize her books and two tennis trophies she won at summer camps. The shelves aren't painted yet, and she's afraid she won't like the color. The misty green shade of the walls appears putrid to her at this moment, and the scent from her unwashed tennis clothes adds a taste of locker room. Yet the growing black hole in the pit of her stomach slowly consumes any remaining joy and adds a sense of life's hurricane spinning out of control.

Audri's patterned bedspread grates against her bare legs where the new dark blue Levi shorts quit and the white ankle socks begin. The shorts cramp her legs and make her feel fatter. Her physical exhaustion, first noticed in her thighs, now extends to every part of her body after today's tennis workout. But she isn't too tired to detect her burning anger at Cheryl, or the Cher-Devil as they like to call her, intertwined with the familiar dark opaque fear closing in on herself.

Audri and Tanika have been best friends since fifth grade. While they enjoyed playing together throughout grade school, the connection escalated when their teacher took Audri's phone as she was passing it to Tanika, wanting to share a photo. Without hesitation, Tanika stood up and told their teacher that Tanika's uncle had "passed," and her phone was nearly dead (at least the nearly dead phone was the truth, even if the dead uncle was not). Audri was helping Tanika contact her mother, and could she be excused to do so? Mrs. Madsen looked intently at Tanika for a moment, then gave the phone back without any argument and allowed her to leave. The teacher trusted Tanika, in part because her mother had just been named principal of the new alternative high school.

Later that same year, when a boy from North Liberty called Tanika the 'N' word, Audri's ferocity was reflected in her crimson cheeks and the sudden movement of her forehand swing across the boy's startled face. The boy wanted to deck Audri. But given her 4 inch height advantage and her strong right tennis arm, he made the wise decision to let it go. These two girls have had each other's back ever since.

Audri pulls up her 'favorites' and calls her friend, but no answer. Her churning stomach elevates concern that Tanika's mother has already found out about skipping school to see the Hawkeye women's tennis match and her phone has been confiscated. *No, her mom's probably still at school*, thinks Audri. *Maybe I should go over there and check on her*.

But Audri's mom told her to stay home until she returns. That would be soon, with just one more house to show a client. And with the showing on this side of town, Audri may not have enough time to get over there and back.

She calls again. No answer. It's frustrating not to be able to reach her BFF under such circumstances. She certainly couldn't discuss this problem with her mom. That would amplify her troubles.

Audri suddenly remembers her history test in first period tomorrow. She quickly calls her mom. Several rings and no answer. Just the voicemail Audri helped her complete.

"Hi mom. Gotta go to Tanika's to review notes for my history test tomorrow. I had to help Mr. Thompson. So I missed a few things in his review. I'll be back in 20."

She feels a little better with that excuse, then grabs her ever present purple backpack to help with the cover story. She slips on her shoes and heads down the stairs, two at a time, focusing on the front door. The worn brown banister feels supportive under her hands, but her desperation rises, needing to know what's happening with her friend.

This afternoon she's grateful for all those cold mornings when her older sister made her wake up early to get in a run before school. As she reaches for the front door knob, her phone rings.

"Hi mom, get my message?"

"Yes, and I'd be happy to pick up the notes on my way home. I'll be driving almost directly by their house."

"Thanks, but I need to go there. Nika doesn't have an extra copy. I'll be quick."

"OK, but be home right after. Your dad'll be home tonight, so we can all eat together. I don't want you to miss it. Oh, please pull a package of chicken out of the freezer and let some hot water drip on it before you leave. I forgot to take it out this morning."

"Yeah, got it".

Audri can't get out of the house fast enough after tossing the chicken into the sink and running a tiny drizzle of water. The trees are in full bloom now and flowers are blossoming everywhere. The big leaves on the sycamore tree in front of the Johnson's house next door appear especially green this year, and she loves the first scent of fresh cut grass. She relaxes a bit, as the smell suggests the promise of summer. Yet the knot in her stomach keeps pressure on her pace.

Tanika answers the door after the first knock.

"Did ya see what that shit posted on Twitter today?" Audri once again could feel that burning mass in her gut that makes her blood boil.

"Oh my god, I'm a dead girl if my mom sees that one! And if not my mom, then my dad! I can't believe she got that pic! I only sent it to you, Sophie, and Angie!"

Tears start running down her cheeks, and Audri follows suit. They give each other a hug, then go up to her bedroom to plot their next move.

They spend some time figuring out how to get Erik, Tanika's neighbor and social media genius, to help them. Hoping their plan will work, Audri finally heads back home.

Wednesday night dinners are a recent invention by Bella, Audri's mother. Ever since her dad, Rick, established his new Italian restaurant downtown, he's been gone most evenings again. And with Bella so involved with real estate, her guilt seems to have provoked new family traditions.

The old dining room table feels comfortable, even given the absence of Sarah, Audri's older sister, who has another study group this evening. It's been a tough semester for her, especially since she takes school so seriously. University classes are getting harder her second year, and she wants to get into law school.

Fortunately for Audri, Alex, her older brother and ally, is at dinner, just home from his baseball practice. She's glad to share his final year in high school, especially since some rad guy friends hang out with him in his newly finished basement bedroom.

Audri also appreciates Alex's caring attitude toward her, although she isn't always excited about his protective tendencies.

Audri blushes slightly, reminiscing about one Friday night a few weeks ago when Mike came to pick her up to go to a movie. Mike pulled up in his old green Subaru Outback and honked for Audri. That put Alex through the ceiling. He walked out, opened up the driver's door and with his most aggrieved face, said, "You will NEVER honk for my sister again, or you will NEVER drive again. Understand???"

Audri later tried to explain Alex's big heart, but Mike never appeared convinced. He never honked his horn again for Audri. In fact, he never asked her out again. Luckily, she didn't like him all that much.

Later, Dad suggested with a smirk on his face that such bullying could be a problem for both boys and urged Alex to find a new way of supporting his sister. He stopped that behavior, but he never lagged in his support. And Audri found ways to reciprocate such affection.

A print of Monet's "Beach at Pourville" hangs on the dining room wall opposite Audri, a favorite of Bella's. Audri shares her mom's love of both Monet and the beach, so she often loses herself in the print when her interest fades with the family interactions.

The wooden dining chairs, with their flattened pads, are feeling hard against Audri's butt. And the wooden slats provide little comfort to her back this evening. The yellow and green flowered tablecloth covers the water stain marks on the auctioned dining room set that was Rick's "treasure" purchased several years ago, before his other restaurant started going downhill.

The worn wooden floors feel rough against Audri's feet as she swings them back and forth. The smell of the chicken casserole makes her mouth water, and she loves the mushrooms in it too. But her mom put bell peppers in with the chicken this time, which diminishes the savoriness of any good dish. She's happy about the fresh green salad with avocado and will have more of that instead.

Her mom and dad are engaged in the same small talk as Rick takes the last swig of his pre-dinner gin and tonic. Bella pours them both some red wine.

After putting down the cocktail glass, Rick picks up his wine glass to test the nose on this vintage. His Italian heritage and love of wines has helped him develop a sensitive palate, especially for reds. He holds up the glass to gaze at the color, swirls the contents around, then buries his nose into the top of the glass, assessing the bouquet. A big smile comes over his face, the first Audri has seen in several days. She, too, smiles as she observes his method of relishing wine.

"I do enjoy this vintage, don't you Bella? I'll be serving this as the special this evening. Nothing like a tasty Sangiovese with a chicken and mushroom dish. I think it pairs nicely." Audri feels her stomach relax as the two of them begin to focus their conversation on wine, one of the few topics they both enjoy discussing. Audri listens to them talk about what they taste, how it lingers and changes, with an after taste that's complex and satisfying.

"So how did it go this morning, Rick?" Bella asks, apparently trying to create some normal conversation.

"Deliveries were late again, and they shorted us on lettuce this time. I keep telling Stuart to try a new produce company, but he has a preference for them. Some connection, I think. You know, same ol' shit . . ."

"Rick, please don't use that language around here, especially when we're eating!"

"Come on, Bella. You know all the kids use it anyway. I'm not teaching them anything they don't already practice!"

"But we don't have to encourage it. We can talk appropriately, even if others don't."

Ah, thinks Audri, *back to 'normal.'*

"In some families, that is appropriate talk, Mom," chimes in Alex with a glimmer of a smile. He loves to push back once in a while, more often with his mom. Hovering eight inches and many pounds over Bella helps him get away with it. He also loves to insert a little humor into the conversation, some distraction from the bickering. Luckily for him, Bella just smiles and lets it go again this evening.

The interactions continue this way for some time, the usual small talk and squabbling. Audri notices a sense of gratitude that the conversation stays focused on others as they eat. She tries to work on a strategy if any of the parentals find out about the photo.

She's distracted by the wrinkles on her dad's forehead that seem to be growing deeper, small ledges, apparently to hold the sweat out of his eye sockets. She perceives sadness in those deep blue ocean reflecting eyes. And his hair appears grayer than usual, mixing with the brown. It's long again, bringing out the waves and curls, which always make her envious.

Why didn't I get his curly thick hair instead of Mom's scraggly brown trailings, wonders Audri?

Bella focuses back on her salad while Alex, still with his white baseball pants and red under jersey, is now gulping down his food as if it were his last meal.

Yet, at this point, such questions about hair feel like a waste of time. Audri veers back to her developing plan.

She shifts between playing with her food, moving it around the plate some, and gulping it down in response to her appetite. It's harder to avoid eating when her mother is focused on her. But when she does eat, it can be challenging to stop.

Every once in a while Bella will tell her to eat rather than play with her food. Tonight, Audri attempts to take several small bites so that the focus stays on other family members and she doesn't over eat. Sometimes she pretends it's a big bite, chewing air long after the food is gone. Her competence is increasing when she doesn't want to eat more and yet not get into another struggle with her mom. Still, she seems to have eaten too much for dinner.

Finally, she breaks the tense silent fog that settles in over the table after the bickering. "May I be excused? I need to start studying for my Spanish test."

Her mom looks over at Audri, her lovely green eyes begging her to stay. But Audri wants to get out of there. Finally, her mom verbally agrees. Audri takes her dishes to the dishwasher, then escapes upstairs towards her sanctuary.

A deep sadness comes over Audri. No, not a sadness, but rather that same dark, heavy, overwhelming feeling of guilt and anxiety, while your whole body grows ten sizes. How could she feel so empty inside when she experiences such a fat physical body? As she reaches the top step, she briefly considers going to her room and lying down on her bed, hoping she might feel better with a little rest. Instead, she steps into the bathroom. She walks over to the toilet and throws up.

Is there more tension than usual? Maybe or maybe not. But throwing up seems easier than usual this evening. Now I can focus on homework and prep for the test without any further distractions.

She opens the bathroom door.

Bella glares deeply into Audri's eyes, concern mixed with upset. Her face looks steely gray, lacking all of life's pigmentation, a tone that provides no relief to her daughter, desperately wanting to grasp solid safety and instead experiences an impenetrable surface.

"Audri, I'm worried sick, and I won't let you go on this way. I'm calling Dr. Salvador tomorrow morning while I'm out. I'll try setting up an appointment for Tuesday after your practice. He told me when I talked with him last that he'd work you in quickly, and I'll carve out some time from work if he can do that."

"No, mom! I just had something stuck in my throat, and ....."

"Audri, stop! We've talked about this before. I told you if this happened again I'd need to have you talk with someone. While he is older, I hear he's also very good. Janet's mom recommends him and says others respect his work too. It's time to make a change before this gets worse. You leave me no option."

Audri's gut tells her that she's backed into a corner and not going to win.

"OK, but just one time!"

"No Audri. If you want to attend tennis camp this summer, you'll go until school starts in the fall, at least. This is about your health and your life - we can't mess around. We'll talk with Dr. Salvador about what to do and how long's enough. You'll have some say, but only one vote out of four, including your dad. This is the first thing he and I have agreed on for some time, and your health is too important to compromise."

With that, Bella turns and tromps down the stairs.

Audri thought the photo was bad. Now an even worse catastrophe has developed. She's ending up having to go to see the 'shrink.'

Chapter 2
Game, Set, Match

E ven without her shelves painted, her bed, desk, and window overlooking Clark Street provides Audri not just a hideout, but a haven; a refuge from the challenges of family and a safe place to gather with friends. She's grateful that she has it all to herself, now that Alex has a new bedroom in the basement and Sarah took over his old room.

Audri usually has everything neatly put away, in contrast to Tanika who only cleans on those occasions when her mom threatens to take away her phone, her lifeblood and connection to the real world. Audri's comfortable here. She turns on her iPad music and picks up her phone. Tanika answers on the first ring.

"Your folks find out anything yet?" Audri notices the anxiety in her stomach just asking the question during the eternal second that it takes for Tanika to answer.

"Nothing yet. All seems fine."

"Any idea how Cher-Devil got ahold of this pic?"

"No. I asked Soph and Ang if they knew. Neither said they gave it to her. And I called Erik, but he didn't answer. I haven't seen him around his place yet. He's probably playing video games and ignoring his phone. He'll do that. If I don't hear from him soon, I'll go knock on his window."

"Do you think he'll help you again? He was awfully upset when you teased him in front of Spanish class."

"I'll flirt with him first. He can't resist that," she said with a smile that Audri knew oh so well.

In the moment, Audri couldn't mention the shrink, even to her best friend.

"OK. Well, let me know when you talk with him."

The next morning is gray and overcast as some spring and many winter days are in Iowa City. It is not the ominous clouds that let you know you're about to get drenched at any moment. It's that depressing, 'we're going to hide all the warm sunlight from you' kind of day. Yet it feels so appropriate given Audri's inner forecast this morning, including that dark gray pit that can't be filled in her gut. And it's May. She's tired of the cloud layer that prevents experiencing sunshine's sweet kiss.

Fortunately, it's warm, so her tennis practice after school could feel comforting. Maybe that bright ball of warmth will appear by then.

Audri's worried about her history test, but she faces it head on. There's some relief when it seems to go well. She studied most of the right stuff, and she guesses it will give her an A-, at least. After class, she's finally able to talk with Tanika as they meet at their lockers.

"I did my best flirt with Erik, and he says he'll try."

"Do you think he'll be able to do it?" asks Audri. By now she's extremely nervous for both of them. "What will your mom say if he can't do it?"

"'I brought you into this world, and I can take you out!' I get that when she's really pissed, and she was adamant about not going to the tournament, given the last C+ on my geometry test. I tried to tell her that everyone did poorly. She doesn't care. As you've experienced, grades top everything else for her. You're so lucky your mom isn't a principal!"

"But that match was a chance of a lifetime!"

"Yeah, my most recent and possibly short lifetime!"

Audri watches her eyes water as the words come out of Tanika's mouth, falling effortlessly onto the faded yellow patterned hallway tile.

While Tanika's parents have never struck her, they can be intense, as both girls know.

Audri wipes Tanika's tears on the sleeve of her white sweatshirt, leaving a little eyeliner as a reminder of this dark moment. She turns and stacks her notebook into the neatly organized locker, under the smaller books, of course. Audri will wash her sweatshirt as soon as she gets home. She grabs her geometry book, and they both head for Mrs. Anderson's class.

At tennis practice, Audri has a hard time keeping her eye on the ball and her mind in the game. As she glances over at Tanika, she seems to have the same challenge.

The sun's shining through and the balminess feels stimulating on her skin. It even seems to lift her heart a little, although her inability to hit her backhand is not supportive of any boost.

Her first serve simply sucks. Fortunately, she's been working on her second serve, and her coach is right about putting some spin on the ball. But today, she doesn't have great placement on it.

Sophie, her doubles partner, performs much better and has saved them several times in the early games. Placed second on their high school squad for doubles, they're under pressure from the third ranked juniors, and Audri isn't about to be replaced. With the best doubles team graduating in a couple of weeks, she's hoping they become the top seed.

She tries to force the photo out of her mind and the chance for Tanika to meet her favorite college player at the college match. She focuses her attention on the ball. But it doesn't seem to last long.

They are down 40 - love, and their opponents are getting in some hard serves. They split the first two sets this afternoon, and Audri and Sophie are down 4-5 in the final set.

Audri crouches down a little lower, shifting her weight to the right, left, then steps to the right a little, as the server has been putting the ball close to the center line. Audri sees the ball coming once again toward the middle, then slams a forehand down the alley for a clear winner.

That helps, she says to herself, smiling slightly.

Sophie then hits a deep cross-court return and Audri moves up to the net, just in time to put away the wimpy response.

OK, feeling better.

The next serve comes to Audri's backhand, and she hits it softly across the court for another winner.

Deuce, yes!

This time Sophie puts the return between the two girls, and an opponent messes up her backhand, putting the ball into the net. The next serve comes to the outside again, but Audri is late and hits the ball out of bounds.

Damn! OK, OK. Concentrate.

Again Sophie saves them with a short sizzling cross-court return.

"Yeah, breathe Audri. We've got this," Sophie whispers as she walks back to mid-court.

Again Audri is shifting her weight, reminding herself to move her feet, taking a deep breath that comes out slowly, and watching for the serve. Her opponent serves down the middle, and Audri hits the outside of the line to win the game.

They continue to play better, winning the next two games to save the match.

"Great shot!" yells Soph, as they move up to congratulate the other team. It was a challenging comeback, but they finally did it.

After the match, Audri walks towards the #1 court to see how Tanika is doing.

She still doesn't seem to be herself today, hitting balls long she normally would get inside the baseline. When she takes off some speed, they seem to go into the net. Although she's losing to the team's #1 singles player, a 6-2, 6-2 match is not her best day. But she seems to be hanging in there, especially when her mind is also apparently elsewhere at times.

After showering, they walk over to the parking lot where Beverly, Tanika's mom, is waiting.

"How did you do today, girls?" she asks.

"I sucked, Mom," replies Tanika, happy to be focused on tennis or school. "But the history test went well, I think."

"Oh good, Baby. And how about you, Audri, how was your workout?"

"It was OK. We saved our ranking and we'll go to regionals."

"Well done," responded Beverly.

"Yeah, but I had trouble concentrating after studying so hard for my history test."

The only thing that would excuse lousy tennis with Beverly is studying and a strong performance on tests. Tanika smiles as she listens to the interaction, knowing her friend's strategy well.

"It'll be great that you both get some tournament experience this year." Other than the heavy focus on grades, Audri appreciates the support she feels from Mrs. Washington. She's always a strong fan for them both.

"How are things at school, Mrs. Washington?" Audri asks, wanting to keep the attention on her.

Apparently she had not found out about the photo, or there would be smoke coming out of her mouth and ears. Audri always chuckles to herself when she imagines such a cartoon picture, especially when Beverly is so delightful 95% of the time. But watch out when she's angry!

Mrs. Washington's father, a longtime assistant offensive coach for the Iowa Hawkeyes, could show up at any moment in her eyes and through her mouth. When Audri heard about him yelling at Tim Dwight, one of the fastest receivers the Iowa Hawkeyes have ever had, she knew how harsh he could get. Tim Dwight for God's sake! The story remains burned into her memory.

Apparently, Tim just sat and took it. And these girls know to do the same when her mom boils over. Otherwise, Beverly is next to a saint in Audri's eyes.

"It's been a solid first year, and I am happy with most of the staff. There're always a few that may not work out. But it takes time to see if we can develop a real team chemistry. Still, I am pleased with what they've done and what the kids have achieved this year. And how is your school going to end, Audri? Will it be a strong year, or am I going to have to have drinks with Bella?" she asked with a big smile on her face.

"No, ma'am. You two will be having champagne to celebrate!" While Beverly never asked her to respond this way, it was fun to fit into a culture of respect that Tanika often used, unless, of course, she and her parents were fighting.

Audri presented a positive view of her grades, which, if she said enough times, may come true. But for now, there were other issues more pressing.

"Call me," she said as she got out of the car. "And thanks for the ride Mrs. Washington."

"You're welcome, Audri. And study hard," laughs Beverly as Audri shuts the car door.

Everything is quiet as Audri goes into the dark house, a relief from the pressures of the day. It's relaxing to have the place to herself. She heads upstairs to her sanctuary, glad it has a window over her desk, able to watch people out for an evening stroll.

She takes off her tennis gear, tosses them into the wash basket, and puts on her mostly comfortable shorts and t-shirt. She moves her backpack to the brown padded desk chair as she flops onto the bed, waiting for Tanika's call. She answers on the first ring.

"How's Eric doing? Was he able to break into her account?" Audri asks nervously, worrying about the answer.

"He's working on it. Not sure whether he'll make it. I should know later this evening. He thinks he has a good idea how to get her password. He is a freakin' genius with these things!"

"OK, well, call me when you know. We're running out of time!"

"Don't I know it! I think I've lost 3 pounds over this."

"I wish I had! I seem to gain weight from nervousness!"

"Damn, Audri. You're so skinny I can't believe it. You'll disappear turning sideways some day!"

"Sweet and not true. But thanks for caring!"

Audri hangs up the phone and begins to go through her papers. She still needs to finish her verb conjugation worksheet for Spanish tomorrow, and it's hard to concentrate. Suddenly, her phone rings again.

"He did it!" screams Tanika. "He got the photo removed from her Twitter feed and attached some type of virus that could infect her phone. Then he put the other one up in its place. What a relief! Now, I just hope it doesn't make its way back to mom."

"I wish I could see Cheryl's face when she discovers it," laughs Audri.

"Yeah, she's going to piss her panties!"

"Well deserved," chuckles Audri. "I'm so happy you thought of that pic of her and Maggie in the reindeer outfits from that Christmas party. That will fit perfectly with her caption of 'Misfits.' But now we're going to have to be sweet to Eric for a long time!"

"Yeah, but it's worth it! He's saved my ass once again!"

"Couldn't have a better neighbor, Nika, unless, of course, it was me!"

"Well, when we go to college, we'll be roommates. That'll be really dope."

"OK, thanks for letting me know. And thanks to Eric. I'll tell him tomorrow. See ya then."

"OK. And study that Spanish. We HAVE to do well on that test Monday!" With that, Audri hangs up and returns to the worksheet.

Audri's mom knocks on her door, then opens it. "I talked with Dr. Salvador this morning. You have an appointment at 4:30 Tuesday afternoon. I'll take you so we can both meet him. Then I'll pick you up afterwards." With that, she closes the door.

All the air collapses out of Audri's sail, and the black hole fills the space. She'd won on the tennis court, but her mom won this match!

Chapter 3
The Game

Fridays at school usually produce some relief, especially today with the photo having been removed.

Audri keeps her eye out for Cheryl, wanting to see if she's discovered the replacement pic.

At the same time, that dark pit in her abdomen feels bigger and more consuming than usual. She's read about black holes, and Audri imagines that's what they must feel like, consuming all the beauty, energy, and light in her life. But she also reflects on the problem solving she and Tanika have done the past two days. That provides a tad bit of comfort.

Audri attempts to pay attention in her graphic design class, which she's enjoying. It's a great place to integrate her interest in computers with some of the pics she shot last year as part of her photography class. And the creative juices stimulate her.

At the same time, she's excited to go watch the annual Varsity - JV baseball practice game this afternoon. She has the day off from tennis, as regionals start tomorrow. Now they just need to find Angelina, who was able to bring her mom's car and give them all a ride over to Mercer Park. She enjoys watching her brother play, and this is the first game of the season. It also gives her time to watch some of his cool friends, maybe even making a connection to some hot guy.

Audri spots Tanika.

"Have you seen Ang or Soph?"

"I saw them after biology. They'll meet us at the car. I know where it's parked. Let's blow this popsicle stand!"

I can't believe she constantly says that! Just because her dad says it, doesn't make it current, chuckles Audri to herself.

The stands are not that big at the baseball field, so it is easy to see who's there. Audri knows most of the students and some of the adults. There are several parents and a few siblings who go to Southwest Junior High next door to the park. She glances around for her mom, but she can't see her yet. Bella probably would come sit near Audri and the group, as she loves all three friends.

Audri's there to see people, enjoy her friends, be seen by others, and cheer on Alex who plays second base.

Her brother's a real student of the game, loving to read about baseball players and how they became great. He's a huge Cubs fan, even though they've not won a World Series Championship in over 100 years. But he's eternally hopeful. Growing up in Iowa City, there is a strong connection to Chicago, only four hours away. People love to watch games at Wrigley Field when not watching them on TV.

Today's game starts a bit slow, and the varsity players seem a little awkward in the field. They're not playing as sharply as they did last year, or at least the end of last year. And people attending become as interesting as the game for Audri. The fifth JV player strikes out to end the top of the first inning, and the Varsity players are up to bat.

The first player fouls out, and the second reaches base on an error. As Alex comes up for his first at bat, Audri feels her pride for him. She loves to see his confidence on the field, and he worked hard last summer to improve his batting. As the third at bat, the coach is obviously feeling better about him too. She hopes he can hear her cheering all the way from the top row of the bleachers where she and her friends love to sit.

There's usually a small breeze the girls can feel when sitting up there, and any breeze helps with the humidity on warm summer afternoons. Some moving air cools the moisture so that it doesn't feel so stifling and dense. She hates that feeling, the world compressing all around her. She also has a clear view of the field and people in the stands, and the scent of cut grass is still in the spring air.

Angelina and Sophie have been talking, but they also get quiet as Alex comes up to bat.

Oh sure, Soph quits talking now, chuckles Audri to herself. *I wonder when she'll admit her crush on Alex!*

Smack. The ball goes flying as Alex sends it over the center field's head and near the fence. Alex, who is fairly fast, rounds first base and heads for second. The center fielder reaches for the ball and throws it to second, but not before Alex arrives with a stand-up double and the other player advances to third.

As a junior, the fact that Santiago is batting clean up is impressive indeed. Audri can feel her heart skip a beat as he swings his bat at the plate. It seems he can feel where the ball is being thrown and then meets it perfectly with his bat.

While Santiago isn't really tall, similar to his father, the team's coach, he's strong and a very consistent player. His dad doesn't seem to show any favoritism about Santiago's playing, at least in practice, which all the guys appreciate, especially

Alex. Not all of Alex's coaches have shown such interest in the players, and it makes the game more fun while also encouraging them to play their best. Alex believes this is going to be a great season.

Santiago steps back as the first ball is inside. He stands up to the plate and swings his bat a couple of times, then readies himself for the next pitch. It is right down the middle, and Santiago swings hard, driving the ball over the left field fence.

OK, thinks Audri, *the team may be a little rusty on the field. But they appear to be strong with the bats*!

While everybody is standing, cheering, or at least clapping, Audri notices one person who sits still, just a quiet clapping coming from his hands. Sitting by himself, *the old man stands out like a sore thumb*, thinks Audri. He's very intent on watching the game and each player, but he never yells or cheers, no matter which team makes a score or a stupendous play. He just watches and observes what happens. Somehow, he seems emotionless and yet interested. He moves from time to time, adjusting the way he's sitting, sometimes leaning forward, sometimes leaning back. Just sitting and watching; it just made no sense to her.

Is he a pervert? Is he here 'watching the boys?' Who's he interested in? He seems too old to be a parent. If he were a grandparent, wouldn't he be here with some other family or cheering for his grandson?

Audri turns back to the game. Two more innings pass quickly with little action. Then Alex is up again in the bottom of the fourth. This time he hits a single to left field, just over the short stop's mitt. With runners on first and second, Santiago walks up to the plate. He moves a little as two balls are thrown, then readies himself again. As the ball sails across the plate, Santiago smashes it to the wall between left and center field, allowing Alex and the other runner to score, with Santiago on second.

"Way to go Alex, fabulous hit Santiago," Audri yells. She shouts as loud as she can. No one can criticize her for not supporting her brother, even when she knows she might hate him later.

She can't seem to help herself, especially when his stories at home will be more entertaining than the game itself. *Maybe I should skip the game and just listen to the 'highlights' at home. But then I can't be with my friends or meet some cute guy by just listening to his entertaining stories. And I do enjoy watching them play.*

She doesn't mean to hate Alex at those times. In fact she loves him and is proud of him. That is the confusing part; she hates him and loves him at the same time.

Damn. How is that possible? How can I feel two such opposite emotions at the same time? Maybe my folks are right. Maybe I do have a real problem. It doesn't seem like it, but right now I couldn't argue with them.

Lucky for her they're not there, and she doesn't have to admit it to them!

As the game ends with each team congratulating the other, the boys begin picking up their equipment and clearing the field. Audri climbs down the bleachers behind her friends. She glances over, but the old man is gone.

When did he leave? She hadn't noticed. *Did the police come and take him away? No, I wouldn't have missed that. Maybe he just snuck off before they could get here,* she thought. Then she turned back to her friends, who had just seen a new, cute player they hadn't noticed before.

"He must be a sophomore," Ang suggests, who seems particularly interested in him. "I've not seen him before, and I didn't see him play. I would have noticed," she says with a smile.

Soph makes some comment, but it's lost on Audri. As they walk to the parking lot, she sees her mother's car. *I guess she did make part of the game.*

Bella waves and asks if they want a ride.

"Ang has her mom's car, and we want to go eat downtown before regionals tomorrow. Can I have $20?" asks Audri with a big smile.

Her mom digs into her purse and hands her two $20s. "Have fun and my treat. But be home at a reasonable time. You need your rest."

"Thanks Mrs. Giovanni!" yells the three friends in unison. The girls find the car and head towards Wedge Pizzeria on Riverside, one of their favorites. As usual, they share a large Dagobah pizza with drinks and laughter. Tonight, Audri finally feels relief and begins to enjoy herself. She's happy to miss dinner at home and the funny stories by Alex. As promised, Audri is home by 10:00 pm and goes straight to her bedroom.

She takes off her clothes, puts on her jammies and crawls into bed. Audri's tired and yet not sleepy. She begins to reminisce about the challenges she's been facing with the photo.

Maybe I could be a detective when I get older. I am getting more confident at this problem solving stuff. I could discover all sorts of interesting things that others may not see. Maybe all this struggle is useful for me. Maybe I'll be the first female Sherlock Holmes!

She might not have known about the history of Mr. Holmes if her father didn't enjoy watching old movies on cable, at least not as an historical figure. She loves following Sherlock's insights. Yes, she and her dad have some fun times together, introducing her to some classic sleuths, even if he doesn't do it intentionally or is even aware of it.

But, she thinks, *I enjoy sitting by him and like having him around late at night while we silently watch a movie, even when little is said.*

At the same time, she feels the emotional distance between them and doesn't know what to do about it. There's more problem solving to be done, and she hopes to be up to the challenge.

To Audri, it seems so easy for Sarah, Dad's favorite. She's focusing on sociology at the university now. But Dad knows she wants to go to law school, and that keeps her in the favored status position. The high achiever, which Dad admires, apparently because he didn't finish college.

Alex and Mom seem to have so much fun, and she always laughs loudest at his jokes. Why did they have a third child, anyway? Why didn't they just quit with their favorite two?

And then they named me "Audri!" What kind of a stupid name is that anyway? It feels more like, 'Oddball. Maybe they should have spelled it, O-d-d-r-i.' Maybe I'll start writing it that way, and they'd get the point. Yes, Oddri it would be from now on! At least maybe it would have a little sting for them. Not like the hurt I'm feeling right now, of course, but maybe a little sting.

Why didn't they name me Sophie? Sophie sounds so delicate, so fashionable. There must be some attractive green print associated with it, not something that doesn't fit in anywhere. How about Tanika? That sounds so powerful, so strong and clever. It sounds a bit like Mozambique, although Nika keeps saying her ancestors actually came from the Ivory Coast.

Or maybe Angelina. Why not Angelina? Angelina sounds so cute and magical. It matches her long dark hair, angelic face, and dark eyes. Why couldn't Audri be so attractive, so appealing to boys? Angelina, like Sarah, seems to just attract the male gender.

If she and Angelina were not such close friends, Audri wouldn't have any idea how much fun it is to flirt with boys and then talk behind their backs about how sucky they act. What fun!

Oh yes, Craig was attracted to Audri, but he's a dork. He doesn't play baseball or basketball, and he's so awkward for such a tall boy. She can't believe he can't dribble the basketball any better than he does. The team could use him if he could run without tripping.

Now Santiago, there's some fire! He has such mysterious eyes, and I love his wavy dark hair. I wish he didn't cut it so short, like his friends. It would be so beautiful if he would let it grow a little longer, especially at his height. And he's so coordinated – no fumbling around the ball field for him! And yet he doesn't seem to take baseball as seriously as Alex and his friends. How can he be so accurate and not take it more seriously?

She can't wait to watch him again this year, to see him shag the balls at shortstop, to flip them to first base with little effort, and to be so accurate every time.

Shag the ball. What kind of stupid term is that?

She hears Alex use that often, but what does it mean? Audri is trying to learn to talk "baseball" to connect with Alex and his cute friends.

Still, she doesn't understand how Santiago plays so well and easily, while Alex works so hard in the backyard or at the elementary school near their house. But then Santiago's father's the coach. Maybe he works hard at other times, and Alex just doesn't know it. Yet, Alex is bothered by how easily baseball seems to come for Santiago, how easily he can watch the pitched ball without being distracted, and how accurately he makes it go where he wants.

What bothers Alex the most, because she hears him telling his friends with a voice that seeps through his bedroom wall while she watches tv downstairs with the volume turned low, is the accuracy of Santiago's hitting. It seems his bat catches the ball, and in a split second sends it in the direction he wants it to go. Others on the team have tried, but they don't seem to get the hang of it. The coach talks about focusing their attention, but there are too many things that distract the boys, especially against the Cedar Rapids Prairie team, the league champion for the past two years.

They are hoping that this year, the Little Hawks will experience less tension and have a better chance. And certainly Santiago will help tremendously.

But Audri knows from Alex that it bothers the other players when Santiago makes it look so easy and is even humble about it.

He is not cocky as Eric had been last year. Eric also was strong, and he let everyone know it. So they were not that disappointed when he moved to Des Moines. In fact, they would rather lose than listen to his bragging.

But for Audri, Santiago is different. And she hopes Alex's team will finally win a conference championship, maybe even go to state. That would be exciting as she plans to get more involved her junior year. She figures she will be more visible and possibly connect with her older brother's friends! Maybe Alex will help her be more popular. Finally, her brain becomes so exhausted from analyzing her world she falls asleep.

Audri feels some anxiety when her alarm goes off early Saturday morning. Fortunately, the regionals are being played at the Hawkeye Tennis Complex, not far away. Audri showers and puts on her neatly ironed tennis outfit. This morning, it feels tight again. She goes downstairs to have a bite, then gathers some snacks for the day.

"Oh Rick, just stop. I don't want to talk about it any more, please. Let's just eat breakfast in peace."

As Audri walks down the stairs, she hears her mother at the kitchen table and knows it's not going to be a jovial morning. *What's the argument about this time?*

Audri has been so focused elsewhere she missed this one, but then it probably isn't much different from the others.

"Morning," Audri stammers as she turns the corner and enters the kitchen. Neither parent looks up from their coffee.

"Hi sweetie," her mother replies. She has on that cute pink dress and black belt that shows off her small waist. Audri loves those shoes that match the belt. She can't wait to figure out a time she can talk her mom into letting her wear them on some hot date. But she'd have to feel a lot prettier before she'd risk wearing such outfits.

"You ready?" asks her mom as she finishes her breakfast.

"Just have to fill another water bottle." As she turns on the tap, she hears a knock at the door.

Bella moves to the front door and opens.

"Oh, don't you two look great! Audri's almost ready," and they all head for the garage. Tanika and Soph settle in the back while Audri rides shotgun as her mom backs out the car, then heads down the street towards campus.

"I'm excited to see you play today, girls" says her mom supportively. "As soon as I am through showing this property, I will be over there. I hope you have a great day!"

"Thanks mom." Bella drives them towards the campus with little conversation, as all are nervous. When they arrive, the girls climb out with their gear, thank Bella, then she heads towards her appointment.

The day is warm and sunny, which feels stimulating, and apparently it helps all three girls win their first match. While Tanika also wins her second, Audri and Soph meet a strong team from their city rivals, West High, who end their hopes. Tanika loses her third match, and the trio are done for the year.

Yet their top singles and doubles players are continuing on, which gives them something more to cheer about. In the end, their team doesn't win regionals, but they're happy to have had some fun and won a few matches. Not bad for sophomores.

They find Bella and Beverly in the stands and convince them to take the girls downtown to eat. The snacks were just not enough at this point. And Audri begins to feel more disappointment from the matches and anxiety about the upcoming appointment on Tuesday. She wants some comfort food, maybe from her dad's restaurant. His rich chocolate cake would be fabulous at the end of what is becoming a disappointing day.

Chapter 4
Queen of Schemes

For a Sunday, this is way too early to be awake, thinks Audri.

She notices her sore body as she turns under the soft sheet with a light blanket. It's a bit chilly this morning. She's happy to have a little weight over her, something tucking her in bed gently and lovingly.

She can see rays coming in under the shade. The sun must be shining, or it wouldn't be this light in her room with the shade drawn.

Today Audri is in no hurry to get up. Then her body begins to tense as she remembers the appointment her mother made with the shrink for Tuesday afternoon.

How's she going to get out of it? This budding detective will have to be even more clever.

Maybe I'll stay in bed for a bit to see what ideas have been seeping in during the night. What's a girl to do? I'll just stay right here until I am sick of it.

YES! THAT'S IT, she realizes. *I'll be sick on Tuesday. Let's see, I don't have any tests that day. In fact, my next one is on Thursday, and I can be better by then. I'll have Tanika and Soph take notes for me, while I miss Monday and Tuesday, possibly even Wednesday to make it believable. I probably should start coming down with something this afternoon, or at least tomorrow morning, so there doesn't seem to be any connection with Tuesday's appointment.*

It could be the stomach flu, which has been going around. That would allow me to throw up, not eat much, and feel awful. This flu has not always included a high fever, so it'll be easier to fake than some illnesses. But I'll need to be warm and very miserable. This will be worth a couple of days, and I can even get some studying done for my test on Thursday.

Audri reaches for her phone to contact her two helpers. She starts with Sophie.

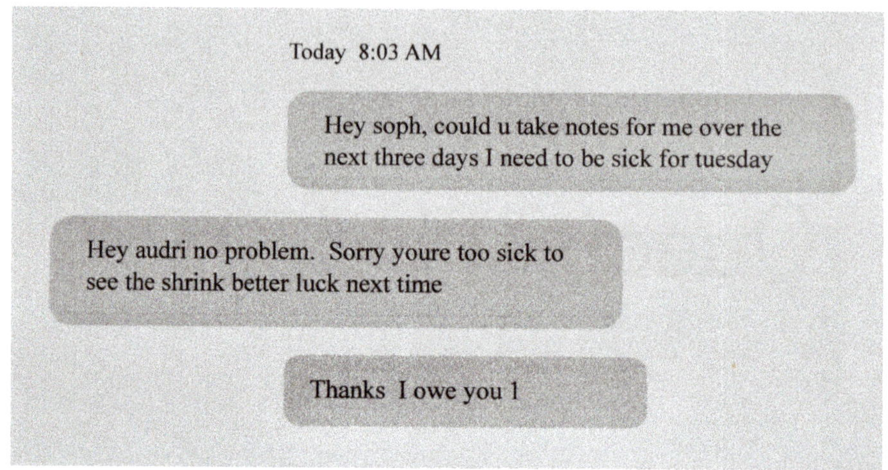

I'll talk details with the others this afternoon when we go downtown to the mall and make arrangements for their help. Soph can cover in English, and Ang can hand in my Algebra assignment. Nika will help with notes, which she can drop off Tuesday afternoon. That'll show Mom how much I want to work, EVEN WHEN I AM SICK! This may work well all the way around!

Tomorrow morning, I'll have to put on an extra blanket under the sheet so I get warm and sweat while acting chilled. Then I can have some water under my bed to pat my head and arms a bit. Yes, I think I can make this work. Sarah's supportive about my not going to a counselor, so I think she'd help without a lot of payback.

Maybe I could do a little ironing for her this evening just in case she needs extra incentive. Yes, I think I can make this work.

Now what have I forgotten? I'll talk with Mom Tuesday morning about canceling with Dr. Salvador. What else could she do? She couldn't send me to his office when I have something that might be contagious.

I have a book I want to read, and I can watch a couple of movies. Then I'll get ready for the test Thursday and go to the game on Friday. This won't get me out of the counseling altogether, but at least it should get me a week to think of another strategy.

Maybe I could work on Dad about how little use this is and how much money he'd be wasting. Yes, I could start on that this morning. I'll help him outside or in the garage. Maybe I could even clean up that mess of papers in the garage to help him be in a better mood and more receptive to my suggestions, too.

With so much figured out, Audri jumps out of bed. Then she realizes she should not have TOO much energy today. She begins to move a little slower.

She makes her bed and picks up the clothes she did not bother to put away last night. She appreciates her room much better when it is neat and tidy.

Then she realizes maybe she should help with breakfast and make sure the dishes are washed, just to get things moving in the right direction. This time her mother won't know she wants anything, and it won't appear to be out of place, but rather part of her routine.

She walks into the kitchen and finds Alex fixing himself a bowl of cereal for breakfast.

Why am I the only one who seems to think of preparing breakfast for more than one person?

She begins to say something, but then just takes a gulp and stuffs it down. Instead, she gets out the orange juice and begins making coffee. Sarah will want some too, she realizes, and makes 12 cups instead of eight, just to be on the safe side.

She finds the bagels her mother brought home the other night, and gets out the cream cheese and jam. She puts them all on the table in the screen porch, then gets plates, knives, and glasses. The coffee is finished as her father comes into the kitchen, so Audri pours him a cup and hands it to him.

"Thanks, Sweetie," he says, sipping on the hot brew. "Tastes great as usual. I taught you well how to make a tasty cup of java," he says, smiling.

Yeah, Mom had nothing to do with showing her how to measure and clarifying the proportions that most people appreciate and the strength that her dad prefers, thinks Audri.

She starts to say something, and then again swallows it along with some juice. She pulls out some vitamins from the cupboard, hands one to her dad, takes one herself, then puts the bottle on the table.

"Hey, don't leave the cupboard open," shouts her dad. "Someone may hit it and get hurt."

Audri walks past her father and shuts the cupboard, noticing his arm could have reached it without moving more than a step. Suddenly, the juice seems filling and her hunger's gone. She starts to head for her bedroom when she remembers her plan and turns around.

"Is strawberry jam OK, Dad, or would you prefer orange marmalade?" asks Audri as sweetly as she can muster in her present state of resentment.

"Oh, marmalade would be great," he answers.

Audri goes back to the fridge and pulls out the preserve, taking it out to the table. She also grabs napkins along the way. Then she comes back in to toast bagels.

As she gets the bagels in the toaster, her mom walks in with Sarah on her heels. "We smelled the coffee," her mom says somewhat laughingly. "Got plenty for two sleepyheads?"

"Sure, Mom. I knew you'd want some too, Sis, so I made extra." Audri gets down two more cups and pours coffee for both of them, handing them to Mom and Sarah. "I also put out toppings for the bagels you brought home, Mom."

Bella and Sarah get their bagels and head out to the porch with their coffee. At this point, Alex comes back into the kitchen with a big smile.

"I'd like a cranberry orange one," shouts Alex as he walks out to the porch.

Yes, and I know right where I want to put it, thinks Audri!

But instead, she slices another and toasts it as well. Bella comes in for creamer and Sarah comes back in to get juice for everyone.

How is it that only females are here in the kitchen while the boys are out drinking and eating at the table?

She lets the thought go and puts the other bagel on a plate. Then the women take the food out and sit down. All focus on their breakfast.

Audri, while munching on half a bagel with a hint of jam, begins to review her strategy. As they finish, Bella and Audri clear items off the table and take them into the house. Bella begins to wash off the plates as Rick heads for the garage. Audri follows her dad to figure out what she might say to plant a few seeds regarding the futility of counseling for her.

Rick opens the garage door and begins to clear a few boxes in front of the lawn mower. "Want me to mow the front lawn," asks Audri?

"Sure, that would be great," replies her dad. "I can clean off the back lawn and get it ready while you do that. Sarah and I are going to watch the Cubs game this afternoon, so I want to finish this quickly."

"Well, since I am so 'crazy' that I have to see a shrink, I might as well work," Audri throws out for her dad. She isn't sure if he'll bite at this, but she'll keep trying if that doesn't work.

"Yeah, I know what you mean. I thought your mom was going to try getting us all to go to the counselor. But she seems to feel it would be best to start with you," her dad adds.

"I just hate to see you waste all that money on something so useless, Dad," Audri says in a somewhat pleading voice. She tries to sound sincere, hoping her dad becomes sympathetic.

"Oh, don't worry, Audri. Our insurance will cover most of it, at least for the first 10 or 20 sessions, depending on what the doctor says. We only have to pay 20% for those, so it isn't that much."

Another miscalculation! I can't afford those right now. I have to start getting these right, she thinks, feeling increased tension in her stomach!

"Well, I'm glad of that," responds Audri with a hint of sarcasm given her disappointment, yet not so much that her dad notices. But then these days, that would take quite a bit.

She moves the mower out of the garage and into the front yard.

Well, on to the next step, she says to herself with some disgust. *And now I'm stuck mowing*! *This sucks*!!

After she finishes the front lawn, she rolls the mower around to her dad. He's finished picking up sticks and is ready for it as she comes around the house. He thanks her for mowing the front, but the gratitude falls off her as she's deep in thought about her oncoming 'illness.' She leaves the mower for her dad and heads toward her room.

As she passes through the kitchen, she asks her mom about going to the mall. Bella agrees. Audri gives a silent sigh of relief. She doesn't want to spend more time with her mom right now. She needs to think by herself and with friends.

She goes up to her room, tosses her essay notes in her recycle bin now that they're typed, then calls Tanika to see when they could meet. The other three will be at Audri's in about 15 minutes, with a ride offer from Nika's dad who is going that way.

She grabs her jacket as she heads for the front door to wait outside and think. It's a lovely day, and she's glad to have the opportunity to hang out with her friends. But her heart remains heavy thinking about the appointment and her necessary illness. She needs to pull this one off, or everything could get even worse.

Before Audri has time to plan, Nika's dad pulls up. Audri hops in and they head for the mall. Audri finds Tanika in better spirits than she was last night, when the disappointment of regionals was lingering. As they arrive, the girls get out and Nika's dad leaves, wishing them a fun time. They walk around, looking at clothes and who's at the mall today.

Soph soon spots a new guy she wants to get to know, and Ang starts teasing her about being "in love" again already.

They have an enjoyable time examining clothes they'd want for summer, although they don't enjoy this mall as much any more. Since the new Coral Ridge Mall opened near the interstate, the downtown mall has continued to suffer. But it's easy to reach, and they appreciate the tradition. They try on a couple of items, but no one has any money today, so buying is not going to happen. Still, looking and trying are much of the fun, as they enjoy hanging out together.

They get an iced tea and sit for a minute. Audri explains her strategy to her three friends, asking if they will help with the homework. Of course they'll help, they all reply.

Then Soph tells her, "I'm not so sure it'll be worth it. The plan will only put off the inevitable, so what's the point?"

"The point," responds Audri, rather indignant, "is that it gives me time to get out of this all together. But I need more space to think of a better long term strategy, and a way around all of this completely. Right now Mom is rather set on this Dr. Salvador, and I don't want to go. I mean he's an old man, a former professor, and probably not even from this country. What would he understand of adolescents here and my troubles? What could he possibly know that would be of any use and value to me? Who is this guy, anyway? He's probably so old he wouldn't even understand me or my life. Why don't they make it illegal for old people to be counselors to adolescents? If they can remember anything at all, they certainly can't remember what it's like to be this age. And who would want to remember adolescence during the Dark Ages anyway? I'm sure he is at least that old! I've not been able to figure a way out of this shit, and I need more time."

"I'm not sure it's worth the work. And I don't see your mom giving up on this too easily!" says Ang.

"But I have to try," responded Audri. "I have to try!"

"Well, I'll help you. But I don't think it's worth the trouble and risks. What will your mom do if she finds out you're faking the illness just to get out of this?" asks Sophie, with even more strength in her voice.

"I'm sure I can pull this one off," says Audri. She tries to sound convincing, but even she's beginning to have doubts. She hasn't been all that successful getting out of things recently, despite her outstanding record in the past. Her mother seems to be watching all this closely.

As she says this, Derek, the center for the junior varsity basketball team walks by with Eddie, one of the guards. The girls all quit talking and smile at them. They wave but keep walking. So the girls turn back to their discussion.

"You know you've not been all that great gettin' out of things lately," suggests Ang.

She seems to be supportive of Audri, yet the words cut right through her.

She's right, and Audri hates to admit it. What'll happen to her career as a detective if she fails to figure out solutions with her mother?

"I mean, I don't want to sound lame, but it's not your best time with her these days," continues Ang.

Audri knows in her heart they're right, and she hates to face it. She hates defeat, and this appears to be the worst one in a long time. Much worse than yesterday at regionals.

She's usually so inventive at creative scheming, having fun, and appearing successful at the same time. She wonders if she's losing her touch, and more effort doesn't seem to help. She suddenly feels regret about coming to the mall, meeting her friends, and most of all sharing her strategy.

Why aren't they more supportive? Her eyes water, but she fights to hold back the leak. She's determined not to cry in public!

"Let's go to Blick's," suggested Audri, trying to change the subject. "I need some new art pencils."

"So what are you going to do," asks Tanika? "Do you want our help? You know we'll help if you want!"

"I guess I'll think about it and call you tomorrow. I'm just not sure right now. I hate giving up, but this doesn't seem to be my best plan," says Audri softly.

"No, you've had better ones than this, that's for sure," adds Soph, trying to cheer up the sadness in her voice. "You're the queen of schemes, and this is only a temporary setback," she declares with great enthusiasm and a graceful curtsy.

Still, the support doesn't help to overcome the sadness and tension Audri's feeling about the session on Tuesday. Maybe she really will be sick. She's starting to feel nauseous just thinking about the session!

The four girls spend the afternoon wandering around the stores, then walk over to Film Scene to watch an afternoon movie. As they leave the theater, Audri remembers enjoying the show, though she can't remember much of it. Her mind's somewhere else, and even the movie couldn't distract her enough to focus on it.

Angelina's mother picks them up after the movie and drops them all off at their houses. Audri goes upstairs to her bedroom and lies down on her bed. She considers reading, but then just falls onto the bed instead.

I'll have to make a decision soon. Well, I guess I have until morning. She watches another movie she can't remember, finally slipping into her jammies. After a little more debate, reading, and scheming, she falls into a restless sleep.

The next morning, she still doesn't feel hopeful. The strategy doesn't seem as if it will change anything beyond a temporary reprieve. Maybe she should just get the whole damn thing over with.

Maybe I could go there, tell the guy a few healthy responses, and he'll say I'm 'cured.' OK, maybe that would be better. Yes, I know how to play 'well' even better than playing 'sick.' I might not know how to talk as a counselor does. But it won't take me long to figure out how to be a successful client. Even if I have to go a few times, I'll find out the right way to talk with him so this guy will tell Mom how 'well' I'm doing and how healthy I am. This might help me become the perfect child, despite how successful the other two are. Rather than being the 'sick' child who had to see a counselor, I will turn this into the child who is 'certified' as healthy. Do Sarah or Alex have that? No way!

Yes, I'll turn this around as I have so many other situations. I'll prove Angi's words correct: I am the 'Queen of Schemes,' and this one will solidify my reign!

Chapter 5

Intruder Introductions

Audri can't believe how quickly two days can pass. She tries to keep herself focused on her many assignments and finals. She has the test on Thursday, and even that doesn't seem as awful as the damn counseling appointment.

How is it Tuesday already? And school's almost over! When Bella mentioned this morning that she'd pick Audri up after practice, Audri at first felt pleased. Then horror swept over her body that her mother was just making sure she made it to the appointment!

What a witch, thinks Audri. *Like casting a spell over me and making sure it sticks!*

But Audri's still confident of her new plan. In fact she's looking forward just a bit to outsmarting this "old fart," as Sophie called him.

Well, old age just might make it easier for me. Yes, he just might be a pushover, Audri begins to consider.

Her confidence grows, and she's starting to believe everything might turn out well. Outside the family, it usually does for Audri.

After school, Audri walks out the side door by the courts, and there's her mother, on time and waiting.

That's OK, thinks Audri, *I'll get the best of this guy yet. I'm doing alright.*

She reassures herself, and yet there's something nagging, something she can't put her finger on just yet. She keeps having this thought about what if ...

What if this old guy gets the best of ME??? No, she thinks, regaining her confidence. *No. I'll be the healthiest client this guy's ever seen. I'll have the whole thing finished in about two sessions. Maybe even one! Some old guy can't be that smart! He isn't even working at the university any more! I'll figure my way out of this one too!*

Neither she nor her mother says much as she gets into the car. There's the usual 'hi' from both, but Audri wants to think, and her mom doesn't seem interested in pressing her to talk. They drive over to East Court Street, away from the school and towards the office, turning right on Muscatine.

"I do hope this helps you, Audri. I really do," her mom says, being the first to break the silence as she turns left onto East Burlington.

Audri hears her, but she's more intent on where this office is located and how she'll finish all this in just one session, three at the most. She watches as they pass Dodge and turn left onto Linn Street. After another block, her mother slows the car and turns left into a small parking lot. Bella stops the car and opens her door first. Then she hesitates before getting out and turns towards Audri.

"I'll walk you in and introduce you. I've talked with Dr. Salvador on the phone, but I've not met him face to face. He seems very pleasant and said he looks forward to meeting you. I think you'll like him. And if it doesn't work after several sessions..."

"You said three, mom, just three sessions," Audri retorts.

"No, I said if this guy doesn't work out, then we'll search for someone else. I'm not sure three is a fair opportunity. But we can talk about it as we go. I just want you to give him a chance, Audri, and I want you to participate, to really try. We're just wanting to help you, sweetie, and I don't know what else to do. Will you try, Audri? Will you really share with him? You don't seem to talk with us any more, and I think you need someone. I just hope you can connect with him."

"Yeah, I'll give it a try," Audri responds. She's trying to sound as honest and sincere as she can when she doesn't mean it. She only hopes her mother doesn't catch this one, as she has with others these days. "I'll talk with him," attempting to be more convincing.

They get out of the car, leaving the familiar smell behind them. It's an older BMW with well 'loved' spots, although her mother tries to keep it clean. Audri likes it somehow, and now it's the last familiar thing she experiences before going into the pit, the corner where her mother is trapping her with no exit! It all feels so strange, and Audri doesn't like it one bit.

The small building contains only a few offices, and Audri notices a small sign with black block print and a name, "Alberto Salvador, Ph.D." The entrance to his office is down the hall near the back of the building.

She checks out the other doors along the hallway with the hope that she'd find an acceptable office she could say she was visiting if she runs into a friend. There's an attorney's office first, then an insurance company, and then some management company. None of these will do. And then she spots her escape – a dentist's office. She memorized the name: E. Wyland, DDS. Yes, this will be her new dentist, and she's happy to find him. Or is he a she? Audri will need to check the first name on the Internet. She doesn't want any more mistakes!

They enter Dr. Salvador's office, but there's no receptionist. There're just a few chairs and magazines.

There's a Time Magazine on top of one scattered pile, with a Sports Illustrated on the other. The latter appears more tattered, which speaks well of his clients. Maybe some cute guy comes in, maybe her age. Or maybe, even worse, someone she knows that will tell everyone what she's doing here!

She made her friends promise not to tell anyone. She trusts them. But what about someone who doesn't like her? What about Cheryl? What would she do then? Cheryl's crazy enough to be here, too!

As Audri starts worrying and begins scheming, the inside door opens and an old man walks out. He's wearing an old plain light blue corduroy shirt, rolled up twice on the sleeves, and a pair of dark blue slacks. He has darker skin, with peppered hair, more on the gray than the black side. His dark eyes seem somewhat friendly, but Audri immediately figures this is a counseling ploy. He's wearing a pair of loafers that appear well worn, and his belly strains at the buttoned shirt. He smiles as he looks at Audri, then Bella, and holds out his hand.

"My name is Alberto Salvador," he says as he focuses first on Bella. "You must be Mrs. Giovanni and Audri."

He shakes Bella's hand first, then holds it out towards Audri. She shakes it limply to be polite and doesn't put much feeling into it. Yet she wants to appear like she's cooperating, so she suddenly adds a little energy towards the end.

"Yes, I'm Bella, Dr. Salvador, and this is Audri. I told you a little bit about us over the phone." Bella begins to continue, but Dr. Salvador interrupts the flow.

"Yes, great to meet you, Audri." Somehow he not only smiles with his lips, but his eyes too. She isn't expecting this and feels a bit taken off guard. Then she pulls herself together and focuses on her objective, searching for a way to finish all this crap quickly.

Dr. Salvador turns again to Bella. "Will you stay and wait, or will you come back for Audri?" he asks her with a smile.

Why is he smiling so much? What does that all mean? Have they cooked up a plan I don't know about? Yeah, Mom may just do that at this point.

Audri realizes she will have to be extra careful here.

"No, I have some errands to run. I will return when you're finished. What time do you think I should be back, Dr. Salvador?

"Oh, you can call me Alberto, if you don't mind. I am not big on titles. It just creates more distance and structure that I don't think is all that useful. Well, I usually like to take longer on the first session in order to get to know a person. I'm not that consistent at time limits anyway, as it's difficult to schedule endings. But I would say about an hour and a half. Would 6:00 work all right for you?" he asks.

AN HOUR AND A HALF! What the hell am I going to talk about for that long, Audri thinks?

"Yes, that should be fine. I'll meet you here at 6:00, Audri," Bella says as she turns toward her. With that, she turns again, about to leave the office, abandoning her poor baby into the hands of some stranger who wants to talk FOREVER.

"Oh," jumps in Dr. Salvador. "By the way, I have a back door where Audri can leave. If you just drive around to the back of the building when you return," suggests Alberto. "You'll see the door on the east end. That way people don't see others leave, and many seem to prefer it. Is that alright with you, Audri?"

ALL RIGHT, she thinks, *IT'S QUITE ALRIGHT! At least he's smart enough to think of a back door escape for people!* "Yes, that's fine with me," she says with some relief.

Bella leaves with that agreement, and Alberto suggests they go into his office. There is something familiar about this old man, but she can't put her finger on it. He doesn't seem all that smart, anyway, so she's feeling more confident that her strategy will work. Besides, an hour and a half should give her plenty of time to prove how healthy she is on her first visit. Maybe all this will work even better than she had hoped.

The office isn't big. It has an old brown desk along one wall on the left side of the room, with two chairs and a small couch or loveseat on the other side between the chairs. They appear to be a bit worn.

He doesn't seem to be rich. Or maybe he's making loads of money but doesn't waste any on furniture. Audri isn't sure which.

She glances around cautiously, trying to decide where to sit. The two chairs face each other at either end of the couch, and she doesn't want to sit close. There's another chair at the desk, but to take that one seems rather awkward.

"Why don't you take the chair with your back to the wall, and I'll sit over here in the other one. That way you can keep an eye on what's happening all around the room. I learned that when I lived out West," he says with a smile.

Audri makes herself comfortable in the far chair, glad he's sitting opposite her and not too close.

"Where did you live in the West?" she asks rather inquisitively, not sure if he is talking about cowboy land or simply Western Iowa.

She begins scanning the office as she asks the question, trying to get clues about this man her mother has stuck her with for eternity.

"I lived in Los Angeles for several years, but that was many years ago. I've lived here in Iowa City for some time now."

"Did you grow up in LA? You don't talk like someone from there?" Audri isn't quite sure what someone would sound like who grew up in Los Angeles. But she is hoping she's right. And she needs to talk with some authority. She isn't going to let this guy get the best of her.

"Oh no," he chuckled. "As you astutely can tell from my accent, I was born in another country. In fact, I grew up in Guatemala. Do you know where that is?" he asks with a rather inquisitive look on his face, not seeming to want to put her on the spot while also apparently testing some of her skills.

She remembers studying about the Panama Canal and Central America in history class. Yet, she's not sure of the arrangement of those little countries. She takes a shot at it, anyway. "North of Panama?" she replies, with all the authority she could muster without sounding too arrogant.

She notices the framed papers on the wall, guessing they are degrees or some such thing. But she can't make them out with quick glances.

"Very good," he replies. He seems rather pleased with her response. "Many people put it in South America or even Africa. And not that many people know the relative positions of such small and seemingly insignificant countries compared to the United States. Yes, it's the first country south of Mexico and north of Panama, with a couple of others in between. It's difficult for people to remember the positions of Central American countries unless they have some interest there, which is why it's easy for me, I guess. I still have family there and care about it, especially when it's had such an influence on my life. Have you traveled much??"

"I've been to Chicago quite a bit, and we went to California and Oregon one year. But I will someday, when I can get out of here. I want to go to lots of places."

"Where would you go first? What place would you like to see most of all?"

This seems like a funny question for a "shrink," someone who's supposed to be counseling me, thinks Audri. *What the hell's he trying to pull here?*

"Well, I'd like to see Paris. I've always wanted to go to the top of the Eiffel Tower. Guess that'd be my first choice." This seems like a harmless, healthy answer to Audri.

She decides against saying she really wants to see the dungeons in England or the Guillotine in France. She thinks those responses wouldn't sound so healthy, and she needs to be through with all this *'damn shit.'*

He asks questions about school and friends, all of which seem harmless.

In fact, he doesn't seem to be doing a good job identifying my 'problems' or 'illness,' chuckles Audri internally.

They talk a while about what she likes to do and her favorite movies and books. He's even seen her favorite movie, "Breakfast Club," and liked it. And he's read her favorite books, the Tolkien Trilogy. Or at least he says he has. But then he knows about Bilbo and Gandalf, including the ring. He appears not to be just guessing. She's surprised at how much he knows of movies and novels, especially for such an old fart.

Between answers, Audri is trying to figure out his age, but it's hard to guess. His face is a bit crusty, with wrinkles around his mouth and eyes. There's a warmth and sparkle in his eyes, and she knows she's seen him before, but she can't remember where. Still, she doesn't trust him or the questions he's asking. He's up to something, but Audri isn't sure what yet.

They talk for a while longer, just chatting, comparing some likes and dislikes. Audri wonders if they may be finishing the session when Alberto casually shifts the conversation.

"So tell me a little about yourself," he says. "Tell me more of who you are. What do you like about yourself?"

OK, so here it comes, she thinks. Now she knows what he's doing, and she's ready for him. *He isn't going to outsmart me here.*

"Well, I am the youngest child in my family, with an older brother and sister. My dad owns a new Italian restaurant downtown, and my mom sells real estate. They are great parents, and we all get along. I do well in school, getting mostly A's, and I have three close girl friends."

"I see," he says, sounding a little bit doubtful. "And tell me three ways you would like to change yourself?" he asks.

"I'd really like to improve my backhand in tennis. Umm, and I wish my hair were a little darker." She pauses to appear like she's thinking, and then says, "I can't think of a third. Those are the only things I'd change. I'm mostly satisfied with myself."

This is going well, she observes. *I might be able to finish up by 5:30 and be through with all this!*

"And what about your parents? Anything you would change about them?"

She again appears to be thinking about his question seriously, then replies. "I wish Dad would spend more time with us on weekends. And I wish mom would make my favorite pizza more often. Otherwise they're swell parents."

Yes, I'm getting through this in fine shape, and I'll have him wrapped around my little finger in no time. Then he'll write on a piece of official paper that I am healthy or cured, and I won't have to come back here again!

"How's school going? Any difficulties there? Or is that going as well as it is at home?"

Is there some sarcasm in his voice? Is he playing with me?

She senses something else going on, but she isn't clear about it.

"As I said earlier, I am doing well in school. Getting mostly As, and I am on the honor roll. In fact, my friends and I are all on the honor roll. Great friends. We get along, study hard, and don't use drugs. Everything's pretty much perfect there too."

"Do you help a lot around the house? Do you have regular chores, or do you just pitch in and help on your own?"

Now he's digging at something, but I'll outsmart him here too. I'm doing exceptionally well, and he isn't going to start generating problems where there aren't any!

"No regular chores. Just help when I'm not doing homework. I cooked breakfast the last two Saturdays, without even being asked. And I help my older sister do laundry because of all her homework. She's at the university studying sociology. Then she'll go to law school, hopefully either here or Northwestern. And I help my brother, Alex, too, and go to all his baseball games. He plays second base at City High." she said with great pride.

Yes, this old man can't possibly out smart me, and I think I'll have this stupid counseling wrapped up soon. No wonder Dad doesn't think this is useful.

"Yes, I know Alex. He plays on the team with my grandson, Santiago. He's a very strong player, and I think he just keeps getting better. I believe he'll be solid enough to get a scholarship by the time he graduates. My son, Alex's coach, also thinks he'll be successful."

Audri's mouth drops open! He must've noticed, but she can't help it - she begins losing all composure.

Then she realizes where she's seen him. He was the old man she saw watching the game last Friday! She knew there was something familiar, but she didn't place him there. How could she have missed the connection? And now she finds out he's Santiago's grandfather! This dope of a guy has a shrink for a grandfather!

She begins to make connections she missed before, about his name, his dark hair, his enticing looks too. This old man probably was attractive when he was way younger.

I just can't believe it! How could I end up in the office of Santiago's grandfather and want to be out of it so much? It would be tight if it were Santiago's house, but not some shrink's office! Not some wacko analyzing me and prying into my private life, always searching for some sickness. What am I going to do? I have to complete this shit and just get out of here with a certification of health!

"But enough about Alex and others. Tell me what brings you in here today."

Audri stumbles a bit still, but then catches herself.

"Oh, my mom just wants to make sure I'm a healthy and happy girl. So if you'll give me my certificate of health, I'll be on my way," says Audri with a smile.

Alberto peers at her and chuckles a bit. "Counseling doesn't work that way, unless maybe you're court ordered. Is that how you got here? Your mom didn't mention that part."

"Oh no," Audri says with a laugh. "I'm not in any trouble with the court."

"Well, then, what brings you in?"

"Just checking on my mental health in general. Like many mothers, my mom worries whether I'm doing OK."

"What would your mom say brings you in here?"

"Oh, well, she may think I have an eating problem, just because I throw up when I get something caught in my throat. I think I must have an unusually narrow passage."

"I see," remarks Alberto, peering at her for a moment. It feels to Audri that he's peering right through her, which disturbs her further.

Does he have some evil power I don't know about? What the fuck is going on with him?

"Is there always something stuck in your throat when you throw up? And have you seen a physician about that?" asks Alberto as he finally continues with more questions.

"Yeah, my mom took me to some throat specialist. But I don't think he knew what he was doing. He did an exam and x-ray and said it was fine. But I know how it feels."

"How often do you throw up?"

"Oh, maybe once every few months."

"How often would your mother say that you throw up?"

"Well, she would say more. She hears me coughing when I get something caught, and she thinks I'm throwing up. But really I'm just clearing my throat in the bathroom. She can't actually see."

"You don't think your mom knows the difference?"

"No. She's too busy with her work, laughing at Alex, or arguing with Dad to notice."

"I see," responds the old man, again peering into her. "And when you throw up, is it just what's in your throat or your stomach too?"

"Mostly just what's in my throat. Once in a while it's my stomach, too. But not very often."

"Is your throat sore afterwards?"

"Sometimes, because food gets stuck there, which seems to irritate it."

"Or the acid in your stomach that can burn. Do you drink water and make sure you get plenty of electrolytes so your body doesn't get depleted? That's especially important when you play tennis, too."

"Oh yes, I make sure of that. I'm careful about both. I take good care of my body and try to drink a lot of perfectly nourishing liquids."

"So you're as perfect taking care of your body as you are in your family and in school?"

"Oh yes. I do it all very well."

"You know, perfection can be perfectly difficult, especially when it involves giving up yourself for others or struggling for control. How important is control in your life, Audri?"

"Oh, that comes pretty easy to me. I don't have to worry much about that."

"I see. And how do you work to keep control?"

"I have a creative mind, and it's pretty active most of the time."

"When you're focused on maintaining control using your mind, how do you connect with your body? How do you keep grounded in your physical being?"

"Huh? What do ya mean?"

"Well, with so much energy going to your brain, thinking about ways to get or stay in control of your life, what keeps you connected to your body?"

"Ah, I don't know. Guess I haven't thought about it much. But I'm sure I'm pretty good at it. I'm still moving around." Audri begins to laugh at her clever response.

"Do you do it by vomiting?"

"What?" Audri's mouth again drops open, although this time she remembers how to close it. "No, I don't think that's true at all. I just get things stuck in my narrow throat."

"I see. Well, our time is about up, and this might be an appropriate place to stop. But I'd like you to think about two questions this week if you would. First, I'd like you to think about how you'd want to be as an adult if it were completely up to you – if no other people were telling you how to shape yourself or what you should do. A second thing I'd like you to think about is one thing you would change about yourself if it were completely up to you. Would you think about these two questions for me? Then maybe we could meet again at 4:30 next Tuesday. How would that work for you??"

"Next. . . week?" Audri can hardly get the words out of her mouth. "But I told you, everything's fine with me. I don't really need any help. Don't you see that? My mom just wants to make sure, and I've told you everything is perfect. I don't think I need to come back. I mean, don't you think I am healthy and happy? Don't you think I am fine?"

Audri's at a loss of what to say. She feels so off balance as she realizes who he is that she's losing track of her whole strategy.

And now he wants to make another appointment. This isn't part of my plan!

But Audri can't find an easy way out without risking her mom being angry and not letting her go to the summer tennis camp.

"I know you're healthy and happy. I am not suggesting you're sick. And all of us face a few challenges in life. I think maybe I can help you with some changes that would be useful to you, and I would like to explore those a little more. But we don't need to meet. And you can quit at any time. It's up to you and your parents. Let's just try it a couple more times. Then if you find it's not helpful, I'll recommend someone else to your mom. How about that?"

Audri feels trapped in a corner again, talking about two more sessions. But she doesn't want to upset the parentals and be grounded or lose her phone. She'll have to agree. And she's not happy about that.

"OK, we can try it a couple of times. What can it hurt? I don't have anything better to do on a Tuesday afternoon anyway, except improve my tennis," she says with much exasperation.

She's losing control of the situation, and she hates it. Maybe a little sports guilt will help?

Now she just wants to end it so she can figure out how to get back in control and take charge of this situation. He's thrown her a 'curveball,' as her brother would say, and she'll have it figured out before they meet again. That she promises herself!

"Oh, and we don't have to talk at the games." Alberto just brushes aside the attempted guilt, off-centering Audri even more. "I just go to watch the boys play, and we can pretend we don't know each other. I may say hello just to be pleasant, as friendly strangers would do. No one has to know you're coming here. I always keep my clients' identity and information confidential."

At least he is gracious about not letting anyone else know. And she likes the smile in his eyes. She wonders if her eyes smile like his and seem so happy. She'll have to look in the mirror when she gets home to check it out.

"You know what I like best about you so far?" he asks.

Again she doesn't know what to say. She just stares at him with her mouth closed so she doesn't gawk.

"I like the smile and sparkle in your eyes! It shows so much life inside you, so much I'm guessing doesn't always get out. I hope you never lose that."

This is too much. She just says thanks and goodbye, then walks out the back door. She doesn't care whether her mother is waiting or not. She'll sit on a rock and pull herself together. She has to get out of this office so she can think. Everything's just too much for her in here.

She's happy when she walks outside and sees her mother waiting in the getaway car. She opens the door and falls into the front seat.

"How did everything go, Audri?" her mom asks pleasantly.

"Fine," replies Audri as she gazes out the window and falls deeply into planning.

Chapter 6

The Right Answers

On her way home, Audri continues to feel stunned and remains quiet. Given the short drive, her mother appears anxious to engage in conversation, but Audri's lips are sealed.

"Want to share anything about your time with Dr. Salvador?" asks her mother as she pulls out onto Linn Street. After several blocks, they turn right onto Washington, and she finds a place to park. "I have to drop off the checkbook to your dad. I'll be right back."

"K," replies Audri. This distraught girl stares out the car window watching people move along the sidewalk, then glances over towards her real dentist's office. In this moment, the remembered pain of the needle to deaden the drilling on her last cavity doesn't seem to have been as painful as being out maneuvered by this old man.

Her mom suddenly opens the car door and settles into the seat, turns on the engine and pulls out onto the street. Just as quickly, she reignites the conversation. "Did you like him all right? He seems rather pleasant to me."

Audri isn't sure if Mom is asking or selling, which is a common style for her, even in casual conversations.

"OK, I guess," Audri says with a shrug. She can't decide what to say about him. She doesn't want to piss off her mom or shift to some other therapist. Everything might just get worse. She figures this old man will be easier to out maneuver than someone much younger. And she still isn't sure what went wrong in convincing the old man how healthy she is. She does notice less resentment right now, maybe because she's too stunned. More than anything, she's just confused, especially about her feelings.

What kind of questions was he asking? What was he really after with such odd conversations? Did he know about Oddri, this feeling of being so strange? Was he making fun of me, or were they just common counseling questions I don't understand? How do I tell him what I want to be? How do I know? And does it really matter to him?

The short drive seems extra long to Audri this afternoon. She wonders if Bella's taking some extended route. She hasn't been paying attention, but simply watching trees and houses slowly pass by with her active mind deep in review.

Is her mother driving slower than usual? Taking Audri "for a ride?" Sarah and Alex had warned her about going "for a ride" with their father. That meant they were in trouble for something, especially if he asked you to go alone. Is Audri caught just when she needs time to think and sort things out?

They finally pull into the driveway, waiting an eternity for the garage door to finish opening. As the car comes to a stop in the garage, Audri pops open the door. "Thanks for the ride," mutters Audri, then disappears into the house. She bounds up the stairs two at a time and into her bedroom, shutting the door behind her and flopping onto her bed.

Audri has asked herself questions regarding what she wants to be when she grows up, but she's seldom shared answers with anyone. She'd hint at it with her mother, and she shares aspects she doesn't like about herself with her '*Les Quatre Mousquetaires*' (her favorite term for their own Four Musketeers, including Tanika, Soph, and Ang). Yet most of her sharing was about what was wrong with her rather than what she wanted to be like. She wasn't even sure, maybe didn't even know herself. This was going to take serious effort.

How do I talk with him without saying anything? How can I participate without revealing anything personal?

That could be a possibility, but it felt like dangerous ground with her mom. She needs some assistance in figuring this all out, but she's not sure where she'd get it. Maybe Sophie could help. She spent some time earlier in the year with the school counselor about careers. Audri picks up the phone and texts her partner.

There was no answer to Audri's attempt. She opens her Favorites and presses Sophie's number. There again is no answer, and she decides not to leave a message.

Maybe Soph isn't home yet? But damn, I want to talk to her!

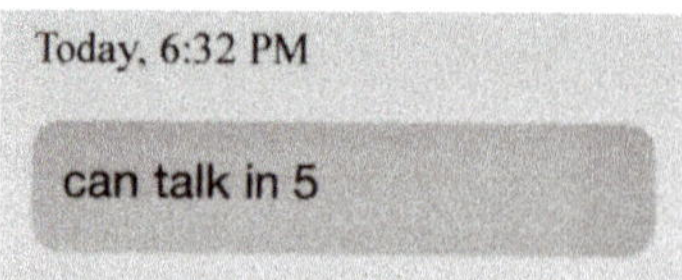

At last a response. Yet Audri feels a panic in her stomach. Every second now life feels weighted in lead, moving slower than ever.

Audri shuttles from thinking about the question of how she wants to be to a panic in her stomach that intensifies with each tick of the clock. She's drowning in her own consternation with no apparent lifeline.

Audri jumps when her phone rings. At last a connection with someone.

"Can we talk about your time with the school counselor earlier this year?" asks Audri without even the courtesy of a hello. But with this group, it's quite common to focus immediately on the important stuff.

"It wasn't too bad. She's pretty nice, and she used to play tennis in high school too. I think she's cool, if you have to be stuck in a counselor's office."

"What did you two talk about? What kinds of questions did she ask you?" inquires Audri.

"We talked about different skills and interests I had and the results of my career test. I guess I did well, and she wanted to know what type of career I'd like to pursue. We also talked about different colleges and universities. Some offer scholarships that I might apply for, including tennis."

"Did she ask what's your heart's biggest desire to be as an adult?"

Soph hesitates for a minute. "What? Hell no!"

"Man, I don't get this guy. I think he's out to lunch. We didn't talk much about eating."

"Guess you lucked out," chuckles Sophie. "Maybe he doesn't know." She laughs more. "Besides, I figure it's costing your folks money, so why not go. I think that's the best way to get even!" Soph laughs out loud at her creative revenge.

Audri doesn't feel great about using the sessions to make them 'pay' in that way. Besides, she'd rather have the money to spend on other things.

"No, I'm sure Mom told him. Thanks for the help anyway. OK, well, I better study before I'm in more trouble. See ya tomorrow. Thanks."

"Yeah, have a good one."

With that, Audri hangs up and puts her phone on the white table next to the bed. Her stomach is churning, her head's spinning. Such upset and confusion is annoying. She's beginning to feel at a loss of how to out maneuver this old man. She closes her eyes and falls into another mental swirl.

Amidst the dancing in her head, Audri ponders the question Alberto asked, wondering what she should say next week.

What's the correct answer? What do I need to say to demonstrate that I'm healthy? Telling him I want to be President of the United States sounds healthy, but maybe a bit arrogant. A professional tennis player is safe, yet not realistic? Maybe I could sweet-talk him, like with Dad, while figuring out the correct answer?

These thoughts keep rolling around and around in her mind, almost like the antique pinball machine her dad once showed her, flipping the ball back and forth from one bumper to another, hitting some poles, but not getting many points.

Audri jumps as a knock radiates from the door. Sarah opens it and asks with a smile, "Did you get my wash done? I need that shirt tonight, and Marsha needs her jeans back."

In all the confusion, Audri forgot to get her sister's wash done as she had promised in exchange for her help with homework two weeks ago. She still has another week's worth.

"Sorry," she says and grabbing her phone she gets up and follows Sarah into her room, pulls out the dirties from her basket, and heads to the laundry room. "I'll get it finished now," calling back as she goes down the stairs towards the basement laundry room.

After filling and starting the machine, she sits on the floor, hoping the washer noise will provide her some new insight. She slumps down as the thrashing of the machine begins to grind away. The constant chugging noise sometimes helps Audri think, but right now it's just bothering her. Today, everything bothers her! She puts her hands to her ears, but that isn't enough.

Audri goes upstairs and out back to the screened porch. It's warm and a bit muggy, but pleasant for this time of year. She smells the perfumed scent of jasmine growing just beyond the porch, which usually has a calming effect. Some humidity also might moisten her brain and help her creativity.

Audri adjusts her body into her favorite chair and takes a deep breath. She begins to feel her body relax, getting more comfortable, and asks herself what she wants to do in life.

She thinks traveling would be fun, and she wants a high income. She considers getting married and maybe children. She certainly wouldn't want more than two, as a third child can feel lost in a family. She knows that well.

Yet she hasn't focused on a particular career. Maybe teaching? A detective? These ideas roll around in her brain for some time, eventually dozing off from exhaustion.

After a brief nap, Alex comes out of the door with his mitt and a ball. "Hey, what'z up? How did your time with the shrink go?"

Geez, he knows too? This just keeps getting worse.

"Fine," she responds rather emphatically and sarcastically as she rises from the chair and stomps back into the house.

While moving towards the stairs, she decides to see if Sarah could help her with this one. Maybe her college experience could expand Audri's possibilities.

Audri goes down to put the clothes in the dryer, then returns to Sarah's room.

It may help if Sarah knows the clothes are nearly finished.

She stands in the open doorway, watching Sarah at her desk. "Clothes should be done in about 45, and then I'll iron the shirt you want. Sorry I forgot. This counseling shit has been on my mind," says Audri sullenly.

"Oh, thanks Dri. So how did the session go?" asks Sarah supportively.

Audri likes it when Sarah calls her by her nickname. Somehow it feels affectionate and caring, especially today.

"He's OK, but I don't get what he's doing. I don't want to go there, and I certainly don't want kids at school to find out! I can't figure out a way to get out of this crap, but I don't want to piss Mom off either. You know anything about counselors?" Audri asks with great hope.

"Na, not much," Sarah replies. "My friend, Lisa, went to one last semester. You could ask her. She also had some eating issues."

"God, does the whole world know? Sorry, I'm just frustrated with all this!"

"Mom's just worried. You know secrets don't last long in this family. They present the same challenge as unwrapped Christmas presents just waiting to be discovered."

"Do you think Lisa would mind talking? I really need some help. I don't know anyone else, except Soph, who's no help. She just saw a school counselor. Could I call her?" asks Audri.

"I'm going to see her at study group tonight. I'll give her your number and ask her to call you."

"Cool. Thanks." Audri backs out of the doorway and heads to her room.

Her body tingles a bit with the sense of new possibilities. She rubs her face with her hands, hoping to continue developing some ideas. After a while, she goes back to the dryer, pulls out the shirt to iron, and finally gets everything done. She takes it all up to Sarah's room and thanks her again for the help.

During dinner that night, Audri attempts to engage in more conversation at the table, wanting to act and feel more "normal." Besides, her mom focuses on her less when she's talkative. Afterwards, she spends some time studying, then goes to bed early.

The next three days are filled with school and homework. While the question is present, it also takes a back seat to more pressing issues, which helps Audri feel more settled. She does talk with Lisa, but she's about as much help as Soph.

Saturday is Sophie's birthday party, and *Les Mousquetaires* are hosting. The three advisors have done some planning, with a few surprises for the guest of honor, but nothing for the memory books. Audri has fun, and the four of them stay the night at Sophie's house.

Around 2:00 am, Audri finally falls into a relaxing sleep. Enjoying herself for a time helps her mood considerably.

The four girls finally begin stirring about 9:30, and Soph's mom calls them for breakfast. Audri eats a bit and has a small coffee. Soph's mom is a dear, but she's no barista.

Audri texts her mom, asking her to be picked up at 11:00.

As her mom pulls up in front, Audri thanks the girls as well as Soph's parents, then goes out and gets in the car.

"How was the party?" her mom asks with a smile.

"It was fun. Everyone seemed to have a great time."

"You still hungry? How about a yogurt from Aspen?"

"Yeah, great. But could we go to Yotopia? They have my favorite toppings."

"Sure." With that, her mom heads towards Clinton Street, finds a parking spot, and they go inside. They both get a small serving with a few toppings, then find an empty table.

"How's school going? You going to be ready for finals?" asks her mom with a smile.

"It's going good, and I think I'm pretty ready," chuckles Audri, with mixed feelings about her mom. Little is initiated after that from either distracted party.

Monday and Tuesday pass quickly again. Audri can't believe how fast days pass when she wants them to go slowly. Even Monday evening goes rather quickly. She finishes her book that evening for lit class on Wednesday. She isn't entirely clear what it said, but she can honestly report she finished her reading all the same.

Then it's Terrible Tuesday again. She's facing the same sense of being cornered, and this time she has no plan at all. She doesn't know the answer to the question or how to get it right, and she could 'fail' counseling! After just the first session, she could fail!

And this from an old man who probably can't even remember what it was like to be in his 'teens!'

What could he know? How could he be helpful? Is he in it only for the money? From the looks of his couch and shoes, he needs the money! Am I his only client? What should I do when I see him in public again?

She had a hard time not watching him at the last game. Surely it'd be more difficult this time! Would she tell her friends about the connection to Santiago? They all rather like the 'hot' junior, but would they like him if they found out he's the grandson of a shrink?

Maybe I should spread the word! I might not be able to get this old man, yet I could make his grandson miserable. But how can I do that? Santiago is a dope of a guy, and I kind of like him.

Maybe his grandfather could tell him what a great girl I am, how terrific it'd be if he would ask me out. Could I slip him such a hint? If I can't get out of the sessions all together, maybe at least something good could come out of them, like have Santiago notice me finally.

But why would he notice a 'crazy" woman? Why would he bother if I'm 'seeing a counselor?' Such things were not that highly rated at school, and I'm sure he'd see this as no exception, even if it is his grandfather.

She's lost. That's all there is to it. She's lost!

After school, Audri goes outside to find her mother waiting once again. Audri opens the door, slides into the front seat, then buckles her seat belt to be driven to the dungeon of the 'Dragon.'

And she's dragon', too. She's no energy left to face this old man. Once again she feels the brick wall in her face, and once again she can't breathe.

"You alright dear?"

"Oh, just having some trouble breathing this afternoon. Guess the hay fever season is coming on."

"If you are having a panic attack, it's a good thing we're on the way to the counselor," jokes her mother.

Audri frankly finds no humor in her mom's comment and just sits in the seat looking straight ahead.

"I think he can fix that too. Just breathe for him dear, and let him see your difficulty," continues her mom, half chuckling.

Again Audri fails to see any humor in her mother's sick jokes!

Is she now trying to be a comedian? She's too old for that.

But Audri doesn't want to interact enough to inform her. She'll just let her find out for herself, just as she's let Audri do so many times! Once again she holds back her comment.

All of a sudden they are there, at the dungeon. She's going to face her dragon, and suddenly her knees feel weak. Still, she can walk, and she makes it into his office with Bella 'standing guard' as she walks behind Audri, like a guard walking her to her cell. Or the death chamber.

Again, no one's in the waiting room. They sit for only a moment before he appears in the doorway, breathing fire, from Audri's perspective.

"Hi Audri. Come on in. It's great to see you again. We should be finished by 5:30 today, Bella. Audri can meet you out back then."

With that, Audri's mother leaves, abandoning her child to enter the dungeon. She hasn't been creative, and now she's walking into what feels like her death sentence.

As she crosses the threshold into Alberto's office, she begins to imagine instead that she's walking onto the tennis court for a championship match. She digs deeply into her competitive spirit to access her bravery as she enters the room. The worst problem is that he still has that smile in his eyes. She liked it at first, but in this instant she's hating it.

Why's he so calm and peaceful? Does it have to do with the death of me? Is he enjoying all this? Well, I'm sure not, thinks Audri. *I'm sure not*!

Chapter 7

Surviving the Dragon

"Did you think about the questions I gave you last week?" asks Alberto as they take their same seats. The room still appears old and worn, as does the old man.

He's wearing a pair of dark blue slacks with a light blue shirt, and seemingly the same loafers he wore last week.

Can't he afford two pairs of shoes? wonders Audri. *At least he can have a little better taste in clothes with all the money he makes! Or maybe I **am** his only client,* she chuckles to herself. *Maybe he wants me back because he can't keep any other clients.*

"Yeah, I thought about it. A lot really. But with so many options, I'm not sure. I can't figure out the best answer. Does that mean I have to stay longer?" asks Audri discouragingly.

"And do you always worry about getting the 'best' answer?" he asks.

There seems to be a bit of a twinkle in his eye with such a question, but Audri isn't sure what that's about. Yet it makes her nervous.

What's he up to? What does he mean by that?

"Well, I try to do well in school. I work hard at it. And at tennis too," she tells him, still trying to understand what he's up to with these questions. She doesn't know, but it bothers her.

She focuses on this old man's face, well tanned, some wrinkles. But still no clue as to what he's searching for when looking at her or what the right answer might be.

"I'm sure you try hard and do well. You seem very bright and on top of everything going on in your life. But sometimes the best answer isn't in your head. It's in your heart."

Audri's having difficulty following him, listening more closely than usual because of his accent, let alone the topic.

She notices nervousness in her stomach. She doesn't like situations where she isn't sure what's right. She wrestles around in her chair, gazes into his dark eyes, then starts rubbing her thumb and forefinger.

"Are you feeling nervous?" he asks. "This may be new to you, and sometimes it's a little challenging for young people until they get used to it. I remember how I felt when I began with my first counselor," he says with a bit of a smile.

There he is, smiling again. Is he making fun of me?

Even his teeth look old, yet they still are rather white against his darker, sun-tanned skin. Yet, his smile is warm.

She relaxes a little in the chair, which is finally beginning to feel more comfortable. It's like the chair won't relax until she does, not allowing her to settle in until her body becomes a little less tense. And now that's starting to happen. She rests her arms on the sides and takes another short breath, more exhausted from her processing than relaxed.

"You went to counseling?" Audri asks, trying not to sound too shocked. "What's wrong with you?"

"Before someone becomes a counselor or therapist, one needs to experience the other side of the relationship. It's difficult to be an empathic therapist if you don't know what it's like being a client. Besides, many of us have some difficulty in our life that can be helped by talking through with a professional."

"Yeah, I suppose so," responds Audri.

"People or families often find it useful to talk through challenges they are experiencing. For example, some adults have difficulties with employers or co-workers they want to discuss, sometimes because they don't notice their own responses or patterns. Others have challenges with family interactions that they want to change and are not sure how."

"OK, but I don't think there's anything wrong with me. And I don't want to talk through my challenges. I just want to go to school, play tennis, and have fun. Anything wrong with that?" asks Audri, now feeling indignant.

"No, nothing's wrong with that at all. But why does your mother want you to be here? Does she see a challenge you disagree about?"

"Why do you do that? Why do you look so intently at me like that?" asks Audri somewhat frustrated.

"I'm just trying to feel into your response and get a sense of anything else that might be going on with you. I want to know more, and sometimes you can get a feeling for that."

"What kind of sense? Do you think I'm lying?" asks Audri, her annoyance increasing.

"Do you think you're lying? Even unintentionally? Is there something else going on that even you might not notice?" responds Alberto slowly and calmly.

"No! And besides, lots of my friends throw up sometimes. It's very common."

"And do you want to be like your friends?"

"Doesn't everyone?"

"No, not everyone. Sometimes people decide to make very different choices from their friends, especially if other people's choices aren't helpful for them."

Again, Alberto remains calm and soft spoken, even with Audri's growing agitation. His unusual response throws Audri off even more. She's used to people responding to agitation with their own aggravated response.

Audri feels the irritation in her gut and confusion in her head. She isn't sure what to say any more and is frustrated that this old man continues to get the best of her. She just stares at him for a few minutes, then says, "I like my friends. They're great!"

"It sounds like you make many great choices, which is often true of people who do well in life. And yet, there can be an area, even just one choice, or one issue that plagues them. That is their challenge. When they address it directly, they do much better than simply ignoring it or pretending it's not there. That's all. Besides, there's a big difference between challenges and being mentally ill or crazy."

Audri's stare remains focused on him, refusing to respond. At this point, she realizes she possesses no idea what to say.

"Do you have a sense of what your life is about, what your passion is? Or have you not found it yet?" His face softens as he asks these questions, and his eyes get even brighter.

"I think I'm here to bug my folks," she says rather abruptly. The words just come out. They slip out of the front door while she is not paying attention. All this gibberish about purpose and passion is confusing her, and now she's sharing responses she doesn't mean to be expressing.

She doesn't want him to get the wrong idea about her, to think there might be something wrong. She realizes she needs to monitor her words more closely from now on.

Alberto chuckles at her response. "Yes, I think my son and daughter both felt like that was their job when they were young. And they did an admirable undertaking at times! But I am talking more about you and what excites you, what motivates you to get out of bed, to share your ideas and experiences with your best friend?"

Audri stops to ponder for a moment.

Should I be honest with this guy? Can I trust him? Should I talk about the empty feeling I get from time to time, much more often than any enthusiasm? In fact, resentment describes my feelings more often than excitement or passion. But should I tell him, trust him with my feelings, my truth?

She tried to share her sense of doom with her dad one night. But his focus remained on getting the restaurant started. He ignored her feeble attempt to share.

She also wanted to tell her mother on several occasions. Bella just seemed to get upset and tell her she's a lovely girl and shouldn't worry about such things. Her mom kept saying she was far too young to have such thoughts, but that's the way she feels at times.

What should I do? How can I describe the emptiness, this absence of any light in my life? It's like someone shoved my insides in a closet and closed the door! I can't feel anything except the damp darkness!

Alberto paused like he was searching for an answer, took a breath, then continued.

"Sometimes it takes a while to find your passion, what you want to do more than anything else. The important thing is to understand that you can access more sources of information than you often realize. But we can talk more about that later. I'm getting ahead of myself. Let's talk about the question I asked you to think about during the week. Do you mind?"

Why is he asking my permission? Obviously he's in charge, and I have to go along, whether I like it or not. And right now I don't!

"Why do you ask if I mind? You're going to do it anyway, aren't you?" Audri's getting more upset and resents his 'playing' with her. She doesn't mean to sound so frustrated, but it's building and just slipped out again. She's having real difficulty controlling the situation and him!

"No, I wouldn't actually. We could talk about something else. For example, we could discuss what's bothering you about the question."

"If I do that, then you'll see me as sick, and I'll just have to spend more time here. So I don't think honesty pays off all that much right now, quite frankly!" Audri certainly didn't intend to be so frank and honest, but she's running out of ideas about how to appear healthy and keep control.

"Is that why you think you're here? You think you are 'sick' in some way?" he asks with concern in his voice.

"Of course. Isn't that why people send kids to counselors?" retorts Audri.

"Well, some may see it that way. And some kids do have serious problems. But that isn't my view of you. Not at all. In fact, if that's your concern, let me put it to rest right now. Audri, I have no sense of you being 'mentally sick,' and that isn't why I think you're here. I suspect there are some aspects to your life that are bothering you, and at least one that isn't healthy. I thought maybe we could talk them through."

Audri shifts in her chair, wanting the irritation to cease in order to get back to feeling healthy.

Alberto continues.

"Sometimes I can help young people see an issue in a different way, just as my teacher helped me see life differently many years ago. But it's not about being sick or mentally ill, not that at all. My worry is that if you continue some patterns over a long period of time, they become much more difficult to change and can have serious long term consequences. I believe that's your mom's concern too."

Alberto shares a caring smile with mouth and eyes, as if his heart is speaking from both parts of his body.

Audri begins to relax and thaw, but just a tad.

"So how can you help me? If I am not sick, why does everybody think I need help?" asks Audri, trying to hold back the tears she begins to feel building.

"Do you want to talk about the emptiness you feel? When you feel it, what do you do?"

"What emptiness?" responds Audri, experiencing sudden vulnerability and anger. "Who told you I felt emptiness?" she asks rather indignantly, feeling exposed and shocked in her body.

"Oh, just a guess. Maybe I'm wrong. Maybe it's just other kids who feel it, like some of the clients that I've worked with. You may be different, and I may be inaccurate about that."

Again he smiles with his whole face, not in a laughing way, but with warmth, as if the smile embraces her and holds her comfortably in her chair, as a mother cradles her child in loving admiration.

"So, how would you want to create yourself if it were completely up to you? What would you want to be like?" he asks again.

"Well, I'd like to have dark, thick hair. And I'd want to be beautiful so the boys liked me, and girls too. And I'd want to be the smartest kid in school, but still be popular and fun. I'd like to feel happy inside, because I knew my parents loved me, and others liked me. And I'd have oodles of money and be able to play tennis very well, and have beautiful clothes. That is how I'd make myself."

"And if you were to begin with one thing, just one thing to change about yourself, what would it be? Of all those lovely parts of yourself, where would you start?"

"I don't know," responds Audri as she tries to think about such odd questions. "I guess I'd start with being beautiful, or maybe smart. Maybe even the money, which can help with the other two. What does it matter, cause I can't change any of those," retorts Audri who is noticing a sense of rawness.

"And what would all those give you? If you had all three, what would that provide you?" asks Alberto, gazing intently into Audri's eyes.

She isn't sure what she should say. They would be comforting to have, yet the empty feeling still would be there. It wouldn't help with that at all. She doesn't know how to respond to what feels like a tricky question.

Should I say what I really feel, or tell him the correct answer? But I'm not sure what the correct answer is. Can I trust him? Will he share this with others? Damn, I hate this!

She feels stuck again, but it's not like being in a corner. It's more like knowing the truth and not knowing how to say it, expressing it out loud to an old man who is shifting from knowing so little to understanding more than she imagined.

"It would make me popular. People....would.... like me," she replies.

"And would the emptiness go away with all of these," he asks? "Would all these fill you up and make you feel whole?"

Now he's digging deep, and Audri isn't sure she likes the direction this is going. *Does he have the right to ask such questions?*

Audri begins to cry. She isn't sure why she's crying, but she can't hold back the tears any longer. And surprisingly, she feels a release, even in front of this stranger, this old man from the ballgame and Santiago's grandfather. None of that matters now.

Audri feels some comfort as she cries for a change, even if it makes her appear 'sick.' And she feels her body letting go of some stress, frustration she's been holding in for the past few weeks. She also begins to believe maybe, just maybe, there's someone who can understand her life struggles. But she doubts it's him.

"Yes, the emptiness hurts, doesn't it," says Alberto softly. "No matter how hard we try to fill ourselves up with objects and people, try to make ourselves perfect, the emptiness hurts."

Audri lowers her head to her hands and releases the tear drops. She wasn't counting on this, and now she doesn't care much what he thinks. She just feels like crying.

She knows he's peering at her, and she worries for a moment about his possible judgment or criticism. More directly, she's aware of the emptiness and hurt inside. She doesn't know what else to do. And he just watches her, with what Audri begins to feel are loving eyes and an open heart.

After a time, she looks up at him, tears still running down her cheeks. She isn't angry that he watches her, but rather confused. Most adults would either criticize or comfort her at times like this, but he does neither. He just watches through his supportive eyes, an eagle keeping close watch on a little one without being able to help it fly.

She feels like she's stumbling around, not sure what to do, with this old man guarding over her without touching or wiping away the tears. Just watching and protecting her in this big, overstuffed nest of a chair.

"There's a tissue box on the table next to you if you want one," Alberto finally introjects.

Audri grabs a couple of tissues and wipes the tears and blows her nose.

"So what do I do with this emptiness? How do I get rid of it," still tears in her eyes and snot in her nose.

He smiles with a soft, loving smile. "You don't have to do anything right now. We've some exploring to do first, some learning about yourself and who you are underneath the emptiness. Then, eventually, it will go away, or rather it will get replaced. But if we try to do that too early, you'll end up trying to fill it again, as you've already tried, and as so many have done before you. Right now it's important just to acknowledge it, to feel into it and get to know it, know that it's there without running away from it. You've done a great job just now."

"Thanks, Doc. I guess."

"I really mean that Audri. You stayed with it rather than running or distracting, which is what most do when they become aware of it. Staying with the awareness is a challenging thing, especially for adults who've learned to cover it up. Of course, I think you're stronger than most adults, which is why you're still here. I don't think you're aware of that just yet, but it feels very true to me. That's why I wanted to see you again. It felt like you were strong enough to do this kind of work and in a good place for it."

Alberto peers again into Audri's eyes, a look full of support and hope. She glances at him, then around the room, feeling too much intensity with the eye gazing. Again, she begins to rub her thumb and forefinger. Alberto glances at her hand, then continues.

"You do that with your hands when you're nervous?" Alberto asks.

"Yeah, sometimes," Audri responds as she quits rubbing them for the moment.

"These feelings or holes occur for a reason, but not because you've done anything wrong. We're helped in developing them without even knowing it, others supporting us to do what they've done. For next week, I would like you to do two things. First, I'd like you to pay attention to the hole when it occurs, just noticing when it comes and how you feel when it's present. The other thing is I'd like you to continue with the question I gave you last week. But rather than focus on what you want to do or achieve, I'd like to know who you would like to BE as a person. Will you do that?

"Sure," responds Audri. She blows her nose again, then takes a couple more tissues from the box and wipes her eyes and cheeks.

"How are you feeling? Want to talk any more today, or do you feel like that's enough for now?"

"I think I've had enough for one day."

"OK, then. I'll see you next Tuesday. You did a great job facing some challenging issues today."

They both rise out of their chairs, and he smiles at Audri once more. He continues his smile as he gazes deeply into her eyes again, and Audri feels her body relax further. Rather than intrusion, his focus is feeling more like a supportive nest.

"Bye, Doc," says Audri as she turns and walks out of the office.

Chapter 8

Dreams and Nightmares

The day begins like a typical Wednesday morning as Audri and Tanika walk along East Court Street on their way to school. Audri's backpack feels a little lighter than usual, as does her body.

"Did you see the new kid hanging out with Santiago yesterday? He was fire!" chuckles Tanika.

"No, missed that. Must have been looking at someone else," giggles Audri with a big smile.

While continuing the conversation, Audri notices the trees and flowers that continue blooming, and the warm sun invites summer to appear. Birds sing that lovely spring song of winter's departure, and she hears a young boy laugh as he gets into the car with his mom, tickling Audri's heart. The day appears a little brighter, sunnier, and warmer to Audri. And she feels a little more relaxed inside. It's a lovely morning to be walking with her best friend, prepared for classes ahead.

As the two girls approach the south door of the school, Audri tells Tanika how surprised she is at Alberto's insightfulness, even when he's pushy, avoiding the part about crying. Just as she reaches for the handle with her right hand while gazing at Tanika on her left, the door opens by an arm Audri didn't notice on her other side. She steps back and turns to look.

"Hey there, Audri, how's it going today?" asks Santiago as he smiles while holding the door for these two young women.

Audri tries not to hold her mouth open even though frozen in space, staring with shock into his beautiful eyes.

"She's good," responds Tanika with a chuckle. "She just can't talk much this early in the morning. She doesn't do mornings well," and continues to giggle as she walks through the door. "Thanks for being such a gentleman." The words fade away as she continues down the hall by herself, glancing back at Audri with another big grin.

Audri can hear the chuckles as she finally gets a "good" out of her mouth and walks through the open door, followed by a soft "thanks." Audri's still mystified that Santiago even knows her name, and her heart is pounding so loudly she can't think straight. She wants to say something clever, but "how are you?" is all she can muster out of her mouth.

"I see you at the ball games cheering for Alex and the team. I know he appreciates the support. He says so," continues Santiago as they walk down the hall. "That's cool you care so much."

"Thanks," is all Audri again can get out of her dry mouth, feeling her tingling stomach and hoping her shaking is not noticeable to others.

"Well, have a great time in class," responds Santiago as he turns right towards his classroom, walking past Cheryl who has been watching them stroll down the hall together.

Tanika is standing a little ahead by her locker, watching the show while pretending to adjust her books. All Audri can see is Santiago walking away and remembering that beautiful smile.

Audri saunters towards her locker, exchanges a few books, and still unable to speak. Then she and Tanika continue to first period.

"Way to go girl," smiles Tanika with the biggest grin Audri has seen in a while. "I didn't know he even knew your name!"

"Me either," laughs Audri, with a smile that continues clear down her body to her big toes, which tingle.

"But did you see that dick, Cheryl? She looked like the Devil with daggers in her eyes!" continues Tanika laughing at her own description.

"What? No. Was she around?" asks Audri with a bit of astonishment.

"Oh man, if she could have thrown those daggers, you'd be a dead girl right now! I don't know if that was about our photo switch or the coolest junior in school chatting you down the hall!"

"Oh, she's super basic anyway! Forget that dick!" At last Audri's mouth and words are back, just in time for math class.

As the two settle into their seats, Mrs. Anderson passes out a pop quiz. Audri gasps a bit to herself. Then she breathes again, grateful she not only completed her assignment last night but also reviewed the chapter afterwards to take her mind off the session. The test seems to go well, and she reminisces about the hallway stroll as others complete their exam.

During second period, she gets engaged in her computer project, creating a collage of her favorite photographs in a way she imagines creates a unique appealing arrangement. She likes the way her photo of moss on the tree stump came out, and she enjoys the nature arrangement that's developing. It appears the project is coming together ahead of schedule, which will give her time to play with details before it's due next Tuesday.

Oh, next Tuesday. *I wonder what we'll talk about next session. I hope I don't cry again. It makes me feel so little! So childish! Maybe I could talk about this project and how much I'm enjoying it. That might make me look healthier!*

While the next session is almost a week away, it's never far from Audri's mind.

Audri leaves fourth period to drop off books at her locker, then heads for the cafeteria to have lunch with the gang. She finds them getting into line, and she hustles to catch up.

As she begins to tell them about her new collage project, she notices Tanika and Soph staring towards a table halfway across the lunch room. Audri turns, and she too becomes silent.

There, near the corner, is Cheryl flirting elaborately with Santiago. Even from that distance, Audri can see that Cheryl's top button is open, exposing more of her voluptuous breasts. She's smiling her sexiest smile, with her arm touching Santiago's hand. And he isn't moving it!

Was he just faking it this morning? Was he making fun of me, by smiling and acting so sweet? I guess he just sucks!!

Audri turns back towards her friends, like she doesn't care, or at least trying to pretend she doesn't. Her friends turn towards Audri, fumbling for the right words to say.

"Guess he's a bitch too," Audri finally says. She holds back the tears, turning her attention to the lunch line and asks, "What are they going to kill us with today?"

She forces a chuckle, and they move towards the service area, grabbing trays and focusing on food. A lovely morning suddenly turns to shit, and Audri no longer feels hungry.

"I don't really think I want anything to eat. I just want to work on my project some more."

Audri wasn't sure anything would feel worse than going to counseling these days. But once again, she's wrong. She turns, puts back her tray, and walks towards the door, followed by two of her faithful *Mousquetaires.*

As the three girls walk past the vending machines, they buy a snack, then push open the door to take in the fresh outdoor air.

Thin clouds now cover the sky, which feels perfect to Audri. Her internal sunshine has faded too. She notices the pain in her chest, surprised that she cares so much about both the open door and his flirting with Cher-Devil. Again tears come to her eyes, and she breathes hard to stop them.

"So sorry, Audri," Soph whispers, finally breaking the deadly silence. "I didn't even know he liked that dick."

"Never could trust her, never will!" adds Tanika. "But I thought Santiago had better taste than that!"

"I can't believe both things could happen in one morning!" whispers Audri as tears trickle over her eyelids.

"It's actually not too surprising, given that the witch saw him talking to you so sweetly as you two strolled down the hall. I'm sure she's just getting back at us for the photo, and you know she isn't that creative, just conniving!"

Sophie quickly adds, "And she probably doesn't even care about him. She just wants to piss you off or hurt you back. That's her only gift, besides her looks!"

"And even those are questionable," chuckles Tanika. "If her mom didn't buy her expensive clothes and get her hair all done up, she would be a third rate street walker!" All three girls start to laugh at Nika's comment, and finally the tears are subsiding.

"I'm grateful to have such loyal friends as you two!" Audri whispers as she wraps her arms around them both, melting into a group hug.

"And what about me?" asks Ang as she walks out the door. "I don't want to miss a group hug!" Soph and Nika open their arms to let her into the circle of musketeers. Like the original group, this one too has great loyalty for each other.

"Are we ripping on the Cher-Devil?" laughs Ang. "I saw what she was doing in the lunchroom. I was saving you slow pokes a place to sit, so I had to finish a few bites and get rid of my dishes. But you missed the part where Santiago pulled his hand away, gathered his tray and left the table. It was rather hilarious, especially the look on that witch's face. I'm sorry, that is an abasement to witches!" which made them all laugh.

Ang says that mostly for Soph, who sometimes feels a connection to white witch powers. But the group doesn't talk much about it, as it makes Ang feel uncomfortable. Yet her loyalty to Soph encourages her to make such comments out loud, even if she doesn't have the same affinity. She does have the best vocabulary, however.

"So where did he go after he left the table?" asks Audri, letting her curiosity rise to her mouth.

"He took a couple of last bites as he walked across the lunch room, put away his stuff, and left. I don't know where he was going, but he didn't seem at all interested in her."

"I guess he does have better taste than that," chuckles Nika again. "Even if he's fooled briefly, he isn't fooled for long. I think more people are beginning to see right through her."

"I think there still are boys on the football team that would like to see through her!" laughs Soph. "But then some of them don't seem to care past those boobs!"

Again, they all let out a squeal and pass around a high five. Audri begins to feel better with the support of her friends. It feels comforting when all four are together at times like these.

The bell rings for the end of lunch, and the girls break up their circle to head back for afternoon classes.

While the clouds still linger, Audri's internal environment feels a little brighter and lighter. She goes through the afternoon classes with some ease and yet there still feels like a dampening of the wonderful feeling she experienced walking down the hall this morning. It was such a delightful surprise, and one girl can change all of that within hours of the event.

That evening, pleasant dinner conversation gets passed around with Bella and Alex, talking about work, school, and baseball practice. After clearing her dishes, Audri heads back up to her sanctuary.

She lies down on her bed rather than studying for her test in Spanish the next day. She notices the hole in her gut. Then remembers the request from Doc. She feels into the vast emptiness.

How is there such vastness with the limited space of my stomach and gut? This makes no sense to me. Maybe because I feel so fat? Is the fatness also the vastness? This black hole seems to extend forever! Is there some dark, magical extension of time and space? I don't get it!

Even if it's only the size of a soccer ball, it seems like the hole is endless at the same time. But most of all, it makes Audri feel empty, alone, and certainly not enough. Even with the other parts attached to her body, full of bone, muscle, blood, nerves, and processed food, she still feels an emptiness that makes the rest of her world feel useless, meaningless. And that's the part she hates the most. That's the part that dominates at times like these.

Why couldn't I be so appealing that Santiago would not even stay at the same table as the Cher-Devil of Iowa. Why does this emptiness over take everything else in my life? Why can't I be more interesting and appealing? Why couldn't people like me more?

The tears reemerge, sliding down her cheeks. She's glad to be alone, not showing this ugly side of her to anyone else. It's bad enough that she has to feel it, experience it, even know it exists.

If it weren't for her compulsive desire to do well, she would have remained on the bed and cried herself to sleep. But she needed to study, and she hates paying attention to that place anyway.

Doing something practical and focusing on school may help shift her attention and ignore her pain.

She slides off her bed and moves over to her desk. She grabs her Spanish book and begins to study for her test tomorrow. And the shift in focus is successful once again. The pain subsides, her attention is on something she can control, and she begins to feel better about herself.

Why bother focusing on something I can't discard when I can pay attention to what I do well. It feels much better to achieve some success, which helps me feel better inside. I think Doc has it wrong. I think it's better to cover the hole than focus on it. That feels too discouraging.

The next few days bring more success in Audri's life. She focuses on school work and hanging out with her *Mousquetaires* on the weekend. Not only is she prepared for her classes, she's also ready for Doc. She's done her assignment, and now she knows the right answers too. The sunlight is coming back, and once again the hole fades into the background.

Chapter 9

Concluding Counseling

By the time Audri reaches Alberto's office, she's feeling more confident about her correct answers. She's figured them out and will soon be finished. While she's starting to like the old man, she still doesn't want to be 'in counseling.' So she's happy to be concluding all this.

Just after she sits down in the waiting area, Doc opens the door and invites her in. She enters the room, glances around at all the boring things on the desk and wall, then sits in her chair, feeling more comfortable today as she prepares for her end game.

"How was your week, Audri? Did you think about the questions I asked you last session?"

"Oh yes. I paid attention to the emptiness last Wednesday. It was awful as usual. But in the process of noticing, as you suggested, I figured out how to distract myself and put my energy into school success. So I transformed the hole into accomplishment, and that's productive."

Audri is feeling rather articulate and healthy, glad to be showing her strong side to Doc.

"I see," said Alberto. "Please tell me more about what happened last Wednesday."

Apparently he isn't totally convinced by my brilliant solution.

Audri starts telling the story about feeling relaxed walking to school with Tanika, then interacting with Santiago and how nice he was, leaving out the part of the pounding heart and shaky body, of course.

That would be too intimate for him to hear about his grandson, Audri reflects to herself.

She goes on to tell him about Cher-Devil flirting with Santiago, how Audri and her friends were surprised by his attraction, and then later that night how she noticed the empty feeling inside, leaving out a few unimportant details in the middle. After a while, she got busy with her homework.

Alberto cocks his head to the right as he listens while sitting quietly for a minute, then shifts his weight in his chair before saying anything.

"Tell me about the turning point from feeling relaxed walking to school to the empty feeling that night in your room. When did the change become obvious to you?"

"I guess it was when Cher-Devil, as we like to call her, was flirting with Santiago. I'm not attracted to him or anything, but I was surprised by his choice of friends. I guess it just made me feel bad for him."

"How would feeling bad for Santiago's choice make you feel empty? What's the relationship between those two feelings?"

"Ah, not sure. Um . . . you know, I guess I just kinda feel bad for a kid that doesn't have more observant powers than that."

"But how would that make you feel empty? What does that have to do with you?"

Audri leans forward in her chair, resting her forearms on the sides. "This isn't about me. This is about poor Santiago falling for Cher-Devil. It's just unfortunate that he doesn't have more sense and better taste. I would think you could help him with that." Audri begins to let go of the building anxiety as she tries to focus the discussion back on Doc and his grandson.

"So, when somebody you don't know very well and you're not attracted to makes a bad choice, that makes you feel empty? I seem to be overlooking an important connection here. Could you help me understand the missing piece?"

"I guess I just feel bad for people who don't see who other people are behind their masks, that's all."

"Oh, well that's an excellent insight. I commend you for knowing about masks that we all tend to wear. But I still don't understand how your empathy for Santiago creates an empty feeling in you. Are you sure there isn't more connection between you and Cher-Devil or Santiago?"

Audri chuckles a bit inside as she listens to the old man refer to Cheryl that way. It's like Audri just hit a winning volley!

"Well, my friends and I don't like Cher-Devil at all. We're like arch enemies."

"In the end, when we get triggered by something, get upset with someone, it almost always includes some issue about ourselves, some hurt that we've not been seeing that gets stimulated all over again. What is it about Cheryl, that's the girl's given name, right? What is it about her flirting with Santiago that relates to some issue with you? What bothers you about it that connects to you?"

Audri wants to interrupt Alberto, trying to get the focus back on Santiago or

Cheryl. She doesn't really want the focus to be on her, and yet there's something that tells her to just listen. Maybe Alberto knows something that could be useful to her?

Alberto continues. "People act in ways all the time that don't affect us, yet someone else can be very hurt by it because it stimulates an old hurt in them. That's the key issue here. How does all this bring up something in you that hurts, that makes you feel empty?"

Audri sits quietly for a moment. She feels puzzled by Doc's question. Her hands begin to fidget, rubbing her thumb and forefinger. She knows one missing piece and doesn't want to admit her attraction to Santiago. At the same time, she isn't clear just how it impacts her. She takes a deep breath and lets it out.

"OK, maybe there is a teensy bit of attraction to Santiago. He is kinda cute. But he hardly knows me, and I'm sure none of my friends have told him anything."

"I so admire your honesty, Audri. That will be important in your own growth. Not just telling me, but your ability to say the truth to yourself and even out loud to others. It will help you immensely over the years. But getting back to this issue. What is it about Cheryl's flirting that would bring up your own emptiness? What do you feel inside when some girl goes after someone to whom you feel a teensy bit of attraction?"

Audri ponders his question. She doesn't want to dig further into the hurt, and yet Doc feels supportive of her at the same time. She wants to change the subject, as she often tries with her parents, which typically works. But she has a sense it's not going to be successful here. And her increasing discomfort becomes obvious.

Is there something I can tell him instead? Could I make something up he'd believe? How do I get out of this without explaining the whole shitty situation? Can I trust him? How can I tell him the truth about myself?

"Maybe there is a little bit more than a teensy attraction. And it hurts when I would like to be friends, but he starts falling for the Devil."

"So you feel some jealousy of the girl he's paying attention to? Tell me more about what goes on in your head when that happens? What do you say to yourself?"

"I don't want to talk about this Doc. He doesn't really matter anyway."

Alberto leans forward in his chair, his arms on his knees. "No, he doesn't matter here. What matters are the thoughts you say to yourself when something like this happens. What matters is what brings on the emptiness. What matters are the stories you've made up about yourself that you keep repeating. This is your own mask to yourself. Please tell me one of the worst judgments that you say to yourself in these moments."

Again, Audri pauses. Again she tries to figure a way out.

Will he tell mom or others? What if he tells this to Santiago? Then he will never like me! Hell, no one will ever like me!

"Well, ah, I guess I tell myself that I am not that attractive, that some people don't like me."

"That's a great start. Want to dig a little deeper today, or wait for later? We could talk about it another week, month, or even later in life when you keep experiencing the emptiness because you don't want to change. These judgments we tell ourselves aren't true. But we hold them as truth, beating ourselves with them, over and over. I can't pull them out of you. But I am happy to listen and shine a light on the truth of who you are."

"I tell myself I'm unlovable!"

The words just jump out of her mouth before she has a chance to stuff them down further. She didn't mean to speak them. But out they came. And now the terror must surely show on Audri's face. Audri stares at Alberto.

How did he get me to say that? Why did I say that out loud? Now he won't like me either!

Again, Audri feels like her mouth is gaping open and frozen in time. Her eyes squint a bit as she lowers her eyebrows, gazing at him suspiciously.

"And no matter how much others tell you they love you, you don't believe them because of this inner belief of yours. Correct? Even if it isn't true, you hold on to it that way and reinforce it with actions by others like Cheryl and Santiago. And it stimulates the old wound. That's why it hurts. And that brings back all the emptiness when the love goes away. But now we can begin to work directly with these core issues."

The shock, both of the words slipping out of her mouth and Alberto's response permeates Audri's body while simultaneously feeling some relief. Luckily, she notices both.

Alberto gazes at her with a warm smile on his face.

He knows it and he's still here. Did mom pay him to stay here? To like me? Yet it doesn't feel that way to me.

Thoughts just keep rolling around in Audri's head, once so full of answers and now just spinning with questions.

"What . . . what's . . . what's working with my core issues?"

Audri asks the question, not feeling sure of herself and needing to say some different words. To inject a different focus into the conversation.

"Great question, Audri. These are the core beliefs about ourselves that we hide from others, often even from ourselves, believing that if anyone knew them, we wouldn't be liked, or even worse, not be loved. These typically are negative views we hold about ourselves, such as 'I am unlovable.' It isn't just that we are not loved, but that there is nothing inside worth loving. And everyone I know and have worked with on such core beliefs has a similar issue they hold deeply inside."

"So such a belief doesn't make me crazy?" Audri asks.

"Heavens no, Audri! That makes you 'normal,'" chuckles Alberto. "Welcome to our world!"

Audri lets out a sigh as she relaxes more in her chair. The relief of sharing the belief about herself and have Doc still connect with her puts her whole body more at ease, even as a few tears wet her eyes. She grabs a tissue and wipes away a drop.

Her face relaxes as she takes a breath, feeling her whole body release some tension.

"But how do I deal with this? Why do I feel empty every time it comes up?"

"Two more great questions, and a further indication you are ready to create a change in your life. For just as we can change our mental beliefs, like there's really no tooth fairy, we can change these core beliefs too."

"Wait, THERE'S NO TOOTH FAIRY??" exclaims Audri with a bit of a smile, wanting to break the tension she feels. Alex has been an outstanding model with such responses and tension relaxers. Audri has learned from her brother, but she seldom demonstrates his timing until today.

Alberto begins to laugh out loud and smacks the arm of his chair with his hand. "I love your quick wit, young woman! It will continue to serve you well, especially when you can create some distance and begin to laugh with yourself and others about the way we live in this world - the crazy things we say and do in life and don't see until we look with a different gaze."

Audri relaxes her shoulders and tilts slightly towards Alberto, resting her arms on the sides of the chair.

"I can laugh sometimes, even when I want to cry. Right now, I just feel rather tender."

"Totally understandable," Alberto says, releasing his own smile. "You've just shared a very deep judgment you hold. And it's scary when you risk vocalizing it, believing no one will like you afterwards. I want you to know that I admire and like you even more as you share such a vulnerable belief. You're a very bright and brave young woman. And expressing this judgment out loud and finding that the world does not come tumbling down is a courageous step. I deeply respect you for that."

"Still, I don't know how to change it," she says, throwing her hands up in the air. "I don't want to live the rest of my life this way," Audri says in her soft and vulnerable voice, tears again welling up in her eyes.

"It is not a quick change, in part because you've held onto this belief for many years with lots of experiences to reinforce it. It'll take some time to shift such a fundamental piece. I will help shine a light so you can see that such beliefs only survive in the darkness, never being challenged by ourselves and not allowing any alternative views or experiences to release them."

"But I keep experiencing this belief as true. Events keep happening that tell me it's true."

Again, Audri wipes away more escaping tears.

"If we hold a narrow perspective of what is possible, we don't see anything beyond that. We're like race horses with blinders. You know those small leather patches that are placed on race horses' heads so they can't see anything on the side? Those are helpful so horses don't get distracted or scared and stay focused on the path straight ahead. But they also limit vision, not allowing views of things beyond that. They keep a view much narrower."

"But I'm not wearing any blinders. I have nothing in front of my eyes."

"Dear Audri, we all have some sort of blinders. We view the world in a particular way. And if we don't question our limits, our boundaries, we never see the blinders."

Alberto pauses for a moment, as if to consider what to say next.

"Think about the discovery of gravity, or the world being round. No one could envision those possibilities with the belief limitations they held at the time. Not until people began to change their views, to hold another possibility, could they begin to see how gravity works and how the world is a revolving sphere."

"OK, I get the gravity and round earth stuff. We all know that now. I don't get how people ever believed otherwise."

"Oh yes, once we have shifted our perspective, it often is easy to see it and challenging to see how people didn't believe it. But allowing for greater possibilities is an essential part of any shift."

"But I know those things now. What blinders do I still hold? What do I still not see?"

"How about that we in fact are composed of love, and it's the energy fields that hold our physical form in place rather than the physical form holding our energetics in place?"

"What??" exclaims Audri. "What are you talking about?"

Audri's eyes are wide open, except where her eyebrows curl downward above her nose as she shares her disbelief in what Alberto is saying, shifting farther back in her chair.

"I'm talking about a very different view of who we are as human beings," replies Alberto.

"But what does a different perspective have to do with being love and energy things?"

Alberto chuckles a bit with Audri's description, then continues.

"There have been thousands of people who have had near-death experiences. While their reports differ in ways, there are some common aspects they share about insights they gained during the occurrence. One of the insights many people discover is that we do not just feel love in our lives as an emotion, but that our being is composed of love. It is the fundamental substance that we're made of."

Alberto pauses, leaning to his side, then continues.

"Some see it as a bright energetic light in our chests, and it may appear in different colors. When we close off our hearts because of hurts and pain, we have a more difficult time experiencing ourselves that way because it's a more subtle energy. As we grow, we focus more and more on the denser energies of our world and let go of any sense of what we may experience as babies. In some cases, people begin to see themselves in such contracted ways that they shift from being love to seeing themselves as unlovable."

"OK, I'm starting to think you're the crazy one here! Do people really believe this stuff?"

"Many people who go through these experiences change their lives completely, focusing on a very different way of living, and continue to say we are love. They challenge the belief that without feeling love from others, there can be no love in our lives. In fact, one common core belief in this world is that love comes mainly from the outside, from parents, family, friends, or God. And while all of these are possibilities, there may be another option too. It may be that we ARE love and just don't see it because of our belief systems, because of the blinders we wear over a closed heart."

"That would be awesome if it were true. But I just don't feel that way."

Audri again raises her hand in frustration.

"That isn't my experience," replies Audri, again with water floating around her bottom eye lids. "That isn't my experience at all!"

"I understand, because I felt the same way when I heard this idea suggested from my first teacher. And it didn't sound any more true to me then as it doesn't to you now. I understand," says Alberto, taking a deep breath. Then a slight smile appears on his face. "In fact, I was about the same age you are when I met my teacher and began to shift some of my fundamental beliefs. Given your vulnerable share about your self-judgment today, I'll tell you more about myself and my journey when we meet next time."

Audri leans forward in her chair again. "Hold on, you're going to make me wait a week for this? This is why I hate to watch a TV series!"

"I know. I hate waiting sometimes, too. But we're out of time. And that may be enough for one session."

"OK, Doc. But I'm not happy about waiting to hear your story," Audri says with a scant smile.

She takes a big breath and wipes her eyes. Then, she gets up, hesitates a moment as she looks at Alberto's eyes again, then turns and leaves the office. "See you next week, Doc, but only for the story," she says with a slight chuckle.

Chapter 10

Exploring Possibilities

As Audri steps outside, she sees her mother again waiting for her. Audri opens up the front door and moves easily into the passenger seat. She closes the door and smiles at her mom.

"Your dad's working tonight, Alex has practice, and Sarah's at work. How about if we get a sandwich at The Red Avocado, then pick up some items at the Co-op before going home?" asks Bella.

"Yeah, that'd be great," replies Audri. "I'm hungry, and I haven't eaten there for a while."

The scent in the car is more comforting than usual to Audri, who feels both unsettled and agreeable at the same time. It's strange what a contrast such feelings are and yet beginning to feel all right with Audri, too. In fact, she seems to begin noticing contrasts that have occurred many times in the past, when Audri had a more difficult time staying aware of both simultaneously.

Bella starts the engine and turns right onto Lynn Street, right again on Washington, then spots a parking spot near the little restaurant, a favorite for them both.

Bella likes the sandwiches, and Audri likes the homemade veggie burger. Although Audri is not vegetarian, she doesn't like eating much red meat. Veggie burgers are tasty and settle better in her stomach than "real" burgers. So she's happy with her mom's suggestion.

"You look happy today. How did your session go with Dr. Salvador this afternoon? You seem better than last week," Bella comments. "You beginning to feel more comfortable with him?"

"He's a different kind of guy. I didn't think I was going to like him. Today was challenging, yet kind of interesting too."

"Do you want to talk about it? We don't have to, but I am happy to talk if you want. It's up to you," suggested Bella.

Audri knows her mother wants to talk, but she also senses it would be alright if she didn't. While her mother often makes such offers, this time it feels like Bella means what she says.

"Well, it is hard to explain," responds Audri. "We talked about several issues. More than I can remember. They kind of swirl together at the moment."

Audri orders the burger and a tropical drink, while her mother orders her favorite avocado sandwich on wheat bread and a fruit tea. Then they find a place to sit outside, as it's one of those beautiful, warm spring early evenings in Iowa City.

People seem to be coming from the park just up the street, and others are in and out of the Co-op around the corner, carrying their reusable bags stuffed full of goodies.

As they sit there, Audri settles into a more peaceful place, although she isn't clear just why. But she likes the feeling and just sits there, paying attention to it for a moment.

"Mom, what do you think happens when we die?" asks Audri as she breaks the silence. "Do you think any part of us exists after death?"

"Wow, where did that come from? Is that what you and Dr. Salvador talked about today?" Bella pauses and looks intently at her daughter. "Audri, you're not thinking of suicide, are you?" asks Bella in a sudden panic.

Audri chuckles a little. "No, Mom. It's not about that at all. I just wonder what happens when our body dies. Is life here all there is for us?"

"Well, I don't know. Certainly many Christians believe in a soul that goes to heaven. Your dad still seems attached to Catholic beliefs, even though he doesn't go to church. But I've never felt comfortable with a religious explanation about death and a life after. I did read a fascinating book about near-death experiences once, and there seems to be something else based on their reports. And their experience also seems to greatly impact their lives. I guess I find what they say more comforting than most, and yet some argue that they didn't really die. So I am not sure. What do you think about death? What do you think happens?" Bella asks, returning the volley back to Audri.

"Alberto says he thinks there is an energetic light that's inside each of us, that we're composed of love. It's hard for me to believe that, especially with all the killing and violence that goes on in this country and around the world. And yet, I'd like to. I'd like to hope it's true. He said some of those going through a near-death experience report that at our core, we are love."

A young man with long, tangled hair tied into a rough ponytail brings out the sandwich and burger. He smiles as he puts them down and asks, "Would you like anything else?"

Audri wants to say, 'just a clear sense that we are composed of love.' But she thinks better of it. She likes to dream of such comments, but she doesn't actually say them. When her dad makes such jokes or comments, it often embarrasses her. So she seldom copies his style. Still, she loves to think about such remarks.

One day, she thinks, *I'll say them to people, even if only to see the effect of catching people so off guard.*

Today, the comments seem more amusing in her mind than in reality, however.

"No thanks. The food's delicious, and I think this'll do us," says her mother instead.

"Way down deep, Mom, have you ever felt unlovable?" asks Audri, continuing to explore the topic with her mom.

"Wow, there's another shocker. OK, let me consider that for a moment. You've had some powerful discussions with this guy. Are you alright with that? Does it feel at all disturbing to you?" Bella takes a bite from her sandwich.

"That's the funny thing. It's kind of hard in the moment. But it's starting to feel that in some odd way it's helpful."

After chewing, Belle continues. "This sure doesn't sound like a traditional approach to counseling. But I don't see any harm in it at this point, especially if you feel like it might be useful."

"If what he says is true, it feels like a much more positive way to see myself. I don't know. I guess I need to see where it goes," replies Audri, finally taking a bite of her burger.

"Yeah, I guess I do too. And I'm liking the discussions it brings up between you and me. I like that for sure."

"But do you have some inner negative belief about yourself? Is there a deep fear of something being wrong with you, or a sense of emptiness when that deep fear comes up?" Audri asks, continuing with the earlier question and her chewing.

"Mmm, ah . . . I need to think about that a bit. That isn't an easy one to answer with a sandwich in my mouth," replies Bella with a slight smile. Then Bella takes another bite.

"OK, maybe this isn't the best place to ask this, but I'd like to know. Am I the only one who feels such defects?"

Bella hesitates as she finishes chewing, then responds. "Oh, I can assure you that you're not the only one who sees themselves as defective. There certainly are times I feel that, but I'm not sure how to describe what the issue would be for me. May I ask if you are clear about the issue for you? Would you want to share that with me?" asks Bella, ever hopeful, with a curious wrinkle on her forehead.

"Well, it's not easy. Ah... what comes up for me when I feel the emptiness inside is... that I feel unlovable, like, ah, no one would love me if they really knew me."

"Oh, sweetheart, that just makes me want to cry! You know your dad and I love you so much. I don't see you that way at all! Is that how you feel?" Bella asks with tears forming in her eyes.

"Well, yeah, sometimes, when I'm... really down. Unloveable and broken. Then it feels like I need to be perfect in order for others to like me, especially to love me."

Now Audri also has tears in her eyes, both wiping them with their napkins.

Bella drops her napkin and reaches over to softly wrap Audri's hand in both of hers. She gazes deeply into Audri's eyes, a bit like Alberto does when he has something lovingly to say to Audri.

"My dear Audri. I know I get busy and don't always show it. But I love you with all my heart, dear one! And I hope you're in a place right now to let that sink deeply into your being. I so care and love you, and I always will, even when I don't take the time to show it or tell you. You're very important in my life. And I want you to always remember that."

Bella and Audri look at each other for a moment, tears slowly running down their cheeks, and then they let go of hands to wipe the tears away.

"I hope these sessions are positive for you and not just digging into negative aspects," continues Bella.

"It actually feels like a relief to say it out loud to someone who cares about me. Not just because he's family. Do you pay him to like me, Mom?" asks Audri, still wanting some reassurance that Alberto's reactions are authentic and not just because he is getting money to help her.

"No Audri. You must be doing that yourself," her mother says with a smile. "We just pay him to listen and assist you. I'm sure his reactions have to do with you, not any money we give him."

They both eat in silence for a few minutes. Audri takes another bite while also feeling happy with their conversation and wanting to connect more with Mom. And she's feeling more comfort in the silence too.

Such solace still feels odd to Audri. Yet, she also feels a bit overwhelmed and drained.

Usually not talking bothers her, like she should fill up the empty space outside as she tries to do inside. But today, she's in a happier place, letting the conversation and space just be.

There's something about resting after such intensity that feels relaxing to her. *This is very odd*, she thinks. *Yet, I kind of like it. Maybe this is the new Oddri!*

She and Bella both take another bite of their meal.

"He isn't as strange as I first thought," says Audri, finally breaking the silence, feeling the tension and comfort, yet still wanting to discuss these issues further with her mom. "In fact, I kind of like him. I'm not sure if he can help me, or if I even need help. But he's rather supportive. I guess I don't mind going, although I don't know if I need to go very long. We'll see, huh mom?"

"Yeah, let's just see how it goes. He does seem pleasant, and I'm grateful for the conversations you two are having and what it creates with us. I think it'd be useful to spend more time with just the two of us talking as well. I've let some of that go as I've gotten busier. But I'd like to change that. I'd like to have more of these kinds of conversations."

"Yeah, me too, Mom."

"As we're talking, what comes up for me is the fear of being lost. I think that's my deepest fear. And it does feel like a relief to say it out loud to someone else who cares." Bella adds.

She gives Audri a smile, which for the first time in a while feels like it's full of love for Audri.

Bella then takes the last bite of sandwich. Audri finishes her burger, then takes the last sip of her drink as Bella finishes her iced tea. Bella leaves money for the bill and a tip, and they both get up to leave. They walk over to the Co-op to finish some shopping.

"Thanks for saying that Mom. It feels good not to be the only one with such fears."

"Hey, I admire your courage to take the lead in such discussions! You seem more solid in your presence this afternoon, like you're settling into yourself or something," shares Bella with a smile.

She reaches her arm out and puts it around Audri's small waist as they head over to the Co-op to get a few fresh vegetables and cheese. They talk more about what they have been missing in their interactions and gratitude for this reconnection. They continue this discussion as they walk back to the car and drive home.

When they arrive, Audri helps take in the groceries and puts them in the kitchen. Her mother comes in to put them away, and Audri again assists. Then she turns to her mom, puts her arms around her and says,

"Thanks, Mom. I love you."

"Love you too, dear."

Audri turns and goes upstairs to her room.

The next afternoon, Audri is sitting on the floor with her back against Sophie's bed, as *Les Quatre Mousquetaires* are sitting around, relaxing and happy the school year's nearing the end.

Tanika and Ang are sitting with backs to the wall, and Soph is stretched out on the floor, her arm cupping her head.

Classes end in just over two weeks. The girls are talking about final year book signatures, followed by Alex's big graduation the next morning. Then the big party that evening. They still are hoping Alex will get them invited to the party of the year.

They agree that it has been a moderately good year, but they are looking forward to being juniors.

Audri glances at the others for a minute, then interjects a new topic for discussion.

"What do you think happens when you die? Do you think there's anything for us after death?"

"Wow, Audri, you sure know how to put a damper on a relaxing afternoon," smiles Angi as she moves down to stretch out with her back on the floor, her leg lifted over her other bent knee, apparently not that interested in responding to the question.

"What brings this up, Audri? You feel like you have a brain tumor again?" laughs Tanika, teasing Audri about some of her exaggerated fears of illnesses.

"No, just been thinking about what happens. Mom and I were talking about near-death experiences from a book she read, and I wonder if they know something we don't."

"Well, possibly," says Soph. "There certainly are a lot of things that happen we can't explain, like powers people have to see and know information other people don't."

"Come on, Soph. Don't bring up all that witch stuff again," complains Ang. "You know that freaks me out."

"No, I was thinking about people who can see and know about what's happening at a distance. My dad was telling me about the CIA and a program they had using people to spy on others from a long distance, and apparently some of them got pretty accurate," responds Soph.

"I think our spirit goes to heaven or hell, depending on how good we've been and whether we follow Jesus," chimes in Ang again. "That's it. We only get one chance, and we need to be faithful in this life."

"I don't think it's that simple," responds Soph. "I actually think we may live many lives, and the issue is how much we learn and how we treat other people."

"I don't know. I think I'm with Angi on this one," Tanika adds. "I think this life is about the choices we make to follow the teachings of the Bible and believe in God."

"But what if we had a light inside us that's connected to a higher power? What if we're made from God's love, but we just didn't see it because we covered up that connection?" asks Audri. "Maybe we are much more connected than we realize because we let go and no one ever helps us understand that light and connection? What if we don't know about it because we get so focused on our fears that we let go of that part of ourselves?"

"Geez, Audri, have you been drinking or smoking something? What's gotten into you?" complains Ang. This is crazy talk. If we're not going to talk about what we're going to wear to the parties, I'm going home. I don't want to waste my time talking about all this crap."

"Come on, Ang, we're just talking about some interesting ideas here. Don't get so upset over a little conversation," coaxes Sophie.

"I'd better get home anyway. It's getting close to dinner, and I have some homework to get finished. I'll see you guys tomorrow."

With that, Ang picks up her backpack and leaves.

The other three look at each other.

"I didn't think she'd be that sensitive," says Audri softly as she heard the front door shut. "I'm sorry to bring it up."

"I think she just has a hard time because her mom is so religious and makes them go to that fundamentalist church all the time. I actually don't think she believes all that, but she feels stuck in the middle," adds Soph.

"I get where she's coming from too," says Tanika. "My folks don't go to church all the time. But they still are fairly conservative about religious beliefs. It's not easy when you don't believe it all and not sure what you actually do believe."

"I don't know just what I believe either," chuckles Audri. "That's partly why I want to talk about it. I guess I didn't realize how sensitive Ang can be. I'll be more careful from now on."

Audri gets a text from her mom telling her to come home for dinner. Tanika and Audri get up to leave after hugs all around. Besides, there will be lots of time for conversations over the summer.

During the next few days, Audri keeps thinking about her conversations with Alberto, her mom, and her friends. She gets her homework finished for Thursday, and they end up going to a movie on Friday. It turns out to be more fun that Audri expected, even with the strange ideas bouncing around in her head.

Life seems fairly normal with the group. But Audri senses some tension still between Ang and her. She asks at one point if everything is OK between them. Ang says it is. Yet it still feels like there is some distance from Audri's point of view. She hopes she can let it go until another day.

Chapter 11
Transforming Teachers

"So, tell me about your first teacher, Doc," says Audri as she settles into her chair the next Tuesday. The words could hardly get out of her mouth fast enough, excited as she is to hear about this old man's experiences.

Alberto pauses and looks deeply into Audri's eyes, as if peering through her while leaning back in his own chair. "First, let's talk a little about your week. How did it go for you?"

"Well, I talked a bit with Mom about death and who we are. She got a little anxious that I was suicidal at first. But as we continued our conversation, she seemed to feel more at ease. I don't think she's all that comfortable discussing such topics. And I caught her off guard."

"I'm glad she isn't worried about you taking your own life and understands what you are asking. Most parents would worry about such possibilities, and, at the same time, are not prepared to talk about them. That's part of the problem, because so many adolescents are curious about these questions from time to time. Yet most adults don't want to discuss them or simply give the same pat answers they were given. But it's great the two of you can talk. So what else went on this week?" Alberto asks.

"I talked some about it with my friends too, but that didn't go so well. Some of my friends don't seem to like to talk about death, especially if it challenges their religious beliefs. But that's OK for now. I think we're in a good place. But tell me your story. It's been such a challenge for me this week, waiting to hear how this happened for you."

Alberto takes a deep breath, then he begins.

"I was born in Satellite, a suburb of Guatemala city. My mother was Mayan and my father was Guatemalan. So I was a Ladino, a person of mixed race. When I was

14, I was running with some friends who were getting into trouble. My mother began to worry about what would happen to me if I continued to hang out with them. So that summer she sent me back to San Cristóbal Verapaz, close to the beautiful Chicoj Lake, where her people were from.

"I spent the summer with my grandparents in their old village. I was a bit nervous because of my mixed race, but it turned out to be a wonderful summer. I had fun playing soccer with cousins, enjoyed lots of family gatherings and parties, and made some new friends."

"That sounds great, and you got some good soccer practice in, too. Not a bad summer."

"No, it turned out to be enjoyable in many ways. And while there, I also met an old man, a teacher. Someone most people ignored. I would see him wandering around his garden because he lived close to my grandparents' house. Later, I'd see him in the hills when we went for hikes. He was gathering plants and putting them in a pouch."

"Was he a little light in the head, Doc? He sounds rather odd," chuckles Audri. Alberto smiles and continues.

"Yes, he was odd, in some important ways. One day, I became very ill, with a high fever and chills, frequently throwing up. The only doctor in this little town was away visiting family. So my grandmother sent for the old man. He came and spent three long days trying to help me get better. He gave me an awful tasting tea to drink with a smell that matched the taste. And he'd put warm rocks on my body, moving them around to different places. We also talked about myself and about life, even whether there was anything more to me than my physical body."

"Was he a medicine man? Is that what you'd call him?"

"That was what many called him. And he had a certain respect in the village too. Then one night, while still quite sick, I had a dream. It wasn't just an ordinary dream. It felt like I was living this dream. It was very real with all sorts of colors. I saw myself as an older man, sitting in a big chair, wearing a traditional suit and tie, talking with people, both adults and adolescents. They would come into an office, then go, and others would come. I would teach them about themselves, about energies of the body and spirit, and about the ball of light each of us has in our chests. I could see it in myself, experiencing an amazing love, and in each person who came into the room to sit with me. As they came in, they appeared to have smaller or dimmer balls of light, as if covered with something, making the light faint. But over time, as they left, their lights were bigger and brighter."

Audri shifts in her seat, but her attention never wavers. "That's an amazing dream Doc. So what happened next?"

"I asked the old man about my dream the next day. He just gave me some plants to chew on, placed others on my chest with more hot rocks. Sometimes he would put his hands, which often were hot themselves, on different parts of my body, especially my stomach and chest, and just hold them there for a while. During all this, we would talk. He would ask about my own ball of light, whether I could see it or feel it. I told him no, I couldn't do either. 'But that doesn't mean they're not there,' he kept saying."

"Did you ever learn to see them," asked Audri.

"Oh yes, see and feel them. But it took quite a while, because I wasn't very confident in what he said at first. I had lots of doubts about him, about me, about my dream."

"How did you get rid of the doubts?"

"You pay attention. Then, you eventually choose whether you want to live your life by doubts, giving them all the power over you, or live by exploration and increasing confidence in yourself. But it's not a defensive confidence. Rather, it's one you feel in your body, your emotions, and most of all at your core, your essence. It's experiencing that light that makes the difference."

"Can you teach me that, Doc?"

"I can show you the path. But each person must explore, discover, and make the connection themselves. And it takes a lot of audacity to stay with it, to not get too distracted."

"So what happened next?"

"After several days of this, I felt much better and wanted to play with my friends. But the old man asked me to help him carry some items to the top of the mountain outside my village. My grandmother told me I should go, as he had helped me recover from my illness. So we left the next morning, me carrying his backpack filled with plants, food, and some utensils.

"Because I still didn't have a lot of energy, the walk was slow. Along the way, he talked about energy and people. I asked if everyone had this light, and he said they did. But there are many ways people cover or mask it. In particular, people cover the light from painful experiences, which lead them to create defenses and shut down or cover their hearts for protection.

"I recall us discussing what kind of person I wanted to be, the kind of critical voices I had in my head, especially about myself, and the worst judgments about me I would say to myself. We also talked about how my judgments distance me from others and how they are about my issues I don't want to see."

"OK, I see some connection here. At least you listened closely to him!" laughs Audri with a bit of a smile in her eyes and relief on her face.

She shifted again in her chair, with her eyes remaining on Alberto, wondering what he would share with her next.

"Yes, I listened and remembered quite a bit from our interactions. He then showed me how to pay attention to energy of the body, emotions, mental thoughts, and about the energy of plants and animals around me. I asked him if I could learn all this. He assured me I could if I were committed enough. We would stop and rest on rocks by the path, practicing with plants nearby. But I couldn't see anything at the time except a slight fuzzy haze. That's the beginning, he said, but I would need to spend the time expanding it."

"So you could see energy right from the beginning?"

"Well, the beginning of the aura around a plant or person. But it took a lot of time and practice to see more. Feeling it typically comes more easily. That is often what is first available that people miss because they only think it counts if we can't see it."

"You think I could learn to see it too?"

"Quite possibly. But I would suggest you begin with feeling. That helps in many ways."

"Then what happened?" asked Audri.

"We continued our walk, and by the end of the day, we finally reached the top of the mountain. We stayed in a hut owned by a man he knew, and we got ready to go to bed. The man sat on the side of his bed and looked deeply into my eyes. Then he asked me to tell him again about that dream. What did I see?

"I relayed the dream again as well as I remembered it. He peered at me and asked, 'what does this dream mean to you?' I said I didn't know, which is why I was asking him. 'But you must find out for yourself. You must get clear about your own vision and guidance.' And with that, he lowered his body and went to sleep.

"That was it? He wouldn't tell you?"

"I didn't understand then. But it's best for young people to wrestle with it and figure it out on their own. I lay awake much of the night, trying to figure out what it meant to me. But I was at a loss. While gathering plants the next day and all the way down the mountain the third day, I kept asking him, and he kept telling me to be in silence, to listen for myself. He talked about meditation, and we practiced a walking meditation on the way down. Then we stopped, sat on some rocks again, and he had me do a heart opening meditation. By the time we got to the bottom, I told him I thought I was a teacher, working with people to see their own light. 'Excellent,' he said. 'Now you just have to figure out where.'

"Wow, that's cool. And did you become a teacher?"

"Yes, and a counselor too. Much later, I realized I was visualizing counseling sessions, but I didn't have the term for it at the time."

Again, Audri shifts in her chair, changing her position and crossing her legs. All the while, her eyes focus on Alberto's face, waiting for the next part.

"What did you do after that?"

"We walked back through the village towards his little house. Just before entering, he turned and looked deeply into my eyes again. He essentially told me, 'Most people don't understand who they are or their contribution to the world. They just stumble into it if they find it at all, like wandering down a road and ending up in a city. It is a real gift to know your essence and use it as your guide, especially early in life. Take care of these gifts, and they'll serve you well. I've given you what I can. Now it's time for you to find your own way. And other teachers who will help you along your path. If you follow your inner guide, you'll always be happy. If you don't, you'll never be satisfied. The choice is yours. I wish you the best.' With that, he ducked into his house."

Alberto pauses and looks again into Audri's eyes, as if searching for something. Since she doesn't know what he's searching for, she just stares back at him.

"So what did you do?" she asks after a little time, still wondering what he's seeking.

"It was about time to go back to my parents. Soon after my trip to the mountain, I packed up my suitcase and rode back on the old bus. After arriving home, I told my family about my adventures and the illness, but I didn't say much about the old man. I told them how he helped me get better and how I helped him carry items up the mountain. But I didn't talk about the dream or his teachings. I needed to let them settle inside me for a while. But I never forgot it or what he told me. I just didn't know what to do with them at the time."

Alberto took a deep breath, then slowly released it.

"About a month after returning home, my mother came into my bedroom one night just after I got into bed. She sat on the side of my bed and stroked my head. 'So who was your teacher," she asked? With tears filling my eyes, I asked how she knew. She said she could just feel the difference in me, that I felt like a 'Cib', which is the Mayan term for warrior."

"Warrior? Did he teach you how to fight and defend yourself?" asks Audri with a confused look on her face.

"Oh no. She meant like someone who is strong and stands their ground in a spiritual sense. It's more like a Shaman than a traditional fighter. Then I went on to tell her about the old man, about what he had taught me, and about the dream. 'What do you think it means,' I asked her. 'You'll discover the meaning,' she said. I told her that's what he said too, and she just nodded. 'The importance of knowing such answers is learning to listen to your inner guide and following the heart decisions. Follow your heart and pay attention to your passion. It becomes clear when you stay with it.' We didn't talk much about it for a long time, but I knew she was watching me. She would not say much, except let my mind be still so I can hear the heart's wisdom."

"And is that what you did?" asks Audri intently.

She hates it when people don't finish an exciting story, but lets the ending linger. Now, she's anxious to know what he did to learn and follow his path, how he came to the United States, and whether he followed his heart.

"Yes, most of the time. There were instances when I would emulate my friends or pursue interests in acquiring objects. But each time I would not be happy. Don't get me wrong, I enjoy having a nice home, comfortable things, and having fun. But they did not help me feel content or peaceful. And I kept coming back to the dream and my inner guide."

"But how would you know? How did you learn to listen to your inner guide? Did you just guess, or were there signs?"

Audri could feel numerous questions coming into her mind, yet Alberto appeared in no rush to provide answers.

"Great questions. The quick answer is that I kept coming back, but no path is a straight line. There is a little trick, which the old man shared with me, and it took a while to sink in. The trick is to still the body, emotions, and mind so we can listen to the subtle self or true self. We usually are so busy doing, talking, and paying attention to many thoughts in our heads that it's difficult to hear this part of you, this part that we hear as infants before we focus more and more on the denser energies of the physical body and the world around us. Yet it's always there, always guiding and sharing.

"What's always there? What is guiding?"

"The subtle energies and true self, like intuition. It's always available to us when we don't keep our focus just on the physical and mental parts of our being. We typically have a difficult time stopping the physical activity and mental thoughts to listen deeply. When we do hear the subtle information, there are all sorts of messages and signs. When we don't pay attention or listen, there are only signs when we reflect back. So the trick is to quiet the other energies so our subtle hearing improves. Does that make sense to you?"

Audri wants to understand. She knows what the words mean technically. And she has some idea of subtle. But dense and different types of energies are confusing her. They don't make much sense.

"I get some of it. But to tell you the truth, I don't understand about dense energies. This is who I am," says Audri, holding out both arms in the air. "My body, my emotions, my mind. This is me. Audri. What else is there if not this body and mind? This is who I am."

"And when someone dies, what happens to the body and emotions? What happens to the mind?" Alberto inquires.

"Well, they all die, too. That's the end, I guess. But I don't like to talk about death much. It starts to scare me. Unless, of course, I get curious about something, like our talk of near-death experiences and information."

"Great. Curiosity is essential to begin seeing life and our world differently," he responds.

"But I don't really understand your question," adds Audri.

"So what runs the body? What gives it life and death? What happens when someone has a near-death experience and leaves the body? Who is the observer of the body then?"

"I don't know about those times. What happens?" asks Audri, feeling both curiosity about the answer and frustration that she doesn't really understand what Alberto is saying.

"People report being able to see the body, like an observer, someone else who can exit the body to see what is going on by watching it from the outside. The essence of who they are can leave the body and observe it. Others can simply learn to leave their body, or they jump out during times of crisis, such as extreme physical or emotional pain. We're able to do many things, because there's more to us than a body and mind.

"There's an essence, an energy or light that runs the body, that keeps it all going. And it's the essence that also knows the path that brings our greatest happiness, even maybe a life purpose. But it's a subtle energy, less obvious than our physical world or thoughts. That's where we can access other information when we listen carefully. Does that interest you?" Alberto asks.

"I don't know. I've tried many things, but I don't know about this one," responds Audri, wanting to say yes but also attempting to be honest about it.

"Let's try something. Let's clap our hands together 10 times, then rub them very hard."

He begins clapping, and she joins in quickly. After striking them many times, they rub their hands hard and fast.

"Now, hold them close together but apart slightly. What do you feel?" Alberto asks.

"They're hot," she replies.

"Excellent. Now stop, and just feel your hands, holding them close without touching. What do you experience?"

Alberto is doing the same thing. So Audri doesn't feel as funny as she imagines she might appear doing some stupid kid's game.

"They're kind of tingly, and I feel heat between them," Audri comments.

She can sense a kind of prickle in her hands, and the warmth is quite noticeable.

"Now, pull them slightly further apart, then bring them closer together slowly. Don't let them touch, but just pay attention to how they feel as they separate and then approach each other. Close your eyes, and focus on your palms for a minute. What do you experience now," he asks?

Audri smiles as she begins to feel something like soft strands of something, maybe like taffy, or a very thin elastic, between her hands. She opens her eyes for a minute, but she can't see anything. Then she closes them again and focuses on the sensation between her hands. She can feel the pull between her hands as she separates them further, and the feeling gets stronger as she brings her hands closer together. She becomes rather fascinated by her experience that's so simple and strange at the same time.

"Has the feeling been there before?" Alberto asked. "Have you noticed it before, or did it just begin for the first time today?"

"Well, it's probably been there before. But I've never noticed it. Never paid attention to it before now," Audri replies.

"Exactly," said Alberto. "The energy is always there. But we don't pay attention to it until we focus intently on it, letting our physical and mental sensations move to the background. Then we can pay attention to the more subtle aspects in the process. The same is true of the subtle self or essence. It is always there, but we don't learn to pay attention to it.

"We aren't taught to listen. But today you know. Now it's important to start listening to yourself if you seriously want to be in touch with it. Because underneath what feels like emptiness is the essence. When we're so used to paying attention to pain and the physical world, we are not aware of the more subtle parts. We believe we're empty because we don't pay attention to the subtle self, the essence of who we are."

Alberto stops for a moment, as if to consider what to say next.

"If we have such a part of us, do you think it would be important to listen to it? Does it seem to you something worthwhile to know?" asks Alberto.

"Well, yeah. It kind of seems important. But I don't think I've ever felt it," says Audri, rather hesitantly. "At least, I don't remember ever feeling it."

"Are you willing to try? If you could let go of the emptiness inside, the black hole, would it be worth trying?"

"Yes, of course it would. It'd be very worthwhile if I could let go of the emptiness I feel. It's awful and overwhelming," responds Audri with a stronger response.

"OK. Now I want to share one other thing for you to practice during this coming week."

Audri leans back in her chair, still focused on Alberto. She feels the tension in her body, as if she's in class and not sure she's going to understand the next idea being presented.

"I want to share a process of creating more space with your thoughts and emotions. When thoughts enter our mind, we grab hold of them and sail away. It's automatic and reactive. It's like they are a ship that helps us sail away into one direction or another. The problem isn't that thoughts enter our mind. That process can be important. But if we don't pay close attention to the process, then we automatically grab hold and journey with each thought without ever giving ourselves a choice. An opportunity to observe them but not get carried away by our thoughts, emotions, or activities. When we step back and observe all of them, we put ourselves in a place of choice rather than simple reactions."

"What?" says Audri, with a quizzical look on her face, shrugging her shoulders and raising both hands in the air. "I don't get it."

"Why don't we spend a few minutes exploring this idea. Relax your hands on your lap and your body in the chair."

Audri rests her hands on her thighs after shifting her body around in the chair to find the most comfortable position. Alberto also rests his hands on his legs.

"Now take a slow deep breath. Then gradually close your eyes on the exhale."

Alberto also inhales, letting his exhale be slow and steady.

"Keep inhaling deeply and slowly, just observing your breath, focusing on it."

Again, Alberto takes in and releases his breath slowly.

"When a thought enters, watch it, thank it, then let it go. If an emotion arises, do the same. If you get carried away, just come back to the breath," Alberto shares in a calm, soft voice.

Audri sits in her chair, paying attention to her breath, then remembers a book she left at school. She wonders if she needs to go back and get it. Then she remembers Doc's suggestion and comes back to her breath, letting the thought fade away. Then she thinks about signing yearbooks soon and how fun that will be, relaxing and writing sometimes caring, sometimes funny sayings in people's books.

"I can't do this," Audri shares as she opens her eyes. "I can't just focus on my breath."

"And how was your serve the first time you tried it?" asks Alberto.

"It sucked too," laughs Audri.

"Exactly. This also is a skill that takes some practice, especially when we get stressed or overwhelmed. It's like feeling the pressure in tennis or baseball. You need to have great reflexes with lots of practice for times like those. Letting go of thoughts and emotions is also a skill that needs to be practiced and developed."

"OK, that makes sense."

"Will you practice the meditation this week that we just practiced? Just do five minutes every day. Even when it doesn't feel like you are getting anywhere. Set the time aside to practice. Will you do that?" asks Alberto.

"Yeah, I'll give it a try. But I'm not sure how successful I'll be. My mind's rather busy some days," chuckles Audri again.

Alberto joins in her laugh. "I know what you mean. I see some of that in here. By itself that isn't a problem. You have a quick mind and quick wit. The biggest downside is that it doesn't give you choices when you may want or need them. I just want to help you develop a choice skill with your thoughts and emotions. It's an amazing gift when it gets as strong as your serve must be."

"OK, Doc. I'll do it," responds Audri with a bit more conviction this time.

"Great. Then I'll see you here next Tuesday.

"Alright, Doc. I'll be here," she responds. "But only to practice a couple of new things."

She smiles, rises from her chair, and walks to the door. Then she turns around and walks back to him as he stands up from his chair. She wraps her arms around him, and she could feel his heart as he encloses her in his big arms. She feels hopeful about herself and her life for the first time in many years. It's comfortable just being hugged by this strange old man with a big heart.

Chapter 12

Exploring the Unknown

It's after 7 AM when Audri wakes on Saturday morning. She lies in bed listening to the birds outside and watches the morning light peek underneath her blinds, waking her world. She loves the feel of her black bamboo sheets in the coolness of the morning. It's warm enough not to need a blanket, yet cool enough that the sheets provide support and comfort. They provide enough heat to stay warm, yet there is a cool hint of security.

It feels like a parent who furnishes some structure, which provides security, and yet allows enough distance that a young girl can begin to experience adulthood, a real person that counts in the world. Audri yearns for that feeling and basks in it this morning.

While relishing such comfort, she also reflects on her sitting meditation over the past few days. They haven't gone well. Her experiences have been an interesting time to reflect about life. But she hasn't been successful in the 'letting go' process. She easily gets carried away by the 'thought ship,' having difficulty simply observing. Still, she continues to practice, hoping to improve a new skill.

Audri, half reluctantly, gets out of bed. She considers trying another sitting meditation. Instead, she puts on her running clothes, grabs her favorite Brooks shoes, and slips downstairs. No one else seems to be stirring yet. So she decides to go jogging by herself. She ties her laces and goes outside. With tennis camp starting soon, she wants to stay in solid shape.

It's a beautiful spring morning. The kind that warms the ground and stimulates flowers to blossom. Audri notices the violets blooming in the grass, one of her favorite flowers.

Maybe I'll pick a small bunch when I get back to put in my room. But first I want to get in a long run.

She's been running about four to five miles, and today she feels like running at least that long. Maybe farther. She stretches her legs, wanting to avoid a pulled muscle. She feels a little tightness in her left leg that she hadn't noticed before.

Funny how you feel little pains when you pay attention, she thinks.

She does some extra stretching with that leg, then begins to run down Clark Street. She isn't sure which way she wants to run, although she kind of likes going past the river.

Maybe today I'll run through City Park.

She and Sarah measured the distance with the car one day. She recalls that it was about two and a half miles over to the park tennis courts, plus a similar amount to get back.

If I run along the river a bit too and through campus, it would add at least another mile, making six or maybe seven in all. I'm not sure I would make the whole thing. But I'll head in that direction and see how it goes.

Besides, she likes to run past the little train in the City Park. Her parents used to take them all there to ride it when they were young.

The trees and flowers are in full bloom. She loves the fragrance in the air, especially from the lilacs this time of year. It's been an inviting spring. And it still isn't too hot or humid. It's one of those rare springs where it actually warms gradually rather than winter one week and summer the next, with a couple of warmup days in between.

She loves this weather before it gets so hot and humid you feel like you just stepped out of the shower every time you go outside. She heads down Burlington, then Muscatine, and finally down Dubuque to cross the bridge.

On these days, running's easier when you're not held back with all the moisture in the air, making your body feel heavier. On mornings like this, it's like running without weights on her feet, running free and easily.

This morning, Audri isn't sure whether it's her external body or her inner self that is lighter. Maybe it's both. As she takes each breath, she inhales deeply, hoping for a faint whiff of flowers with each intake of oxygen to feed both her lungs and her joy for the fragrances.

Audri's feeling strong and running well as she reaches the bridge to cross the river. There isn't much traffic this morning. That makes it easier to focus on her running.

So what is running this body, she keeps asking? *What's inside that keeps me alive? Am I actually more than my body and mind? If so, where is this light? Where does it hide?*

She continues to search and ask questions as she crosses the bridge and heads for the park. She runs along the river bank, looking at the water moving slowly and steadily along its path.

She runs for a while without any particular thought in her head. This actually feels like her head is relaxing, even expanding slightly by letting go of the stress that tightens her brain matter. Then the questions arise again.

Does the water know its path? Or does it just follow along the riverbanks? Am I like the water, or do I actually have choices?

Audri heads off through the park, refocuses on her breathing, passes the little train and merry-go-round, past the tennis courts, and up Riverside Drive.

"Hey, Audri," calls Pam, a member of her tennis team running the opposite direction.

Audri was so deep in thought and exploring questions she didn't see her coming.

"Hi Pam. Keep up the good work," she calls as she runs by.

Audri feels her body getting warmer as she charges up the hill, breathing a little heavier, and still running strong. She and Sarah have run this route so many times that it feels familiar, checking out who was out and about on campus during an early weekend morning. Especially around the Union and the Pentacrest.

It feels great to be pushing my body and watching all that's going on in my mind.

She surprises herself as she observes what enters her brain without getting carried away by the thoughts.

It's like I'm just watching them move in and out, leaving space for new ones as the old ones leave. It feels rather odd to just notice thoughts. As if I'm observing all the parts of my life parading in front of the main grandstand, with me as the only bystander.

Audri's used to feeling odd. But all of a sudden that is too much for even her "oddriness." She feels a shudder rushing her body as she gets uncomfortable with the simple perception. Still, she tries to stay with it a while longer. Even letting go of the questions and not getting carried away by the ship. But then, this latter thought carries her away. She chuckles.

She begins to investigate her emotions to see if the same thing goes on there too.

Rather curious. I can feel them come up, but I just look at them. Like the river passing by.

It's the first time she can remember just watching her emotions, rather than getting caught up in them. It's rather unique and odd at the same time. She's moving her body, still running well, and having thoughts and feelings without holding onto them.

So who's the observer, she asks herself? *Who's the one doing this watching?*

While it still feels awkward, she's beginning to be a bit more comfortable with the process as she stays with it and just notices. At the same time, she realizes she's grabbing thoughts as she asks such questions. Again, she focuses on her breath and lets them go.

Just breathe, Audri. Focus on your breath.

About this time, she's nearing the home stretch. She checks her left leg. It seems to be doing fine. So she pushes herself a little more as she heads back down Court and then Clark Street, the finale. She always likes to go faster the last little bit, as if sprinting to the finish line.

"Hey, great run," yells Sarah as she approaches their house. "Why didn't you wake me? I would have run with you this morning."

"I didn't hear anyone, so I figured you were sleeping, and I wasn't sure when you got in last night. Sorry, but I didn't know."

"That's all right. I talked Marsha into running with me this morning. How far did you run this time?"

"Not exactly sure. I went down by City Park, then back through campus, like we often go. I think it was between six and seven, just guessing."

"Excellent run, girl. Way to go. I don't think I can talk Marsha into a run that far. But maybe I won't tell her until we get down to the park. Then she'll have to run back just to get her car! It might work, anyway."

Both young women are stretching, Sarah to warm up, Audri to cool down. It's been a strong run, and while she enjoys jogging with her sister, it's been a great day to go alone this morning and focus on the observer, as Alberto suggested. She hadn't anticipated exercising her mind while she ran. But she's happy with her practice.

It worked out well, she thinks.

"Marsha and I thought we'd catch a show at the Bijou or maybe see what's playing outside at the Pentacrest. Wanna go along?"

"I'll see. We might try to talk mom into taking us to Old Navy this afternoon. I wanna get a new shirt over there. I hear there's a sale on. So I don't know what time we'll get back. But we can talk later. Have a great run," says Audri as she heads for the house.

She's thinking more about a shower than anything else at this point. She feels the wetness and gets a whiff of her odor.

Audri goes upstairs and pulls off her clothes. She puts on her robe, goes into the bathroom, turns on the shower, and waits for it to warm up. She steps into the hot water, again paying attention to what's going on in her body and mind. She experiences the hot sensation pouring over her skin.

It's the same shower, but she notices differences. The fragrance of her shampoo seems stronger and fresher as she washes her body. She feels the sensation of the water dancing on her skin as it rinses her head, arms, and back. It's the same body that took a shower the day before. But this time she's watching what happens, as if from some small observation deck inside her body somewhere. She isn't sure this is what Alberto was talking about. Yet, it's fascinating, nonetheless.

What is the connection between the watcher and my body? My mind? Who's in charge? I don't get this. It all seems a bit strange. Maybe even crazy! And yet I feel calm, rather relaxed. This is an oddiness I like, she says to herself with a bit of a chuckle.

But if others could read my mind, would they lock me up? Am I going mad? And who would make that determination? I certainly don't feel mad! My head feels more at ease than I can remember. Alberto suggests this is helpful, but is it just make-believe? Is it real? Am I just making all this shit up?

Audri begins to feel a bit uneasy, as she can't remember a time in her life when she felt this way. It's confusing. She feels a bit nervous and a little relaxed at the same time.

Audri finally turns off the water after standing under it for several more minutes. Then steps out and dries her body with a soft towel that caresses along the cushiony thread ends.

She focuses on her breath again, catches a whiff of her shampoo. She lets go of the internal debate, puts on her robe, gathers up her running clothes and tosses them into her hamper as she enters her room.

A growl in her stomach tells her to head downstairs for some breakfast. With her phone, of course. She finds some clean clothes and dresses. Overall, what she experiences is a relaxed feeling pervading her whole body.

Her dad's still sitting at the table reading the Press-Citizen and drinking his coffee. She pours some orange juice and finds a bagel in the refrigerator to toast. She's going to eat just half, then decides to have the whole thing, as she notices the growl in her stomach again and a justification with a long run. Besides, she loves the orange cranberry bagel that'll be gone if she doesn't finish it.

She sits down at the table with her father and waits for him to say something. Maybe eventually notice that she's there. But nothing. She sits there like the other half of a pair of strangers, sharing a table at a coffee shop without acknowledging the presence of the other. Audri considers whether to say something. Then lets it go.

Is he pissed off at me, or just alone in his own world?

Just as she is finishing her bagel, she hears her phone chime from an incoming text. It's from Tanika.

Audri puts away her dishes and rushes up to change her clothes, as she needs to look "appealing" for a Mall trip. You never know who'll be there!

Soph and Ang are with Tanika and her mom when they stop for Audri.

The four girls enjoy their time looking through stores, getting a couple of items, then sharing sandwiches for lunch. They keep their eyes out for new boys. But no interesting prospects are spotted today. They talk and laugh. Audri is feeling like her old self again. They discuss possibly going to a movie. But nothing seems interesting. So they decide to rent a couple of movies through cable at Sophie's house.

Audri calls Sarah. She, of course, is not home. She leaves a message on her voice mail, which is only marginally better than not calling at all. Sarah might receive the message eventually. But Audri never knows whether it would be today or after college graduation. Still, she's tried to let her know, anyway, that she was grateful for the invitation. She wants to spend the evening with her friends.

On Sunday, she goes downstairs for some coffee. She says hello to her mom, who responds to her comment, then becomes quiet again. Audri isn't sure what's going on. She knows something is bothering her. She decides to go back upstairs, hoping to gather some information along the way.

She stops and asks Sarah about Mom. But she just shrugs it off.

Audri wonders if she's in trouble again for some reason she hasn't figured out. Sarah's pretty sure Audri hasn't done anything wrong. At least not this time.

Alex and Heidi, his new girlfriend, decided to go to an afternoon movie. So they wanted to borrow Bella's car. Her dad is at the restaurant. This would mean no transportation for Audri, unless she can talk one of her friends into getting a ride if the girls make plans to go somewhere. This always worries Audri a little. But then they can always take the bus as a desperate last resort. Audri has a book she wants to finish. She decides to read now, just in case some great offer comes along this evening.

After a couple of hours with her book, she goes downstairs to get some tea. Bella's sitting at the kitchen table with a mug in front of her.

"Hi, mom. What're you having?" asks Audri, trying to get a clue of how she's feeling.

"Just some tea. Want some? The kettle's still hot."

"Yeah, great. Is there any of that spicy Good Earth tea left?" asks Audri, trying to get some type of conversation going.

"Yeah, I think so. It should be in the tea cupboard. If not, there should be more in the pantry." Bella picks up her mug and has another swallow.

Audri listens closely trying to determine by the type of sip how her mother's feeling. A long slow sip means she's fairly relaxed and OK. A quick, fast sip often means something's bothering her. Unfortunately for Audri, this was a medium sip, meaning it isn't clear how her mother feels. Audri likes those sips least of all.

Audri opens the cupboard and finds the tea she likes. She gets out a bag, grabs a mug, then carefully wraps the string and label around the handle so the bag doesn't slip into the cup while she pours the hot water. She returns to the table and sits across from her mom.

"You have any showings this afternoon?" asks Audri, still trying to figure out what's going on with her mother?

"No, I did the open house yesterday and took today off. I didn't feel all that well this morning. And I didn't want to work both days. It just gets to be too much sometimes."

This isn't going to be easy, thinks Audri.

She tries a more direct tactic. "So is one of us in trouble again? Or are you just worried about work?"

She thinks there might be yet another option, but she wasn't sure what it could be. So she settles on these two. She'll just keep working until she eliminates options that don't fit.

Her mother glances at Audri and chuckles softly, with a shadow of a smile on her face.

"No," she says. "No one's in trouble. Not so far, anyway."

Bella's response provides great relief to Audri, who feels her stomach relax slightly. Still, she has a sense of something else going on with her.

Again, Audri watches internally as even more of her body begins to relax. She hadn't realized how tense she had become when she began to question her mother. Then her mother continues.

"I've been trying to sell a newer listing, and it just doesn't seem to interest people. I've had people come by, and this is usually a great time to get into contract. I'd like to lower the price, but the owners are desperate to sell for as much as possible while also trying to get rid of it. I think they're going through a divorce. But they aren't actually saying anything. They have two young kids and talk about a smaller place. And they're not leaving town or changing jobs. I don't think the kids know, and I worry about how it'll affect them. It's always hard for them to find out. Even when they have an idea of what's going on. But it's not my business. I just wish I knew and could help them. Anyway, just kind of thinking about that and what might happen," says Bella, taking another sip of her tea, holding the mug with both hands, as if it were some precious porcelain antique rather than an old mug from the Java House.

Bella cares about her clients. But these people she didn't seem to know well. Her mom often gets inklings and is deeply committed. But something else felt like it's going on too.

Audri asks a few more questions. There is still an odd sense about the whole conversation. She just can't quite put her finger on it. And her mother doesn't provide any further clues. Finally, Bella says she needs to get some paperwork done and leaves for her office.

Audri tries to let it go, thinking maybe she's just in a loony place with all this watching she's been doing. She decides to go up to her room and call the *Mousquetaires*.

Chapter 13

Digging Deeper

Monday begins with a minor panic. Audri forgot last night to review for her final algebra exam. She studied the material last week. But she intended to review it last night. The conversation with her mom threw her off a bit. And her struggling with Alberto's questions and story got her attention more than the review.

What's going on? I don't miss such prep for tests!

During her first two periods, she sneaks her notes behind books to cram for the exam. She begins to beat herself up for failing to study, then remembers Alberto's comment about 'perfection being perfectly difficult.'

Hum, maybe I'm not perfect, and maybe I don't have to be. But I also don't want a bad grade either!

Audri's body relaxes a bit as she considers Doc's point. She can do well without pushing herself to be flawless.

She takes a deep breath, then focuses on the cramming again. The test goes well enough, given the limited study time. Luckily, her other assignments and tests will still produce at least an A-.

Tuesday goes more smoothly, given that classes basically are over. She looks forward to gathering with girls that evening at Ang's house, wanting lots of laughs and a funny movie.

By the time her mother picks her up after school, she has lots of questions for Alberto.

Bella asks if she would like to go to the new Cottage Bakery and Café near campus after the session, which her daughter thinks would be great. Then Audri gets out of the car and goes inside.

Alberto opens the door as she steps into the waiting room, then proceeds to claim her typical chair as she moves into his office. It's feeling like a comfortable spot. And she has lots on her mind this afternoon.

"You seem to be deep in thought. Have you been thinking about our discussion from last week?" Alberto begins as he settles into his own chair. He again has on a comfortable looking pair of khaki slacks and white linen shirt. He seems settled in the same pair of brown loafers.

Audri chuckles to herself. *Maybe he doesn't have to be perfect either!*

So today the old shoes don't bother Audri. Maybe that's part of her increased comfort. She peers into his eyes and watches a smile settle onto his mouth as she begins to formulate which question to ask first.

The room once again seems filled with his warm energy. She's surprised how comfortable she continues to experience this once avoidant place. Like this is a setting to talk about issues and ideas never before discussed, with caring and honesty never before experienced so completely. It's all still new to Audri. Yet, there's a hint of familiarity she doesn't understand. Right now she's more focused on her questions than anything else.

"What does this essence feel like? Will I feel it? How will I know it when I feel it? Can you tell when I am feeling it? Or am I the only one who knows? If everyone has one, why don't more people talk about it?"

Audri has so many questions that it's difficult to pause for an answer. At the same time, she has a sneaky suspicion he isn't going to provide explanations to all her questions right away. So she might as well throw a bunch out there to see if he will bite on one. She's about to ask another when she thinks better of it and pauses for a moment.

"Sounds like you have been considering these ideas this past week. That's great. And I understand why all the questions. I had many too in the beginning. But first let's talk about your experience. Then we can address your questions. Please give me an overview of what went on during your week?" Alberto asks.

Audri talks about her difficulty in meditating the first few days, then her run on Saturday and how she watched her body, emotions, and thoughts. She shares how challenged she felt initially and how it got easier as she stayed with the movement the next two days. Although even then she experienced challenging times.

"Well done," Alberto exclaims. "You made a great start this week. Many adults have difficulty doing such watching without feeling disconnected or constantly carried away by thoughts. Sounds like you were present and just watched. I find adolescents have an easier time with this than adults. Maybe because they're still learning about themselves and aren't so final about their self definition. But this is an important step for you. So who was doing the watching?" Alberto finally asks.

"That's my question!" Audri replies. "How can I watch myself watch myself? Am I creating a new personality or going crazy?"

"No, you are not going crazy," Alberto assures her. "This is just an observation by the inner self. At this point, millions of people have learned to do this. Once we know we're not just our bodies, our emotions, or our thoughts, we can begin to watch them like a movie. And there's little to no stress or conflict involved. We just see them for what they are, just parts of who we call ourselves."

"But the watcher is an elusive part that no one discusses," blurts out Audri. "And there's still this fear that I am going crazy or something. Or maybe a fear that I am not real!"

"Yes, you're right. Not a lot of people talk about an essence. But that's changing. And the inner fear we experience comes from the loosening of the belief that we are just our bodies and minds. We learn this as we grow up because that's what most adults believe, having lost touch themselves with their own more subtle parts. When we go inside, we may see emptiness or a dark pit, if we look at all. Yet there's an observer too, different from other parts of ourselves. That observer, or essence, is a key part of our larger, greater self."

"But if it's so important, why don't parents talk about it?" pleads Audri.

"Because they have lost touch with it themselves. There's increasing evidence that children experience this in many ways while young. But parents discourage it or sometimes even punish it because it is not taught in science or religion. So they worry about their children not being accepted in a society where social norms don't readily include such possibilities."

"Then why is this so important? If we seem to be getting along fine without it, why worry about it or focus on it?" responds Audri.

"Are we getting along fine without it? Are we doing so well? We're killing each other in mass shootings and war. We fight in families and neighborhoods. We take advantage of people with products that harm humans and the earth, many times admitting it only when forced to do so. And we feel emptiness inside because we have such a narrow belief of who we are as people, or more often a negative view of ourselves," replies Alberto.

"OK, maybe we're not doing the greatest job with each other. But what's the big deal about seeing ourselves as more?" inquires Audri.

"When we get stuck with an issue or problem, the observer can see what's underneath the choices we make or notice choice patterns, sometimes even as we're making them. Backing up and taking a larger perspective can allow us to see different options. Not as a thought or emotion or behavior. But as the chooser. This allows us to see additional choices when we weren't aware we had them. But more on that in a later discussion. What was it like just to watch the thoughts and emotions? Please describe your experience to me."

"It was kind of awkward or strange at first. But then as I settled into it, there was almost a sense of relief. It was like the watching could happen. And it didn't take any energy at all. I didn't have to worry about getting caught up with thoughts or emotions. In fact, I could relax more. It was like a silent cartoon after a while.

Where I could just see them happen, but I didn't hold on. They just kept floating by."

"Yes, so who's the watcher? Is it you or someone else," asks Alberto?

"It doesn't feel like me, but it can't be anyone else. That's the strange thing about it," explains Audri. "So is this the essence? Is this what you call the true self?"

"When you were the observer, what did it feel like? What was your experience of it?" asks Alberto once again.

"I can't describe it well. It was like . . . . like I saw and understood things while feeling them, and . . . . and yet not attached to them at the same time," explains Audri, stumbling, trying to come up with the right words. "In some ways, it feels like my head and body relax."

"That's actually quite a good description," says Alberto.

He has a big smile on his face and looks pleased with her description, which encourages Audri to feel some success.

"It's a difficult thing to explain. But once you begin to feel it, you know the difference. That's what's important."

"But if this is so important, why don't people know about it and talk about it more?" asks Audri, a puzzled look remaining on her face.

"Oh, some have for a long time. But not many. And those people typically have been ignored. As we grow up, we learn to identify with the denser energies, like our bodies and emotions. Our parents get so focused on our learning to move, walk, talk, and go to the bathroom that we eventually ignore the more subtle parts. If parents don't focus on such aspects, then most children don't either. And eventually we see ourselves only as moving bodies that think and feel without much connection to more subtle elements."

"So we limit how we see ourselves? We focus mainly on the physical? Is that what you're saying?" asks Audri.

"Yes, exactly. We typically ignore other abilities. And as we feel anxious, hurt, or in pain, we develop elaborate and complex methods to protect ourselves, a defense mechanism. Then we begin to identify with these protections as who we are, as our whole being. We see ourselves as these defense structures, even sometimes, people argue, impacting the shape of our bodies and minds. In the process, we separate from the essence, no longer aware of its existence. Then, when we do go inside, we just feel pain, emptiness, or numbness, nothing at all, because of the constrictions of the defenses, rather than more subtle joy. If hurt and pain is what we feel, we don't want to look any harder or deeper."

"Yeah, I get that part. I don't like to feel the black hole either. I just want to get rid of it."

"But people don't really know how to do that. So we do all sorts of things to fill ourselves up or cover the pain, further distancing ourselves from our own essence. We keep our minds and bodies busy in order to avoid feeling the contractions inside. Or we numb ourselves with work, activities, accumulating objects, using drugs or alcohol. Or we blame other people, believing they are the cause of our pain. But we don't usually look inside because we don't like what we experience there. And most of us are not courageous enough to explore that environment. But you have that bravery. I suspected that when I first met you," Alberto explains.

"I don't feel all that brave. I just tried something, and it felt easy once I could relax and allow it to happen," replies Audri.

"Yes, easy when you actually do it. But in some ways you were closer, as many adolescents are. You just needed the willingness to try, which turns out to be hard for many, especially when they have been so avoidant of their inner experience. But you did it anyway. Even with the emptiness you so often feel. And you stay with it. That's your audacity, your strength. And that's the power of the essence when you connect to it. This's the force you will know and utilize even more as you get in touch with your true self."

It still seems rather vague and shapeless for Audri. She feels like she's following a path in shifting sands, the wind blowing in different directions, covering up her tracks so she can't tell where she's heading or where she's been. She isn't feeling overly confident about this approach, although she feels more comfortable with the watching. And somehow her trust in Alberto increases at the same time.

"I still don't get why adults don't explore this essence thing? Why don't they talk about it and use it themselves if it's so present?" Audri asks with some frustration.

"It isn't overly present to most adults. It's covered over. In that way, it might as well not consciously exist at all. If we don't believe in ghosts, we don't go looking for them without some experience to suggest they exist. And if a ghost experience is given an alternative explanation, we still avoid searching when we don't hold them as a possibility. Imagine you're outside on a cloudy day. Do you see the Sun?"

"That depends on how thick the clouds are," replies Audri with a little smirk.

"Exactly," Alberto exclaims, with a bit of a smile on his face. He seems pleased with Audri's answer, though she isn't sure why. "When the clouds are thin, what do you see?"

"Well, you can see the sun's form, although it's not as clear. It's like you can perceive it, even look at it's outline briefly, because it isn't as bright as it is otherwise."

"And when the clouds are thicker, what do you see?"

"You don't actually see anything besides the clouds. It still can be bright outside. But you can't even see the outline of the sun."

"Do you know the sun is even there when you can't see it directly?" Alberto asks, with a bigger smile on his face.

"You only see the light in the sky, but not the sun. And it can get dark, like when it rains."

"Yes. It's like the sun doesn't exist. At least in terms of what you see directly. But what if you got in an airplane and went above the clouds? What would it look like?"

Audri remembers taking a flight from Cedar Rapids to Denver, then on to San Francisco when her cousin got married in Napa. It was an exciting time for her, being on her first plane ride. And she wasn't even nervous. She remembers how her view changed as they rose above the gray skies of an Iowa autumn, which can be dark and overcast. Those were depressing days for her, and she was happy to see the bright light of the sun as the plane continued to rise into the blue sky. It was amazing how small the world appeared when she was up so high above the earth's surface.

"It's as bright as a sunny day. It's like there are no clouds at all, with a beautiful blue sky above and a billowy white earth below. And the sun's as bright as ever."

"Now you get it. The essence gets covered by defense systems, those we put into place to protect ourselves. In the process, the sun or essence is covered over, sometimes thickly, as with dark rain clouds. It can appear as if the sun has disappeared altogether or gone away somehow. Yet it's still there, shining as brightly and intensely as ever above the clouds. We just can't see it. The more it's covered, the less we can see. We still see some light, some of its effects, just not the sun directly. But unless we're familiar with the sun and know what's happening, we may see the effects without understanding them. This is how defense mechanisms work as cover."

"But we're all different, aren't we? Our experiences and hurts. They don't seem to be the same for everyone. Aren't our defenses unique?"

"Excellent question. We have different styles or ways of expressing our defense systems. Yet, the overall process seems to have similarities. The more we act like the clouds are our life, the less we remember the sun. What if you had not seen the sun in 50 years? Would you think much about it? And what if from the time you were born, no one ever talked about the sun? If you experienced it a few times after birth, you might remember it for the first few years. But soon the clouds would increase and you don't continue to experience it. If no one else talks about it, would you keep bringing it up? Would you think about it or focus on it if you lost sight of it and never discussed it for decades? It could still be key in our lives. But would you continue to talk about it?"

Audri pauses, thinking about his description and questions. The comparison seems too simplistic, making it difficult for her to accept. And in her mind, all she can think about are the words to the song, *Here Comes the Sun, and I say it's alright,* a song her mom loves to sing in the mornings when she's in a good mood.

Yet the comparison makes so much sense. She shifts her position in the chair, as her body feels uncomfortable. Then again, the discomfort probably exists independent of her sitting position.

"No, people probably wouldn't talk about it. Maybe we'd study it in school. But we probably wouldn't talk about it much. We'd focus on other issues that seem more relevant, even if they're not."

"You're doing extremely well," Alberto replies with a soft and firm voice. He still has a big grin on his face, but it isn't about humor. He just seems pleased. "This comparison hopefully begins to get at some of your questions, which are excellent ones. These are questions I too have wrestled with for some time, and they're important. We don't know all the answers, and there's much to learn. But you're understanding the foundation, which is a critical beginning."

"But when will I be able to know my own essence, actually feel it?" Audri asks, wanting some assurance that it won't take a lifetime to experience.

"It's different for everyone. But I'm certain it won't take long for you. In some ways, you've already begun to know it. It will take time to live from it, and the way and timing are different for us all. The important thing is to stay with the process. The feeling and confidence will come as you continue to explore and practice new ways of seeing, being, and doing."

"What should I do this week?" asks Audri, realizing that their time again is about over.

It's humorous to her that the time now is passing so quickly when it used to drag on forever.

"I think it's important to just watch and listen even more carefully."

"Listen. To what?" asks Audri, with a befuddled look on her face.

"Listen and watch. Watch and listen. You are doing some of both, but it also will be important to practice. Watch yourself and listen to the information that comes in to you. Listen to your body, your heart, your intuition. Listen to all sorts of subtle information. And ask where that information is coming from. Does it feel like a protection, anger, reaction or from a more neutral and peaceful place? Is it coming from your defenses or your essence? Is it from the clouds or the sun? And finally, ask how it's about you rather than focusing on others right now."

"Is information always about me?"

"No, not always. But often we think information is about others when it's usually about aspects we don't want to see in ourselves. For now, just ask how the information might be about you."

Still somewhat confused, Audri gets up to leave. "I'll try," she says. "But I'm not sure I understand the assignment."

"There is no assignment. It's an activity. A learning activity. Do it or don't. It is up to you. This isn't high school. But the school of life. Where you can learn lessons or not learn them. There are no assignments. Only opportunities, which you can take advantage of or let them pass you by. It's always your choice," says Alberto, also getting up from his seat with a smile on his face. "I suggest you play with such opportunities, explore what we discussed, and be curious. That's always helpful in this process."

Audri knows there is some truth to what he's saying. And she hates it. She usually does better with clear, specific assignments.

Chapter 14

The Party

S chool ends for the year on Thursday, with yearbooks to sign, pranks to play, and goodbyes to share before summer vacation.

As she leaves school with Tanika, Audri laughs about others still saying their goodbyes, as if they wouldn't see each other again in this life. But in a smaller town like Iowa City, she'll see most of her school mates during the summer, like it or not. And that means the Cher-Devil too, unfortunately.

She anticipates a lazy, easy going Friday, with some prep for the party tomorrow night and wrapping her homemade book of high school and baseball photos to give to Alex after his graduation ceremony in the morning.

The light dances through the window as Audri struggles to pry open her heavy eyelids on Saturday. The gauzy light, not yet fully morning but bright enough to see a few details on the wall, tells her the day is approaching. But at this dawning, the weight of her upper lids feel too heavy to hold open. So she lets them rest once again on the bottom lashes.

Her body isn't ready to fully face the day. But her mind begins to zip into action. She notices some excitement in her belly as she thinks about the big after-graduation party that Alex invited her and her friends to attend. She knows most of the seniors will be there, but only a select group of junior and sophomores get included. And a little sweet talking with Alex and Heidi on Wednesday seemed to complete an invitation coming their way.

I'll need to iron my dress. And I want those new shoes at the mall. I should've gotten them last Saturday when we were there. Damn, girl, what were you thinking? Maybe Mom will take me over. Or Sarah? And I want to do something nicer with my hair. Maybe Ang will help me fix it up beautifully again.

Audri slowly pulls back her covers and rolls out of bed, catching her foot in the sheet and almost falling to the floor. She stumbles a couple of steps and catches herself. Her mind is moving, but her body is still coming to life.

She finally stands firmly, then turns around to pull the sheet and comforter up to the top edge, fluffing her pillows before finishing her first task of the morning. The other pillows go on top, then off to get some clothes.

I want to get these errands done before taking a shower. I want to feel fresh for Tanika's party tonight.

She puts on her cute tan shorts and a white sleeveless shirt, then pulls out her white shoes. Even when she runs errands, she wants to look attractive.

Audri stops, grabs her phone, sits down on a pillow, sets the timer for 15, then changes it to 10 minutes and pushes start. She takes in a deep breath, intending to still her mind.

She takes a slow, deep breath, then lets the air out with a quiet whooshing sound, followed by yet another deep breath. She sits there, thinking about all the things she wants to get done before the party. She begins to make a mental list, then lets it go. Her mind goes blank for about 2.47 seconds, then she begins on the list again. Another deep breath, another attempt to let her thoughts become balloons that float away. Only to have them drift back with her list written all over them. Feeling discouraged and frustrated, she opens her eyes, turns off her timer, puts on her shoes, and goes downstairs to scrounge up some breakfast.

It's quiet in the kitchen, and the coffee pot is cold. Fearing it's too early to grind coffee, she pulls out some milk, a bowl, cereal, and a spoon for an easy start to her day.

When Sarah shows up, Audri convinces her to go to the mall for new shoes. After Audri cleans her room and Sarah finishes an assignment for school, they get in Sarah's car, then head out for the mall.

The two wander around, examining different shoes and trying on a few. The girls finally settle on a fun new design with a medium heel and a colorful leather top for both stability and style. Audri buys Sarah yogurt as a thank you. Then they drive back home.

Audri gives her sister a big hug after getting out of the car, then walks to the house for a shower. She cleans up her room, wraps Alex's present, then puts on her casual best. She reads for a while before going over to Tanika's place to help with final preparations for the party.

Many of the sophomores attend, with good food, great dancing music, and no boys of interest. Still, hanging out with her friends brings out some good times. And it's a great way to bring in the summer vacation.

The next morning, Audri is up early to help with a quick breakfast, nice clothes, then off to celebrate her brother's high school graduation at the Carver-Hawkeye Arena. Parking is challenging and slow. They finally spot a place and get inside. Dad brought Alex over early and saved seats for the girls.

The event generates a busy, noisy atmosphere as the excitement builds for both graduates and families. Audri has been here before, two years ago, when Sarah went through her graduation, receiving several awards for her academic prowess. Alex already attended the earlier athletic awards ceremony, which was fun to see. Audri attended as well, mostly to see all the cute boys stroll up to get their awards. She feels like she goes through dress-rehearsals for her intended achievements in two more years.

The family cheered for Alex. That was the best part of an otherwise boring ceremony. Beyond that, it was fun to cheer for a few other friends. The speech, on the other hand, would not have been missed if it had been eliminated.

When they get home, everyone goes to their own sanctuaries to relax. Rick heads to his restaurant, Bella to her office, with Sarah and Alex going to their bedrooms in preparation for the next event. Audri goes to the kitchen to get a light lunch. She notices both excitement and some anxiety about tonight's party.

She makes herself a salad, deciding not to add any dressing today. She eats slowly, feeling the tension build in her stomach. She drinks some water, then decides that's too much. She pulls out a couple of crackers, then realizes that's too much. She finishes her salad and puts her dishes in the washer.

As she goes upstairs, she checks to make sure her mom remains in her office. Then she goes to the bathroom and throws up.

Instead of relief, her anxiety continues to increase. But there is nothing more to regurgitate. She leaves the throne and goes to her room.

She notices the warmth and humidity. Audri feels sweaty. She takes off and carefully hangs up her dress, puts her shoes away, and pulls out her clothes for the big party this evening. Then she goes for another shower to clean off the humidity sweat.

As the warm water washes over her body, she breathes slowly a few times. At the moment, she feels in the middle of a war zone. Her old habits fail to provide relief. The new ones remain unfamiliar and unsteady. Nothing provides a sense of security that she seeks. The darkness hovers at a distance. Yet, there exists a space, a measure of safety as it neglects to swoop in and fill the void.

Audri suddenly notices that the empty space, at least for the moment, holds the dark void at bay. It begins to feel a bit like the space in her mind that provides a choice, enough distance to see options. She breathes in again, relief for the choice opening, even if momentary.

The thoughts flow away and the emptiness evolves into a type of comfort. She finishes her shower and takes her time drying her body. Now, everything begins to feel strange with a curiosity undertone.

She slips into her robe and saunters back to her room. She puts her party dress and shoes in a bag, dons some old clothes, then leaves for Sophie's place.

An afternoon of laughing, primping, and getting everyone to look her finest appeals greatly to her after this zone of confusion and change. What she needs right now is another party distraction. And this one promises to be the best party of the year. What a great way to bring on summer fun and let go of school year craziness.

Audri enjoys her afternoon with her *Mousquetaires*. They find some food to eat later in the afternoon so they don't have to consume much at the party. Then all put the final touches on makeup and hair, wanting everyone to look her finest.

"You girls ready to be fire?" asks Audri after the last brush of mascara goes onto her eyelashes.

"Totally," responds Soph with a big smile on her face. "I just hope Justin is there tonight!"

"OK, girls, let's get rockin'," suggests Tanika.

With that, they head for Soph's car. With her new license, her dad's sporty vehicle, and all looking their finest, they head for the Anderson's big house just off Rochester Avenue.

As they get close, they see lots of cars parked in the area already. They find a place to squeeze in between two sloppily parked Volvos and head for the house.

Lots of spiffily dressed adolescents are moving in that direction, as if it were some big game or musical festival. Yet everyone appears too dressy for any bleacher seats.

As *Les Mousquetaires* step through the doorway, led by Sophie, they start to scan the room. Each looks for guys who are attending and which one they might like to spend some time with for a while. They head for the punch bowls and glasses, wondering if there is some indicator as to which one is spiked. They want to know what they're drinking. And the glasses give them something appropriate to do with their hands.

"Alright, let's split up and see who we can find," suggests Tanika. "Remember to signal if you need any help. And I don't want to leave here too early. This place looks like it's poppin'!"

Audri glances around to see if Santiago showed up. Being on the baseball team with lots of seniors would get him an invitation. But he also can be a bit shy at times, even somewhat "anti-social," like Oddri. She wanders around, then goes out back by the pool.

She sips on her drink, trying to look cool. She spots Santiago on the other side of the pool, talking to a couple of guys.

At least he isn't hanging out with Cher-Devil! That's a comforting start to the evening. But I can't just walk over like I'm super basic! Who else is around that I can go talk to near him?

As Audri inspects the crowd, she sees Alex sitting in a chair talking to some girl. They seem to be laughing and enjoying each other's company, but she can't see her face. She walks around the pool some more, then stops dead in her tracks.

It's Cher-Devil!! No fuckin' way! Why is Alex talking to that dick?!

She reaches for her phone, pulls up her Favorites, and taps Alex's number. It rings several times, but no answer. She hangs up and calls again. Still no answer.

Oh Alex, you suck right now!

She taps on his number one more time. Finally, she gets a response.

"Hey, let me call you back later. I'm busy right now," Alex says softy.

"Don't hang up Alex. What the hell are you doing! You know I can't stand that dick!"

The phone goes silent. Audri grunts so loud two guys turn their heads to look at her and begin to chuckle. She turns away and taps his number again.

"Are you OK? 'Cause I'm busy. I'll talk with you later."

"Alex, how can you be hanging out with her? Don't you know what she's like? Does Heidi know? Are you drunk??" Audri inquires with a fair amount of anger behind each question.

"No, haven't had one drink. I'll explain it all later." With that, he hangs up again.

Audri turns around and stares at Santiago's face as he walks up toward her. "Hey, you OK? You look pissed right now."

"Oh, my brother has just put on his idiot cap, apparently with blinders!" grunts Audri, with a scowl on her face. "He's sitting over there, flirting with that dick, Cheryl."

She's having a hard time controlling her combination of anger and excitement. She's feeling the anger so strongly it takes a few seconds to realize how excited she is that Santiago has come to see her while still fuming at Alex. Again, she wonders how she can hold two opposite emotions simultaneously, both so compelling.

"Why don't you like Cheryl? She isn't so bad, despite her need for attention," laughs Santiago. "Do you know her at all?"

"Know her! We've gone to school together since 3rd grade, and she still acts like she owns not only the school, but this whole damn town!"

As she talks, the anger pushes away the excitement, which only makes Audri more frustrated.

This should be a great time. And I have to spend it being mad at Alex and Cher-Devil!

"Yeah, she can act kind of arrogant sometimes. But she's sure great with her grandmother."

Audri hates it when she stands with her mouth gaping open, especially around some hot guy. But at this moment, she can't help herself.

"Ah, ... what do you mean... who's great with her grandmother?" asks Audri, stumbling over her words. She has an idea there must be some type of shocked look on her face, but she doesn't have a clue how to correct what she isn't aware of completely.

"Don't you know? She and Heidi have kind of become friends because they both visit their grandmothers who live at the same retirement home."

"Friends? FRIENDS?? How can that be? That girl's a dick!"

"Look, I'll give you that she isn't nice to others at times. And she acts like the Queen Bee at school. But apparently Heidi says she's a different person when she's with her grandmother at the home. That's the person Heidi likes. Not the one at school."

"Well.... OK, ... maybe she's a little different there. But she's still a dick most of the time. And I don't get why Alex is hanging out and going googly eyed over her!" seethes Audri.

"Whoa there, girl. I don't know what's going on with them tonight. But Heidi was over there earlier, So she's certainly not jealous of their conversation. Maybe just let it go and check in with Alex after the party. Cheryl isn't putting the moves on him. I'm certain of that."

And YOU should know what her moves are like, Audri thinks as she takes a slow deep breath.

"Oh, OK. Maybe you're right," responds Audri with a bit of a sigh and monitoring of her mouth.

"So what are you doing this summer? Playing lots of tennis?"

"Yeah. I start summer camp in a couple of weeks. That'll keep me busy and hopefully up my game a bit for next year."

Just then, two guys come up and grab Santiago, one on each side.

"Come on man, there's a strip beer pong game out back. We can't miss that," pulling Santiago away and heading for the far side of the pool.

"Talk to you later," he shouts, as his friends pulled him further away.

As they leave, Audri hears one of his friends say, "She's only a sophomore. You can do better than that!"

Audri feels a choking in her throat as tears flood her eyes. She glances over at Alex, who's still talking with Cher-Devil. But now Heidi has joined them and appears relaxed.

It seems Santiago was right. That pisses me off even more!

As Audri surveys the crowd, Soph is dancing with Justin. She can't see Ang or Tanika. She turns towards the house to find out how they're doing and to quit staring at the "Happy Threesome" in an apparently enjoyable conversation.

As she enters, Tanika and Ang are talking to a couple of cute guys. So Audri heads upstairs. She finds a bathroom, closes the door and locks it. She feels her body to see if she needs to pee. Instead, she walks over to the toilet, lifts the lid, sticks her finger down her throat, and vomits.

After Audri finishes and flushes, she backs up and sits on the edge of the bathtub. She usually senses more satisfaction after such an episode. But she isn't experiencing much relaxation tonight. As she sits there, she's aware of the black hole settling into her abdomen, that old familiar feeling. She knows people may be waiting for the bathroom. But right now, she feels like shit.

She attempts to get up. Her knees feel shaky. She reaches for the edge of the beige tiled shower wall to brace herself, then stands fully erect. She finally walks over to the door and opens it just in time for a senior she knows from the baseball team to rush in for his turn at the porcelain throne before even closing the door.

Audri wanders back downstairs to see what her friends are doing and whether they're ready to go home. Audri's through with this lame-ass party.

She glances around but finds none of them. There are kids dancing to some stupid hip hop tune. Most times, she loves to dance, feeling into the music and how her body wants to respond. She loves to allow the beat and notes to permeate her being and stimulate the movements. But in her current state, any music seems dumb. Especially when no one asks her to dance.

She finally spots Soph sitting on a newer appearing soft brown couch talking with Justin, who has a freaky look on his face. And Soph doesn't appear much better with that air head grin from ear to ear. Finally, she decides to interrupt the tranced couple.

"Hey, Soph, I'm not feeling well. I called my mom, and she's going to pick me up. Will you let the others know?"

"Oh Audri, don't leave now. The party's really hoppin'. I saw Santiago out back. Go talk to him!"

"Na, my stomach's upset already, and I'm going to go home. Have a great time," responds Audri as she backs up and heads for the front door.

Once she's turned around, she pulls out her phone and dials her mom.

"Could you come pick me up? I'm not feeling well," asks Audri once her mom answers.

"Oh dear, I'm sorry you don't feel well. But I'm out to dinner with friends and we just got our meals. Could you Lyft home and just use my card? Could you manage that?"

"Yeah, sure," responds Audri and ends the call.

She had considered that solution before, but she didn't want to do it without her mom's approval and get into any more trouble. Everything's going well enough with her mom. She wants to keep it that way.

She pulls up her Lyft app to see how long it will take to get a driver. One is about 7 minutes away. That will work. She can be out of this pathetic party soon.

"Hey Audri, I couldn't find you. Where have you been hiding?" inquires a familiar voice behind her.

Audri turns, and there is Santiago staring into her face. Audri immediately worries about her eyes, her mouth, and whether there is any trace of evidence left on her face or clothes from her recent encounter with the throne.

"Oh, just wandering around. How was the beer pong?" she inquires, sans any interest.

"Stupid, as usual. Sorry for letting my friends haul me away and for their sucky comment. They were just being douchebags!"

Audri's body relaxes considerably with Santiago's apology, even with the shock of his appearance and comment.

"Thanks. I get that you want to hang out with them," responds Audri without much energy or persuasion.

"Hey, wanna dance?"

"Na, I'm not feeling well. I'm going to head home," replies Audri, again with no conviction.

"Stomach upset? How about some ginger ale? That usually helps settle my stomach. Come on. I'm sure they'll have something like that here."

He grabs her hand and they go for the kitchen where the greatest variety of drinks is available. Santiago rummages through the tub of soft drinks and pulls out a can. "How do you like it?"

"Straight up, preferably without anything stronger," replies Audri with a hint of a smile.

After Santiago carefully wipes off the top of the can, he opens it and hands it to her. Following a couple of sips, Audri's stomach is starting to settle. The whole Cher-Devil groupie thing is slowly fading into the background. It doesn't hurt that Santiago's sweet gesture and smiling face are in front of her, beginning to distract her from the dark side of the party.

Maybe there's some hope for this event after all.

Audri takes a couple more sips, then the two of them head for the dance floor. She sets the can on a nearby table.

Movement with someone she likes also may help Audri's black hole dissipate along with the memory of Alex hanging out with Cher-Devil.

Chapter 15
Emotional Inquiries

Late on Sunday morning, Audri slowly wakes and begins reminiscing about the party, the interactions with Alex and Cher-Devil, as well as enjoying her time with Santiago. It was the worst and best party of the year for Audri, which pissed and exhilarated her both.

This morning, however, she focuses mostly on how enjoyable it was to experience a tender connection with such a hot guy. That's the first opportunity she's had to spend any time with Santiago, and it feels appealing. She can't tell whether he's attracted to her. But enjoying some fun with him produces inner pleasure and satisfaction. It's just unfortunate it happened at the same party where her brother was such a dork.

Feeling hunger, Audri finally gets up, puts on her robe over her jammies, and goes downstairs to find breakfast, or lunch. At this point, she's not sure which it would be. As she walks into the kitchen, Alex looks up from his muffin and coffee.

"Morning sis. How ya feeling?"

"Doing alright. And you?"

"Not bad. But what was with all the calls last night at the party? You upset about something?"

"It's nothing. It's all good," responds Audri in her flat tone, not wanting to get into a fight this morning. She grabs a cup, pours coffee for herself, opens the refrigerator to find some skim milk, then searches for the low-cal cereal. She sits across the table as Alex continues.

"Then why did you keep calling me? You could see I was in a conversation."

Audri could hold it in no longer. "I just couldn't believe you were so infatuated with Cher-Devil. Especially with Heidi there too? Doesn't your girlfriend care at all about you being focused on such a super basic air head?"

"First of all, Heidi started the conversation. She asked Cheryl about her grandmother, who's been having some difficulty with her medications. When she went to get some water for us, I got to see first hand how much Cheryl cares about her grandma. I wish we had grandparents living. It would be cool to have a nice connection. Anyway, why do you hate Cheryl so? I know she hasn't been that agreeable to you. But you've got a lot of heat around her."

"If you could see how mean she is to us, you'd feel differently about her. Just a month ago she tried to get me and Tanika into…

"Tanika and I," interrupts Alex with Bella's smile on his face.

"Yeah, yeah, Tanika and I got into trouble by posting a photo of us at the Iowa-Michigan women's tennis match, where Tanika's favorite college tennis player had a #1 seed against a solid Iowa team."

"You ditched school and went to that match? Do Mom and Dad know?? I would guess not, 'cuz you're not grounded for the summer!"

"Oh shit! You didn't know, did you! DON'T tell Mom and Dad, or I won't SPEAK to you the rest of your LIFE!"

Alex chuckles a bit as he looks at Audri's red face with a bite of cereal puffing out one cheek. He can't help himself, even with the intensity of the moment.

"Relax, Audri. I'm not going to tattle on you now. I get the other side of Cheryl at school. She does like to have attention on her. But you guys are cool too. So just ignore her."

"That's difficult when she's always trying to mess with my world!"

"Yeah, but ignoring her might be the best revenge!" says Alex with a laugh.

"Huh, I didn't think about that. OK, we'll talk about it. Thanks for the idea." Slowly, Audri cools down as she begins to consider Alex's sage advice.

Audri finishes her cereal and coffee, takes care of her dishes, then goes up to change. She wants to connect with her friends to see how much they enjoyed the party too. And with Alex's suggestion, she's feeling more relaxed about the "Happy Threesome" from last night.

By Tuesday, Audri's feeling positive about going to see Alberto again. As frequently occurs, he's ready for her when she walks in, feeling relaxed about the session and settles once again into her favorite chair. As she glances around the room, nothing seems to have changed, except for the larger pile of papers on his desk. It seems to have multiplied since her last session.

"How are you doing today, Audri?" Alberto sits in his chair, wearing a newer blue shirt with tan slacks and his same old shoes. Or a different pair just as worn.

Audri breaks into a smile as she looks at them.

"Doing well, Doc. We had a fun party on Friday and got to go to the senior party on Saturday. And while I got pissed off for a little while, overall it was lots of fun!"

"Oh? Tell me about what you enjoyed."

"Well, only a few sophomores were invited to the Saturday party. But me and my friends got to go. So that was special. And then I got to dance with this older guy I like, who was nice to me. I don't know if he likes me that much, but it was fun to hang out with him."

Audri decides not to identify this 'older guy,' as she feels anxious about Doc knowing how much she likes him. She tries to talk as if he's some stranger to Alberto.

"My friends had an enjoyable time flirting with guys. And Soph got to spend time with a guy she's attracted to. Overall, it was pretty cool."

"Great. And what pissed you off?"

"Oh, at one point I thought Cher-Devil was hitting on my brother. But it turns out that the dick and Alex's girlfriend were talking about their grandmothers and medications. The two see each other when they visit them at the care center. So it's not that big a deal."

"You thought Cheryl was trying to hit on your brother like she did with Santiago at school?"

"Yeah, trying to get back at me again."

"And what makes you angry about that? What gets triggered when you see her doing that?"

"I don't know. But Alex gave me a great way to get my revenge. Everyone knows that she loves attention. So my friends and I are going to ignore her. Pretend like she doesn't exist. That will help us even the score!" Audri says with a big smile.

"Well, that sounds like a solid plan if revenge is your main purpose."

"Of course that's my purpose. What else is there?"

Alberto peers deeply into Audri's eyes, then says, "Healing yourself and the black hole."

Audri and Alberto stare at each other as she processes his response. Then he continues.

"Such a response will only be a temporary fix. You'll still carry the wound. And there will be other Cheryls in your life."

"Then, what do I do? I don't want to carry this around with me forever. Although I do like the suggested response!"

"As you watch Cheryl getting the attention of guys you like, what comes up in you? Besides the anger, what emotional feeling rises up in you?"

"I'm angry and I'm pissed. I hate her."

"Why do you hate her?"

"Because she is such an arrogant show-off. She'll do anything to get attention, and I don't like people like that. Nobody likes people like that! I don't understand what you mean. This is about Cheryl, not me!"

"Does everyone in the school have the same reaction to Cheryl?"

"No, mostly me, my friends, and other girls. Mostly sophomores."

"Then the reaction is unique to you and a few others. That makes it more personal than universal. So what comes up about you in this emotional reaction of yours?"

"That's not the way it feels to me. She pisses me off. Period. It's not about me. It's about her!"

"The action is about Cheryl. But the emotional response is inside you. We may not like what a person does or you may judge it in some way. But when an emotional hurt gets stimulated inside of us connected to that behavior, there's something we're holding onto about ourselves. For you, it may trigger your belief system, maybe something negative you believe about yourself, which then makes you feel uncomfortable or even upset. Or it triggers a past wound, such as a feeling that no one likes you. That you feel all alone in the world. You focus the upset on Cheryl, because it is easier to look at someone else's behavior than the belief system, judgement, or wound in yourself."

"But I simply notice the behavior in her and feel an immediate reaction. It feels too fast to do all that processing."

"It isn't a typical mental processing. I believe that emotional responses, like your experience with Cheryl, are a way to identify in yourself a past hurt that hasn't healed. That's why they're so valuable rather than something to avoid. We seem to create emotional connections or pathways to know where we're hanging on to hurtful past experiences or painful memories. When we become aware of them, we can heal them. Then, the emotional charge lessens until it goes away completely as we continue to heal. Given your heated response, I'm guessing there's some emotional issue about you that gets triggered by Cheryl. I just want to understand what that is so I might be able to help you begin to heal the belief or experience and let the emotional connection eventually dissipate. So what is it about her behavior that angers you?"

"It's just so damn easy for her to get boys' attention, get them to like her!"

"Does she make you feel less attractive, less desirable than her? Do you feel jealous of her? "

Audri hates it when he tells her the truth, even when there's some relief. "Yes, all of that! I guess I feel some jealousy. That she's much prettier than me. Anyone would hate her."

"No, not anyone. Alex, Heidi, and apparently others don't seem to hate her or have the emotional charge you have. She seems to elicit your belief that you are less attractive, less desirable, less appealing than she is. Less valuable than her. Is that true?"

"Yeah, I guess so. But so what? What does that matter?"

"That matters because wounds get triggered again and again while blaming others. We develop negative beliefs about ourselves from a young age, with a well formed brain synapse connecting to the emotional pain we hold in our bodies. What's important is that we stay with the awareness of the hurt and triggers about ourselves to increase our clarity and lessen the emotional wounds over time."

"Wait, Doc. I'm not following you now." Audri tilts her head to the left and narrows her eyebrows as she looks at Alberto. "Can you walk through that again?"

"Sure. We hold a negative belief about ourselves or some emotional pain about a belief or an experience we've had. For example, you seem to believe you're not attractive to others. So when someone in your life makes it appear that others think another girl is more attractive, that activates the hurt related to your inner belief. Then you get upset at someone else, like Cheryl, because she seems to be so much more attractive. She makes it look so easy to attract boys to her. That perception triggers the hurt in you, the feeling of being less or unattractive. Does that make sense?"

"Yeah, I get that," says Audri as she nods her head.

"Great. Now when you pay attention to your pain, you can investigate what that's about. You begin to see that you feel jealous of Cheryl, when in fact the basic pain is coming from your negative belief about yourself. As you begin to change your belief, that you are less attractive, or your belief becomes less important and doesn't define you as a valued person, the pain also dissipates. In this way, the pain is a gift rather than a burden. But only when you address the internal self-blame or self-belittling because you believe you aren't good enough in some way."

"OK, I'm getting it now. As I let go of these false beliefs, the emotional pains associated with them also diminish." Audri's face brightens, now pleased she is beginning to understand these complex issues.

"Yes, excellent. Some pains may go away immediately and others will take a while because they can be more complex. But the space we give ourselves with insights like the one you gained today will increasingly help the hurt lessen and healing increase."

"But why does Cher-Devil have to be so obnoxious about it? Why does she have to show off and be in my face all the time?"

"Maybe because she feels threatened by you, too? Maybe she's so insecure about her own appearance and boys liking her that she has to go out of her way to prove it, especially with you."

Audri stops to process for a moment what Alberto just threw her way.

"Are you trying to suggest that she's as insecure with her looks and people liking her as I am?" Audri asks with a hint of a smile on her face.

Alberto also breaks into a slight smile with both mouth and eyes. "Your clarity about the connection is a wonderful gift to yourself. If you can begin to be generous to both yourself and Cheryl about the healing of such insecurity, it'll go a long way to releasing the anger and hate that can be so deadly inside your physical and emotional energy fields."

Audri stares at Alberto for a minute more, then takes a slow, deep breath.

"You think that's actually true? If so, it's kind of ironic that I can get so upset about someone who may be more like me than not like me," she says with a slight chuckle.

"That isn't unusual. We often see behaviors in others that we don't want to identify in ourselves. And when we don't see it or like that about ourselves, we judge it harshly in others."

"So now I should love Cheryl?" asks Audri sarcastically.

"No. Just love yourself. Love for others can come from that. When we have unhealed wounds from hurts and self-judgments that show up as anger and hate, we further shut down our hearts from that hurt, both to ourselves and to others. For now, just relax your heart. Begin with yourself. Then it can relax for others. Sometimes immediately or over time. But I recommend you're soft with yourself first."

"That's not easy when I'm upset.

"Which is why now is the perfect time to practice. You don't go into a championship match without practicing along the way. This is a great time to hone this skill, practicing before those tougher moments that are critical for change."

"When I get so pissed, I just want to yell at somebody."

Audri's face begins to turn red just talking about such anger.

"Understandable. The hurts that we feel are real, even if the beliefs are not."

"This sounds appealing. But tell me HOW to be soft with myself? How do I open my heart to myself? I try to like myself. But it's hard with so many things I don't like about me."

"I'm sure there's some love for yourself in you, too. You've been supported in this world in a positive way by family and friends. And you have a caring heart. But you also have deep wounds that you've developed with accompanying belief systems. For example, let's go back to the basic issue of your worst fear, which, as I recall, is that you're unlovable. How does that relate to your fear that you are less attractive or less desirable than Cheryl?"

Audri looks down at the floor to think for a minute. She isn't clear of any direct connection, and yet it seems like there might be one. "I don't know," she finally says with frustration as she looks up.

Alberto takes a breath and pauses while looking at Audri. But he seems to be thinking about his response rather than searching for something inside her. Then he continues.

"Such connections are often not easy to see at first and may take some practice to get clear. But as you exercise the seeking, it gets easier. I know it's uncomfortable, but feel for a minute into your concern about being less desirable than other girls. Do you feel it, that discomfort?"

Audri also pauses for a moment to feel the hurt inside.

"Yeah, kind of."

"What does it feel like?"

"Well, it's this pain in my chest. A long pain line extending from my throat to my stomach, kind of on my left side."

"Good job. Now feel into being unlovable. How might they be connected?"

Audri feels the black hole of unlovability, appearing to extend eternally. She feels it all around her heart and now encapsulates her entire chest and abdomen. She hates it, hates focusing on it.

"I don't want to do this. It feels terrible. I want to get rid of it, not feel more of it."

"I get that, Audri. And I'm sorry to push you to feel this right now. But it's never far away. And I want it to lessen. Sometimes healing is uncomfortable when we inspect the wounds. Like when your parents clean a cut so it won't get infected. Please just stay with me for a few minutes. We won't be at this long. Try asking yourself the question, how are these two related? Let the awareness rise up from the discomfort to your mind so you can get clear. Allow your mind to be empty and ask the question."

Again, Audri feels into the discomfort and pain of these two issues, not liking it any more than last time.

She asks herself the question, *how do I get some clarity out of this shit*.

"Maybe close your eyes and relax into a kind of meditative state, sitting with the question. Then let me know whatever comes up for you."

Audri closes her eyes, then gets curious about what Alberto is doing while her eyes are closed. She tries to sneak a peek and sees his eyes open, looking at her. Alberto smiles at her.

"I know it's a challenge to do this, but just try, please."

She closes her eyes again and stays with this for a few minutes, wanting to know. Yet feeling uncomfortable with the process and the silence too. Her body feels stiff, tense, as she drops her arms to her side.

She stays with it, trying to be patient, then slowly breathes several times. She hears Alberto breathing with her, which feels supportive, even in the pain. As her body relaxes a bit, one thought comes to mind.

"I only feel lovable when someone likes me," shares Audri as she opens her eyes.

"Well done, Audri! That isn't easy, especially with a core issue. And as you become aware of the connection, how does your body respond?"

"Ah, not sure. I guess I'm feeling some relief.... It's like I've solved a puzzle. I feel more relaxed. And some success," Audri says with a bit of a smile. She closes her eyes again. "Now, I feel the black hole move away some."

"Yes, it's done its job for the moment. It's reminded you of another lie in your belief system. That love can only occur when someone else likes you or is attracted to you."

"But how do I know it's a lie? Who says it's a lie?"

"I do. Because I know how these systems work. And they're based on the worst fear we have about ourselves. But that fear is a distortion of who we are based on negative judgments we make up about ourselves and negative feedback from others that we end up taking in as truth. I won't ask you to simply believe me forever because I say that. Yet, I'll ask you to trust me temporarily. Until you've more experience with it. But let's move on to a second step. Close your eyes and focus on your heart again. What do you feel?"

"I guess I am aware of it. I don't feel anything much."

"Try to increase your focus there. Imagine what it looks like, how it's beating, sending life blood to the rest of your body, spreading oxygen to every cell, keeping you alive. Now, just imagine that by you wishing for it, your heart can relax just a little. As you take a deep breath, allow it to beat with a little less effort. Are you able to feel some of that?"

"A little, at least. It's beginning to feel a bit more relaxed."

"Great. Now let's add another piece. Please keep your eyes closed so you can focus on your heart. In addition to the beating and the blood moving in and out, see if you can add a sense of love in your heart, like a warm thick liquid that can spread. This substance moves anywhere you want it to go. Even without veins. Or anything to confine it. For the present, just let it spread through your entire heart, filling every part of it with the power of love that has no clear source. It's simply present and filling.

After a few moments, Audri responds. "OK, I kind of feel it."

"Great! Just stay with it for a few more minutes. Let it get bigger and the feeling get stronger."

Audri sits with the sensation, pleased how it impacts her.

"So what do I do with it?"

"Let your heart soften more, if it will. What happens to the liquid substance?"

Audri tries to let her heart soften and is surprised by the response.

"It gets stronger!"

"Yes. Now as the love liquid gets stronger, let it slowly spread beyond the heart. Let it move out from there to other parts of the body. Maybe include your whole chest or your stomach and intestines. Even your shoulders. Take a minute to let it spread."

Audri focuses on expanding the thick substance. It feels pleasant as it moves further out into the chest and abdomen areas. She, in fact, is surprised how enjoyable it feels as it extends outward.

"What are you aware of now? Do you feel any jealousy of Cheryl?"

Audri stops to notice for a moment. "No. I don't care about Cheryl when I feel this!"

"Yes, well done! This is the softening of the heart or heart opening, allowing this loving feeling to spread through your body. This is the practice I suggest you work into a daily routine and as part of your meditation."

"But can I do this alone? Can I do this without your help?

"Of course you can. And we'll practice here, too. But you're capable of doing this whenever and wherever you want. As you practice, it gets easier. And as a part of the practice, play with accepting who you are. Love who you are, even if there are still changes you want to make. And let go of the need to meet external judgments about appearance or other aspects that are used as sticks to beat yourself because you think you don't measure up to some unobtainable external standard. The secret is not to be the smartest or prettiest, but to be our 'self-lovingest'.

"What do you mean by that, Doc?" asks Audri as she opens her eyes to look at him.

"I mean to be the best Self you can be. The most accepting of you and loving that. You can want and work to be better at parts of your life, like tennis and friendship, while also loving who you are with a completely open heart. There may always be someone better at something. But the question is whether you're as good as you want to be without a comparison to others. Just focus on what you want for yourself, your desire, your intention. Sticking with what you intend with your life goes a long way."

Audri gives Alberto a half-hearted smile. She isn't as confident she can pull this off on a regular basis.

"I'll give it a try."

"That's all I ask. If you just keep at it, this will become easier and more accessible. You may struggle some at first, just like the meditation itself. How's that going, by the way?"

"Some days are good. Some aren't so good. And some days I don't do it at all," chuckles Audri.

"I love your candor, Audri!"

They both get up, knowing the session is about to end. Alberto rises with a smile. Audri gets up with considerable doubt sprinkled with a dusting of determination for change. The dusting helps her manage another small smile too.

Chapter 16

Ups and Downs

B y Sunday, Audri has been practicing a meditation and heart softening session every morning. Today, it goes relatively well again, as it did a couple of days last week. But the previous two days felt like her attempts sucked.

As she sits this morning, she notices that by beginning with the heart softening, the meditation becomes easier. That's something she didn't consider earlier in the week, and Alberto didn't mention. After the meditation, Audri feels more relaxed, as she did on Tuesday at her session.

This feels like a more pleasant way to spend my day, she thinks.

After the sitting, Audri calls Tanika to see about going to the mall, maybe catching a movie too. But Tanika has a family gathering at her uncle's place, so she can't go. Next she tries Ang, but she doesn't answer, and neither does Soph.

After hearing her mom and dad arguing again this morning, she doesn't want to stay around the house. Yet she also doesn't feel like going for a run today or taking the bus to the other side of town. So she decides to walk downtown, maybe catch a movie at the FilmScene, and have some lunch near there. She just wants to remove herself from the house.

Audri picks out comfortable white shorts, her new pink top, and some fun socks. She showers, gets dressed, and heads for the kitchen. As she descends the stairs, she notices that her heart still feels softer, which is delightful.

I think this is the first time such a feeling has continued to last. I kind of like it!

She greets her dad as she walks into the kitchen.

"Hey back at ya. How you doin' this morning?"

"Pretty good. OK if I go downtown, maybe catch a movie?"

"Which movie are you thinking of seeing?" Rick asks as he takes another sip of coffee.

"Brooklyn, probably." Audri watches for her father's reactions, then heads to the counter for a cup of coffee.

"I think your mom saw that with some friends and liked it. Doing anything else today?"

Audri turns back to face her dad. "Na, just hanging out. Maybe get some lunch first. Can I have a twenty?"

"Ah,... OK," Rick replies as he pulls out his wallet and gives her the money.

"Thanks Dad."

Audri grabs her coffee, pulls off a banana from the bunch, then sits in silence to eat with her dad. She allows her shoulders to relax again, wanting to maintain the feeling that started during her meditation. She also checks in and includes a softening of her heart. As she finishes the banana and coffee, she puts the cup in the washer, then tosses her peel into the compost bucket.

"Thanks for the money," she says as she leaves the kitchen.

"Have a great time."

Audri opens the front door and heads for downtown. It's only a mile, and this morning she feels like a stroll as she pays attention to her heart again. It's still feeling soft, and the caffeine only seems to amplify the openness. This surprises her too.

She stops to smell some red roses after she turns onto Summit Street, as her whole body relaxes a bit more. She imagines her feet breathing in the energy of the earth as she takes one step after another along the Summit sidewalk. There's no hurry. Just a meander as she now turns west on Burlington. For Audri, this is an usually slow pace, as she's typically in a hurry to get somewhere.

If anything, today, she's leaving the house and her parents' argument rather than hustling to some destination. And yet, it is mostly just moving. Not so much walking away or to, but a shifting of her body weight as she alternates her steps one foot at a time.

Wow, my heart still feels soft. Amazingly so. It feels different when I don't focus on anything. Some event, some upset. I like this feeling. Wonder how long it will last?

Ang's call startles her, but happy when told that she and Soph will join her. Audri happily suggests they meet at Estela's for some food first, then go to a movie.

Alright! Glad they can come.

Even as she waits for the light to change at Gilbert Street, she does so patiently. She notices her unusually calm mind. She inhales another slow breath, paying attention to her exhale while relaxing her shoulders more.

This is awesome. I like this inner sensation, this peacefulness for a change! I can breathe! And slower breaths are more relaxing.

Audri stops at Estela's to wait for Ang and Soph. Then she decides to find a table inside and wait for them there.

As she enters, she notices Cheryl sitting at a table alone. Audri thinks about leaving, hesitates, then decides to walk over to Cheryl's table instead.

"Guess they'll let any hobo in this place," chuckles Cheryl as she glances up at her.

"You should know," Audri starts to say, wanting to continue with *you got here first*. She thinks better of it, and instead says, "No, wait. Can I sit down and join you?"

Cheryls appears rather puzzled. "I guess so, but why?"

Audri hesitates, then asks, "How's your grandmother?" as she sits down on the other side of the table.

Cheryl gives her a snide look, her eyebrows moving together in a wrinkle. "Wow, low key, girl, even for a brunette!" laughs Cheryl. "What's with you today? Why the hell would you ask about my grandmother?"

Audri just peers into Cheryl's eyes for a few moments, checks in with her heart again, then responds.

" I hear she has been having some difficulties. I'm sorry to hear that. She getting any better?"

Cheryl stops and stares at Audri, a curiosity in her eyes as she brings her eyebrows together again. She appears to be sorting out the true meaning of her question.

"Why do you bring up my grandma? What's going on?"

Audri takes a deep breath, feels briefly into her heart again, then continues.

"I just heard she was having trouble with some medication. I hope she's doing better. If you're visiting her often, she must mean a lot to you."

Still, with a rather shocked look on her face, Cheryl continues to stare at Audri. Finally, she relaxes her face a little and shifts her tone.

"Well,... thanks. They, ah, seem to have found the right dosage, and she's doing better. But how did you know?" asks Cheryl, with her eyes more open than usual and her eyebrows wrinkled above her nose once again.

"My brother told me. I hope that's OK. It's made us realize we wish our grandparents were alive. If I had an ill grandmother, I would worry too when something starts going wrong."

Now Cheryl's whole face softens, and a tiny smile begins to appear on her mouth.

"Yeah, I do worry. She's getting older and more frail. Not sure she has much time left."

"I'm sorry, Cheryl."

"Thanks. Yeah, me too!"

"You must be close. I hope she lives a long time."

"Thanks, Audri. But, I have to ask. Why this sudden change in attitude? You and your friends always seem to be pissed at me."

"Yeah, true. But I don't wanna be so angry or hateful."

"Why? You trying some new tactic?"

"No. No new tactic. But I know you're becoming friends with Heidi and Alex. I'd like to get to know you better, too."

"This is some trick, isn't it! I don't trust this sudden change."

"I don't mean it as any trick. Alex just pointed out that there is a side of you I don't actually know. And I trust his view of people."

"Well,… OK then, I guess. It makes it easier to like your brother. I might even get to like you in time!"

Cheryl laughs at her own comment.

Audri chuckles again as she checks in with her heart. It feels even more relaxed, as does her gut.

"Cool. And I'll certainly be happy not to feel so much tension every time I see you. Even that'll be a relief."

"I don't mean to be distrustful, but will this continue?"

"That's certainly my intention. Can't promise, but I'll try."

Cheryl just stares at Audri for a minute. "Well, OK girl. If you forget, I'll be happy to remind you," Cheryl says with another chuckle.

"Can I ask about one other thing?" says Audri.

"I guess. What is it?"

"I'm just curious. How did you get a hold of that pic of Nika and me at the tennis match?"

"It wasn't that hard. Angelina was looking at it, and I asked to see it. Then I just took a minute to forward it to myself so I could post it. Easy," laughs Cheryl.

"Oh, OK. Yeah, easy enough. Thanks."

"Sure. See ya around." And with that, she gets up, throws away her trash, and leaves the restaurant.

Audri continues to sit and process this recent change in her interactions with Cheryl. She notices a release in her gut, even a little fondness for her identified villain.

This does feel more relaxing! I'm surprised at how much! She's sitting with this feeling when Ang and Soph walk up and join her on the other side of the table.

"Hey, I just saw Cher-Devil walk out? I'm surprised you two are in the same restaurant!" Ang says with a hardy laugh. "You didn't turn around and walk out when you saw her?"

"No, I sat down and talked with her."

"What? What the hell would you two talk about?" asks Ang with a shocked look on her face.

Audri chuckles to herself as Ang's response.

"Well, I actually talked to her about her grandmother."

"Are you shitting us right now?" asks Soph.

"Why the hell would you do that? You can't stand to look at her. And we all back you up when you get pissed at something she does! What's this all about? I don't get it!" Ang responds, raising her voice in the process.

Audri takes a moment to settle into herself again, wanting to be as heartful with Ang and Soph as she was with Cheryl.

"I've been learning about being in a more peaceful place. And how I can begin to see others differently. Alex told me that there's another side to Cheryl that I don't see. So I decided to try it out this morning. It was a spontaneous thing."

"Well, I still don't get it. It sounds like you're trying to make up with her. What the hell, Audri? What are we supposed to think? You want us to be lovey dovey with that dick now?" Ang's face is getting redder, as it does when she gets upset. This bothers Audri. Soph seems to be shocked as well at the whole conversation.

"No, I just want to be less irritated and upset, with her and others," responds Audri.

"What the hell are you talking about? Who are you? I don't know you anymore," chimes in Ang.

"I don't mean to get you upset. I'm just tired of being irritated with her all the time," says Audri.

"But it's not just you!" responds Soph. "We care about you. So we all get upset with her."

"And that's part of my point," Audri adds. "You guys are great at supporting me. But then we all get pissed off. And it's mostly because I'm bothered by her."

"But what about the photo she posted of you and Tanika at the Hawkeye tennis match? She was trying to get you both into trouble!" declares Ang.

"Yeah, but it's like a war with lots of different battles," responds Audri. "If we weren't so mean to her, she wouldn't try to get even. And that's a lot of wasted time and energy on all our parts."

"But we don't care about that. We care about you," says Soph. "Because you have our backs too."

"I try. And you have my back. All three of you do. But wouldn't life be easier if we could ignore her and just do what we want?" Audri asks. "Wouldn't it be great to enjoy our lives and what we do instead of reacting to what others are doing all the time? When I was talking with Alex last week, he suggested we just ignore Cheryl. And that may bother her more than getting upset if she's seeking so much attention. And that got me thinking about how much time we spend tracking her and being pissed off at what she does."

"But she deserves it. She's a dick!" emphasizes Ang, even while softening her voice so others won't easily hear.

"Yeah, I've got to agree with Ang on this. I don't get it either," says Soph.

Audri smiles at their responses. "Yeah, not going to argue about not being that nice to us. And yet, it may have more to do with my jealousy than what Cheryl does."

Soph leans back in her chair and just stares at Audri for a moment. "What are you talking about now, Audri? How could you possibly be jealous of Cher-Devil?"

"It's taken a while to sink in. But Doc suggested the possibility in our last session. That may be why I get so easily irritated at the way she is with boys. I may get jealous because she attracts the attention of boys and makes it look so easy. And that's what I want. But down deep, I believe I'm not attractive. And I'm beginning to think he's onto something there."

"Oh, that's just psychobabble, as my dad would say. I can't imagine you being jealous of that idiot. No fuckin' way!" Ang responds, slapping the table, even with her final comment coming out in almost a whisper.

"Yeah, that was pretty much my response when Doc mentioned it. Though I didn't exactly say those words," Audri continued with a laugh. "But I do get upset easily by her. As I spent some time thinking about his comment, it felt like there was some truth to it. You know how something feels right in your gut, even when you don't want it to be? That's what helped me see Cheryl differently and why I decided to try a different interaction with her today."

"Wow, I'm still shocked. It's hard for me to get my head around you possibly being jealous of her! But I also believe what you tell me. It may just take some time to sink in, not to mention when Tanika hears this!" suggests Soph.

"Yeah, I think she'll be a bit shocked too. Let me tell her, though, will ya?" asks Audri.

"Sure. But..." Angelina's voice tapers off.

"What is it, Ang?"

"Well, it's just that... you know, it's kind of all about you again. In fact, it's often all about you."

Audri now leans back in her chair, surprised and a bit hurt by Angelina's comment. "What do you mean, Ang?"

"I know you have my back. But much of our interactions focus on what's up for you. Or what's happening with you and Tanika. Really, it's seldom about Soph or me. In fact, it never feels like it's about me. And it gets damn tiring."

"Wow, Ang. I didn't know you felt that way." Audri leans closer to the table and her friend. She can see tears swelling up in Angelina's eyes.

"Ya know, if you're going to change the rules about how the Musketeers are going to interact with someone, you might want to check in with the three of us about whether we agree or want to go along. You just do what you want without much thought of us sometimes." The tears are now starting to run down

Angelina's cheeks, which she quickly wipes away.

"I'm sorry, Ang. I'm just trying to figure out some of this shit. I didn't mean to make decisions about all of us without talking to you. I didn't think that far ahead."

"Yeah, that's the trouble sometimes. You just act spontaneously. But your actions impact all of us," adds Soph.

Audri stops to consider for a moment what Soph has just shared with her.

"Ya, you're right. I didn't think it through - again. I'm so sorry."

Audri peers at her two friends for a moment, processing what they have been sharing. Then she decides to check out what Cheryl said about the photo.

"Hey, Ang. I just want to check something else out with you. Nika said she asked you both if you knew how Cheryl got that photo of the two of us at the tennis match. She said neither of you knew. But Cheryl says she borrowed your phone, Ang, when you were looking at the pic and sent it to herself. That true?"

Angelina appeared shocked. Suddenly her face turns red. "Hell no! I did no such thing. She saw it when I was looking at it. But that's all."

"Huh," responds Audri. "She sounded pretty sure of that."

"Don't know what she's talking about. I never sent it to anybody. And she didn't either."

"Oh, OK. Wonder why she'd lie about it?""Oh, you know that dick. She'd lie about anything," responded Ang, her voice getting louder again, expressing her increased anger.

"Are you accusing me of lying? You calling me a liar?" Ang shouts. "You're a dick, too, if you think I'd lie about that. You narcissistic ass. FUCK YOU, ADURI!" Ang responds in a shouting whisper, spit falling onto the table, accompanying her words.

She gets up, glaring at Audri. "You coming Soph, or are you going to stay with this irritating Air Head?"

Soph looks at Aug, then back at Audri, apparently unsure what to choose.

"Since I drove, guess I'd better take her home," Soph offers as an explanation.

She gets up and follows Ang, who is stomping out the door.

Audri looks at them, shocked by Ang's heated response and unsure why she got so angry. She sits there for a few minutes, trying to compose herself and wanting to ignore everyone attempting to hide their stares.

Something feels uneasy about Ang's explanation. Something doesn't feel right. I don't know what to think. Did the questions about how Cheryl got the photo trip the land mine?

She tries to let it go, yet she can't. She's still in shock. She gets up to order some lunch at the counter, but suddenly feels full. She knows she should eat something, then ends up ordering a salmon salad. It looks good when she gets it, yet it isn't easy to eat. Too many words want to come out while the salad is trying to go down.

After finishing much of her lunch, Audri decides maybe a movie will distract her.

She walks over, buys a ticket at the booth, then goes in to find a good seat. Yet, something keeps churning in her stomach, some uneasiness continues to rise up in her. She notices, then distracts herself with action on the screen. It still doesn't divert the feeling completely.

Audri begins to wonder how much she makes everything about herself, ignoring what's most important to her friends.

Am I completely self-absorbed? Do I only care about myself? Is Ang right about my focus? I want to feel more peaceful inside. But I just seem to be creating more conflict with others!

Instead of a relaxing afternoon, Audri feels into the tension of her desire for change. Simultaneously, she feels like making things different just makes life worse. It isn't just affecting her. But now her friends, too.

In addition, she continues to feel uneasy about the discrepancy between how Cheryl and Ang each explained the photo. She wants to believe Ang, and it also feels odd. Yet Cheryl seemed to be so quick to explain how it might have happened and now makes so much sense.

Soon she begins to wonder if her life and her attempts to change both suck!

After Audri gets home, she quietly throws up again, then returns to her sanctuary, hoping her mom didn't notice.

Chapter 17

The Tension of Change

By the time Audri arrives at Alberto's office on Tuesday, she feels like she's drowning in her conflict about change and its impact on others.

Audri feels positive about her conversation with Cheryl, and at the same time suffers from her feeling of betrayal for her best friends.

What else could I do? How do I create the change I want without hurting others? How do I balance that in my life?

As Audri sits down in her regular chair, she notices a hawk outside the window. Such a sighting brightens her at the moment. Yet, the same old room brings back the same old issues.

As she looks at Alberto, he shares once again his caring smile.

"How did things go this week? Any new developments you want to share?"

"Well, I had a conversation with Cheryl, which actually felt successful. It was peaceful, and I thought I did a great job. But that was followed by a disagreement with two of my best friends. And that feels awful!"

"Tell me about the conversation with Cheryl, first."

Audri shares her experience about the meditation, her peacefulness and feelings as she walked downtown on Sunday, followed by her spontaneous talk with Cheryl. She shares her own surprise about how it started and the path that it took without planning.

Alberto pauses to take a breath, then responds.

"It seems like you created a natural outcome with the shift in your perspective about you and the judgment you project onto Cheryl. Well done!"

"Thanks. But it isn't feeling so great today. It seems like I've betrayed my best friends in the process."

"What were your friend's reactions?"

"They both were upset that I changed my relationship with Cheryl without talking it over with them. They see me as selfish, always focusing on myself."

"Is that the way you feel? Do you always focus on yourself?"

"No, I don't think so. But I hate it when Ang and Soph get upset with me."

"And did you throw up afterwards?"

Audri stops and stares at Alberto. She feels the shot of anger in her gut that he would bring up such a topic, making her more uncomfortable.

"Well... I think my salad disagreed with me. I was feeling nauseous."

"You can hide the facts from me. But it doesn't help to hide them from yourself if you want a significant shift in your life."

Audri continues to look at this old man, disliking his directness at this moment. She hesitates, then continues.

"Yeah, OK, I threw up. You satisfied?" Audri replied, attempting to direct her disgust towards Alberto.

"Is that what you do when you lose control elsewhere? When you're stressed?"

Audri's words just stick in her throat, wanting to regurgitate them and clear her passage again. What she really desires is to express her anger. She feels like she has been caught again, and it pisses her off. Like so many other times, she swallows deeply.

"I guess so. I just feel nervous. And it makes me feel better."

"Better in your throat when it burns? Or the self-punishing act of throwing up?"

Again, Audri feels angry with his unnerving questions. Yet, she also knows he cares and isn't trying to punish her with his directness. That makes her feel even more trapped by them.

"I guess some of both. But why do Ang and Soph have to get upset? I did something just before that made me feel good. Why do they have to ruin it?"

"It isn't just about Ang and Soph's reactions. If you're serious about a change in your life, others may not like it. Then you must decide if their liking you is more important than the change you want. Sometimes you can keep your friends through such changes. Sometimes you have to let them go."

"But I love them. I want to remain friends."

"Of course you want to keep great friends. But is their approval more important than the change you're seeking? This is about your commitment to shift behaviors, even when it isn't supported by others. Not everyone is going to like your changes. They're used to the way you were, not where you're headed."

Alberto pauses to take another deep breath and shift positions in his chair.

"What I'm trying to do is help you create other options to allow more freedom for yourself and more peace in your life."

"I want that too. But it seems so difficult right now. It's such a struggle."

"This is the human struggle around change. This is the conflict between who you've been and how you want to make your life different. It's the tension between the comfort of what you have in contrast to what you want. And it's the tension between what you want and other people's reaction to that. You don't get to make that decision for them. If this were all so easy, more of us would have completed it long ago."

"But I don't want to lose my friends. Cheryl isn't worth it."

"This isn't about Cheryl, either. What you're experiencing is the challenge to take a different path than the one you have been walking. We're used to behaving in a certain way, and we develop neural pathways in our brain that make such responses easy and even automatic. For example, if you are used to short, shallow breaths in your upper chest, shifting to slow, deep breaths in your abdomen takes some conscious effort to change that habit. Your body isn't used to that, but it can make the change if you don't continuously fall back into the previous behavior. When you stop throwing up, that also impacts other parts of your life. You learn alternative ways of dealing with stress and control. When you are tired of self-punishing behavior, you find other ways to handle your tension."

"Yeah, I get that. But does it have to be so hard, especially with my friends?"

"That older pattern is easy because you've participated in it for so long. It takes committed awareness and conscious decision making to do it differently for a while, until that becomes more of a habit. Your sensitivity and reaction to Cheryl is like a habit that takes time to change. As you stay with it, the new pattern gets easier and easier. Once you make that change, it can impact how others see, interact, or treat you."

"Well, I'm OK with it taking some time. But why do I have to make my friends upset when I just want to make a simple change?"

"Most responses to people are not simple. A response to Cheryl has implications with your friends, your brother, his girlfriend, and others. Our interactions are complicated webs that we create over a long time. When we change one part of the web, it reverberates throughout the rest of it, like a stone thrown in a calm lake. It creates waves that impact other parts. Changing one behavior is not usually an isolated event. It impacts many other parts of our life.

"But I just wanted to change my interactions with Cheryl. It's not like I am doing some massive overhaul of myself."

"Making a fundamental shift with people in your life like Cheryl often requires a deeper change. That's why I wanted you to look, not just at one thing, but deeper at what else may be related to that behavior, at the lie you tell yourself that drives many behaviors and interactions. And your friends and family may not like the change that you're making. They may want the old you back again. That's what they are used to. Just like you may be used to shallow breaths or throwing up to distract from your problems."

"So it'll take the rest of my life to make one change? That seems excessive!"

"No, I am not saying that. But one change can lead to another, that leads to another. And change isn't usually a simple, isolated event. If you shift your view of Cheryl, that can impact your interactions with her. Changing your interactions with her can impact your friends and family. And these others may not be as happy about your change as you are. It may make them upset. Then you have to decide which is most important, the change you want or the way others want you to remain."

"Can't I just change one core piece and leave it at that?"

"In the end, your behaviors and interactions are manifestations of your basic commitment to your priorities in life, your intentions, and sticking to them. If you don't care about other people, like Cheryl, your behaviors will demonstrate that. If you decide that isn't the way you want to live, if you want to create change, it'll be a struggle for a while as to which priority is most important. You may focus on the change for some time. But there often comes a time you may question that priority, especially if there is pressure from friends not to change. That's when you decide if your change in caring about others truly is more important to you than whether friends like you. That's the struggle, the conflict and priority of behaving differently in contrast to the habits of the past."

"Is there any way to get around that? Is there any way to make it easier?"

Alberto smiles at her in that facial caress. "If you want to change your back hand from one handed to two hands, is it easy? Does it just happen suddenly?"

"No, of course not. You have to work at it."

"Yes, and the same is true of any change. It's as if Life wants to know how committed we are to doing something differently, especially shifting an underlying view of yourself or others. And with a commitment, there are often periods of doubt and questions about such change. When your friends are used to you acting one way, a change in how you behave can throw them off. Some may like it, others may not. If they don't like the new behavior, it can even drive them away to some degree or completely."

"Does Life have a mind of its own? Besides, I thought you were going to make my life easier," responds Audri with a hint of a smile.

"Maybe it's Life. Maybe it's the collective force we create with our relationships and interactions. But I see my task is to help you make your existence what you truly desire or intend, whether it's easy or not. You're free to keep living the way you are now, and there are implications of that choice. Or you can change the lie you believe about yourself, and that change has implications too. If you're committed to anything, there are usually times you may question what you are doing. Do you really want this? Is a change seriously important? Those are the times that can create inner tension about living life differently."

"But how do I turn off the doubts? How do I become more confident in the change and make it permanent?"

"It isn't a matter of turning off the doubts, but rather not getting caught up in them. This again is where meditation can be a useful practice. You can observe the doubts, acknowledging their appearance again, then let them float off like balloons. Let your mind notice their appearance, thank them for showing up and allowing you to recommit to your change, then let them go."

"But doubts are doubts. They make me question everything, especially about myself."

"How do doubts make you question?"

"That's what they do! They raise questions! They make me not trust myself!"

"Do they force you not to trust yourself in some way?"

"Well... maybe not force me. But they're there all the time, and I can't seem to overcome them. They're like a constant in my life."

"You give doubts their power. They're like thoughts in meditation. When you treat them as real, they become so. Thoughts and doubts are simply possibilities, not facts. So don't treat them as such. You can notice them, even be grateful for them, without holding onto them as if you have no option. We don't have a choice when we give up the opportunity to choose. If you treat doubts as a possibility rather than a fact, they remain as a choice rather than a truth, a given."

"How do I hold them as a possibility? That sounds impossible."

"If someone says to you before a tennis match, 'I think you are going to lose this one,' is that a fact or a possibility?"

"Well, before a match it's a possibility."

"And do you trust what that person says?"

"I may, or I may get determined to prove them wrong," responds Audri with a smile.

"Yes, exactly. But if you trust what that person says, are you more likely to lose the match?"

"Yeah, probably. If I doubt myself, I don't play as well."

"But before the match is over, it's still a possibility, not a fact. Did you see the 2009 Wimbledon semi-final match Serena Williams played where she lost the first set, then came back to win? Some call it one of the best women's matches ever. Do you think she had doubts after the first set?"

"I doubt it. She's amazing."

"Yes, but sometimes doubts creep in, even with the best players. The key is not to treat them as truth, not to take them as fact. They are a possibility, and, like you said, sometimes you try to prove the doubt wrong. It doesn't always work. Even the best players lose too. But they don't treat their doubts as fact. They try to focus on what's most important to them. The doubt can come in, and you have to trust what you want most and go after it. You won't always get it. But if you give doubt the power, it's more likely that you won't.

"OK, that makes sense. But sometimes they just feel overwhelming. They're so strong that no other point of view seems to matter."

"That's especially the time to practice trusting your higher knowing, that perspective that reaches beyond the limited view of yourself. The more you practice softening and opening your heart, the easier it gets to do just that. When you open the heart, it is harder for doubts to be treated as truth."

"What the hell are you talking about now? What's higher knowing?"

"The knowing that led you along a different set of choices when you talked with Cheryl."

"How do you know that?"

"From what you described of your experience and the outcome of your interactions."

"OK, help me here. I'm not following you. Be more specific, please."

"Sure. When we get into fear and doubt, our being closes down, our options seem to narrow and be more limited, and we tend to follow the same path we've traveled before. But when we get into our hearts and relax into a more expansive state, our mind and being then expand. In that state, we can step back, be more of the observer, and see different choices. We can have a better sense of what's in the interest of ourselves and others from a more heartful perspective. And we can treat doubts as possibility rather than truth."

"But what does that do for us?"

"In that place, we can connect with a higher knowing within us. That knowing can illuminate new ideas, possibilities, and choices that come from an open heart instead of a closed, contracted one. It's in that place that we can see our fundamental assumption as a lie, giving us another view of ourselves and the world. It's accessing a greater wisdom that comes from the open heart. And it strengthens our own self trust, which is critical in this whole process."

"Is wisdom from an open heart all that different than wisdom from the brain?"

"Yes. In my experience, it is. Heart wisdom is less localized to our individual perspective, more loving towards ourselves and others, and it gives us a larger view of issues or challenges."

"Is that actually what I accessed on Sunday?"

"I'm certain you did. But the only way for you to know and have confidence in such knowing is to continue exploring it. Learning from experience to trust such knowing and a different possible outcome will give you more confidence. It's important that you know it for yourself, not just take my word for it. And that takes some extended practice, just as it does to change a swing in tennis. It's based on self trust rather than trust in someone else."

"But if I got there last Sunday, I'm not sure how. What do I do to repeat that?"

"Keep working with your heart opening meditation. Then, as you begin to feel this opening, relax into it, a more expanded place in and around your heart. It's like falling into a cloud that supports you while feeling soft and expansive. It's difficult to explain to someone who is not familiar with it, like describing the taste of a lemon or coconut to someone who's never experienced the flavor of them. As you continue to explore this process, you'll know that place and get a better sense of how to access the feeling you experienced that morning and maintained on your walk to town."

"I don't know Doc. I'm not confident about that."

"OK, let's try it right now. Get comfortable in your chair with your feet flat on the floor... Now let your body relax and let your eyes close... Take a slow deep breath, then let it out slowly... Now, take another breath, and let your heart relax as you exhale."

Alberto pauses for a moment after each direction, then continues with soft, slow suggestions.

"Again, breathe in, letting your heart relax more with your next slow exhale... Take a fourth slow breath, letting the heart and space around it relax with another slow exhale."

Audri feels the tickle on her arm and wants to scratch it. Instead, she chooses to try letting the itch go and focus once again on her breathing. It feels challenging and inviting both.

"Now, feel that area around your heart... Just let it relax slowly, easily... As you relax into it, notice if the area is more expansive, soft, supportive. Pay attention to how you feel... whether it can open more, whether you feel the love spreading as you did the other day. . . As you feel into the area of your opening heart, ask a question, something you would like to know. Maybe it's an easy one, like 'what do I want to eat for dinner?' Or maybe it's a bigger question, like 'am I unlovable?'... Just wait for that soft, often faint answer."

Audri is breathing and relaxing in her chair that caresses her body while Alberto sits quietly across the room. After some time, Audri opens her eyes and looks at Doc.

"I guess I can do it," Audri says with a faint smile.

"And did you get an answer?"

"Yes. The answer was no, I'm not unlovable."

Suddenly, tears start flowing down her face and around her loving smile as she further relaxes, peering into Alberto's embracing eyes as he leans over and hands her a box of tissues.

"And is that an answer you can trust?"

"Yeah, it feels like it. And then doubts come in again."

"Yes, to test your trust. Rather than doubts being an enemy, possibly you could see them as an opportunity. Like a strong opponent in a tennis match. See if you can view them as an exercise in choice, an opportunity to choose the truth about yourself each time doubts come in. After a while, their power weakens. Every time you make that choice, the opportunity strengthens. Rather than something to avoid, doubts can be like lifting weights, each lift making you stronger, each exercise strengthening the neural pathway in your brain, providing you with a new neural pathway. This keeps power in your choice, not bestowing it onto your doubts. I'm guessing that's what Serena did in that tennis match. And you're in the match of your life. Go for it!"

Audri smiles at Alberto, relaxing into the old soft chair.

They go on to talk about her summer tennis camp and connections in her family. She shares a bit about parental arguments as well as increasing conversations with her mom.

Audri feels more relaxed and enjoys some casual talk with Doc as well. Finally, they near the end of her session.

"OK, Doc. I'll keep practicing. And I get it about friends. I need to do what's best in my life. And if they want to come with me, that's awesome. If they're bothered by my changes, it's sad and OK. That won't be easy, but I get the idea now. And I love the answer I got today. I'll try focusing on the opportunity I have with the doubts."

"See, I knew it. I knew you would start coming up with even better examples of what you can do to make these changes. Great job, Audri!"

"Thanks, Doc. See you next Tuesday."

As they both rise from her chairs, Audri walks over and gives Alberto a hug. She then turns and leaves the office.

Chapter 18

Enough

As school begins in the fall, Audri's excited about her new classes, her work from the summer tennis camp, and a more relaxed atmosphere with Cheryl.

But Ang and Soph have not been the same since the three of them met for lunch, following Audri's shift with the girl who has been such a long time nemesis. The two friends are less available for time with the *Mousquetaires* and often don't return Audri's phone calls.

To Audri, the distance feels like a big gap in the circle of friends, which is disappointing and sad. Yet she's grateful for her continued connection with Tanika.

She continues her work with Doc, practicing the meditations, especially the heart-opening one. It continues to get easier the more she practices. There remain many questions. But she feels more comfortable with the concepts, and she loves joking with him from time to time.

The highlight of the summer, however, was finally getting her driver's license. She hasn't talked her parents into a car yet, but she's able to drive herself when a vehicle is available. And no one seems happier about that than Bella and Rick.

With school starting again, Audri arranged for a later beginning time for her appointment next Tuesday. She's happy to be continuing her time with Doc, and yet the changes they're discussing still do not come easily. Her meditation practice one day is effortless and the next can be as challenging as her first attempts. She feels more competent opening her heart, and yet she still gets mad when hitting a lousy tennis shot or driving behind someone who appears to be in a funeral procession.

One change that delights Audri is the increased sensitivity to energy. She pays attention to it when she sits quietly, especially during the heart opening meditation. There are times she likes to simply be present with the tingling around her body during the meditation as her heart energy expands to fill her chest. She also notices it at times when she runs. That feeling is her favorite way to begin the day, even if such an inner experience only lasts until she reaches the kitchen for breakfast, spotting someone's bowl left on the table for her to clean. Or so it seems.

Audri's up early and ready to go in her new yellow top and jeans, reminding her of a mellow summer. She hears the horn honk in front as she finishes brushing her teeth, grabs her bag and heads out the door to catch a ride with her best friend.

As the oldest, Tanika talked her parents into a car to help transport her younger brother. Convincing her parents was easy, especially with both of them having full time jobs. Basically, it was a slam dunk for that verbal acrobat.

"OK, are you ready to be a full fledged junior?" asks Tanika as Audri opens the door and slides over the frayed hole in the passenger seat. It isn't the most stylish car, this 2008 white Civic. But it's reliable and uses less gas than many.

"Oh yeah! I thought it was going to be a great year, until last week," replies Audri as she looks over at her best friend's bruised right eye and cheek.

She still can't believe two white guys who live in the rural part of the county would attack her friend and little brother at City Park while playing tennis. Audri's especially grateful for her friend's tennis racket, now broken in her bedroom at home after striking both boys, stopping the assault. But tears come to her eyes every time she thinks about Reggie, Tanika's little brother, who suffered a broken arm in the attack.

She also appreciates the Johnson County Sheriff's Department taking such reports even more seriously, since Gutsche's book raised awareness of race relations in the area a couple of years before. But there's still some tension in parts of the county, despite the increased support of many in the city.

Tanika finds a spot and parks. They both head for their first class with Audri's dear friend lagging behind for a change.

"Come on, tiger. We'll face them together. What other girl in this school could walk in with so few injuries after an attack by two boys? Hold your head up high and show 'em!" says Audri as she takes Tanika's arm and opens the door for her, allowing her to walk through first as a hero.

Several students see her enter and start to clap. Then more join in the tribute. Tanika appears a bit taken back, even shy, an unusual response for this extrovert. Audri slows her step, giving Tanika some space, and joins in the clapping, leaving her friend to be the center of attention.

Tanika waves off the clapping, then thanks a couple of people she knows. Others come up and ask if she's feeling alright, and Audri just lets her have time in the spotlight.

She deserves it after feeling so dejected following the attack.

Luckily for Tanika, both her parents are well known and respected in the community. Unlike some kids of color who are more invisible, even in this liberal college enclave of Iowa.

Audri can't change the atmosphere for others. But she certainly can support her best friend during her time of struggle.

Her first reaction when she heard about the attack was to ask Alex and his friends to get revenge. As she sat in meditation the next morning, she realized that would just perpetuate the violence.

Instead, she talked with friends about forming a group called, Enough. They decided they would hold a vigil, inviting all students, especially students of color, to stand together in a ceremony of common support, reifying the words in the Constitution that ALL are created equal, men and women, white people and people of color.

As Audri walks up to Tanika, Soph comes up behind her and pulls on her arm. "What time is the vigil Friday night? I really want to be there."

"It's at 7:00 pm by the tennis courts at City Park, assuming we get the permit from the city today." Audri looks into her eyes and smiles. "I'm so glad you'll be there."

"I know I've been a little distant lately, kind of angry at you. But I love what you are doing for Tanika and her brother. I wouldn't miss it. And I miss you guys. I'm sorry."

"Awesome! Come on, bring it in!" Audri says, as she reaches out her arms. Soph comes in for a forgiving hug.

As they retreat from their hug, Soph looks at Audri with a smile. "I hear Cheryl and everyone is going to be there. What a great show of support for Tanika."

"Yes. It's about time we started making our voices heard for positive change. We women have to stand up, especially as we face the possibility of the first woman being elected President of the United States this fall!"

"Yeah, I hope so. Although some people have surprised me by their distrust of her."

"Still, if not now, when? It's beyond time, if you ask me," replies Audri emphatically. "And I don't like the kind of attitude that's growing in this country about people of color. We need to address our support directly, not just sit back and be complacent. We've done that long enough."

"So, is that where you got the name for this vigil?"

"Yeah. It just came to me one morning. Enough is enough, of all types of prejudice and violence!"

"Ya know, Audri, what Ang and I said in the restaurant this summer may have been a bit of a one sided view of you."

"Actually, Soph, you two helped me see that I can be rather self-absorbed. I'm grateful you two said it out loud. You made me think about it, because I know you care. I think you helped me get a bit out of myself and begin to focus more on others. So, thank you!"

"Well, we were coming more from hurt than concern, as I thought about our conversation. So I'm not sure a 'thank you' is truly appropriate."

"But you were right, no matter the motivation. And it's helped me wake up to this."

"Glad my selfishness can be so helpful. Glad to be of service!" laughs Sophie.

The two girls grab Tanika's arms and walk her down the hall towards class as the other students disappear into their respective rooms. Audri feels delighted that she and Soph are reconnecting, hopefully expanding the friendship circle once again.

At lunch time, Audri calls the city offices to check on the permit for the vigil on Friday.

"Hi, Mrs. Howell. This is Audri Giovanni calling. I wanted to check on our request for a permit this Friday for a vigil in City Park."

"Hi Audri. Yes, it's been approved. There will be a raised platform with a lectern and microphone there, and the city will cover the costs given all the guests who want to be there."

"That's great news. Thanks. Ah, you mean the students who will be there as guests?"

"Well, the sound system will help them hear. But I was talking about the other guests who also would like to give short remarks, including the mayor, a city council member, the superintendent of schools, the university president, and Iowa football coach."

"Ah, oh . . . OK. So will the mayor get the event going?"

"No, I think he is expecting you to introduce it, since it's the students' idea."

"Oh, well, OK. Thanks for letting me know."

"You're welcome. See you Friday, Audri."

Audri turns to Soph as she puts down her phone. "Oh shit! I wanted to organize a small vigil against racial violence in order to support Tanika, her family, and other students of color. Now this has turned into a city wide gathering! You want to introduce it, girl??"

"Who's going to be there?" asks Soph.

"Oh, just the mayor, a city council member, the school superintendent, the university president, and Iowa's football coach!"

"OMG! This is turning into a major production!"

"Yeah, and they're expecting us to introduce it all!"

"With Tanika's dad working for the university and her mom at the school district, this has become a big deal. I think they're reaching out so people talk more about race. Glad you're in charge," laughs Soph.

"Oh girl, you are going to be up there with me, you can count on that!"

Audri finds it difficult to concentrate on her classes during the afternoon. Once school is out, Audri texts Tanika and Soph, asking them to meet her at the tennis courts.

"What's up," asks Soph as Audri approaches the courts.

"I need your help for the vigil on Friday. I want to make some fliers for tomorrow to pass around the school. And I need your collaboration with our introductory speech."

"Our?" asks Soph with a smile. "I'm happy to help make and pass out fliers. But introduce? I think you're on your own there, girl!

"You chicken shit," laughs Audri. "Well, at least help me think about what to say."

"Yeah, that I can do," responds Sophie.

"Hey there, what's up," asks Nika as she approaches the two girls.

"We're making fliers tonight for the vigil. You want to help?" asks Soph.

"You guys are the greatest," responds Tanika with tears suddenly forming in her eyes.

"We love you, Nika. You'd do the same for any of us!" says Audri.

They all get in Tanika's car and head for Soph's place to make a flier and print out 500 of them to pass out in school the next day. As they go into Soph's bedroom, she asks, "So how are you going to introduce this whole thing, Audri?"

"Well, I think I will tell them my name, summarize what happened, then introduce you," chuckles Audri.

"Oh hell, no!" responds Sophie . "I love you all, but I'm not going to speak into that damn microphone! Not in front of those guests! I'll print out all the fliers and help pass them out. Then I hand the ball to you. It's your serve, baby."

"I think it's important to let people know about the attack. But I want to say something more than just describing what happened," Audri continues. "I think we need to talk about the impact of violence and how it just adds to our problems, not solves them."

They talk about more ideas for Audri's introduction. But nothing feels quite right.

Sensing the need to process alone, Audri decides to go home. On the way, she keeps asking herself what she should say, what main point she wants to get across. She wants her friend to know of her support. But it feels like there is something bigger to say, something about violence in general.

As she walks into the house, Audri hears her mom working in the kitchen.

"Hey mom, what would you say at a rally about your best friend getting hurt?"

"Hello to you too," jokes her mother.

"Oh yeah, hi. How are ya?"

"I'm doing well. Got a lot on your mind? How is the planning going for the vigil on Friday?"

"It's going pretty well. Except I don't know what to say for introductions. And now the mayor and others are going to be there. It's turning out much bigger than I anticipated."

"Congratulations, sweetie. You can do it. What's your overall goal with your speech?"

"I want to say something more than just talking about the attack. I want to include something about violence in general, but I can't figure it out."

"Do you want to focus on violence or nonviolence?"

"Oh, well, excellent point. I think I want to emphasize nonviolence."

"Hmm." Bella thinks for a minute as she continues with dinner prep. "How about having the students commit to nonviolence and support each other to talk through and resolve their differences peacefully?"

"Do you think they'd consider that?"

"Well, I think you'd have to motivate them before getting to that point."

"Hmmm. OK, thanks Mom."

Audri goes upstairs, doubts swirling in her head. Then she remembers her discussion with Doc and decides to try this opportunity to use the doubts as options.

It's not easy. Still, a pretty new approach. But she also knows it won't get easier by giving in to them. Eventually, she wants to rid herself of doubts, although she also realizes that probably won't happen this time.

She spends that evening working on her speech. She plans to continue revising it over the next two days. Each time doubts come up, she steps back in an attempt to see a larger view.

The next day, the girls enlist others to help pass out fliers, getting a mixed reaction from some of the students, especially the seniors. But she gives some to Alex's former baseball team mates, and that helps. With Tanika's dad working as a Hawkeye defensive coach, the football players also pay some attention to it.

By the time the vigil is about to begin on Friday, they have a large crowd in attendance. Audri and Soph walk up to the platform that has the lectern and sound system. As they approach the stand, the mayor comes over to shake their hands and congratulate them for initiating this vigil. Then he leads them up onto the platform and suggests they begin.

Audri steps up to the microphone feeling the anxiety in her stomach and trembling in her hand as she drags Soph up to the mic with her. Then she looks out at Tanika, her mom, dad, and Reggie, with his cast on the broken arm. She gazes out over the crowd of several hundred students and town members, takes a deep breath, and remembers Alberto's guidance. She opens her heart further as Soph places her right hand on the back of her heart, as Audri had previously requested.

"Thank you all for coming here this evening. We appreciate the support of Mayor Christensen and the city council members approving this vigil and for the comments they will contribute, as well as Superintendent Polonko, Coach Edwards, and President McKenry from our great university. They all will share their remarks a little later."

"As you all know, a dear friend of ours, Tanika Washington, and her little brother, Reggie, were attacked almost two weeks ago while playing tennis here in City Park," Audri begins. "The two white male perpetrators called them awful names and initiated the physical violence, resulting in Reggie's broken arm and Tanika's badly bruised face. Unfortunately for them, Tanika has a fabulous forehand and backhand, striking them both with her tennis racket several times, convincing the boys to leave. They later wanted to file charges for assault. But two runners, who witnessed the attack, confirmed Tanika and Reggie's self-defense story.

"Significantly, our leaders, police, and community members stood up for these two students. And the boys who assaulted my friends hopefully will get the help they need to be kinder to all people, especially people of color."

"Sadly, we are seeing an increase in racial tension and violence in this country that some say have been around for a long time and are simply coming to the surface. The more I study this issue, the more accurate that seems to be, unfortunately. Especially if that's true, it's important, I think, that we address both in our own home town.

"There are people who encourage violence to perpetuate their perspective. Some even want to physically dominate the conversation. But the US Constitution states that we all are created equal. While this statement may not have applied equally to all when this great document was written, it certainly does and, in my opinion, should do so now.

"If we truly believe that, then we don't have the right to impose ourselves or our views on our equals, especially through intimidation and violence. In addition, violence only adds more problems to our relationships and community. For as many have said, violence perpetuates violence. Not only do people get hurt, but oftentimes there also are legal and financial repercussions due to the physical assault. Such violence typically only solidifies a person's original view while also adding anger, sadness, and a closed heart to the mix. Enough is enough.

"Instead of complicating our differences with violence and the impact of such behaviors, I suggest we seek other ways of resolving our divergence of opinions.

Let's not heap additional complications to an existing challenge or our contrasting views. Let's work together to create a place where we can live in peace and harmony.

"Tonight, I'm asking that we commit to solving our differences without the use of bullying, threats, intimidation, or violence.

"As the great Dr. King said: 'We adopt the means of nonviolence because our end is a community at peace with itself. We will try to persuade with our words, but if our words fail, we will try to persuade with our acts.'

"Two other quotes that I think are appropriate for such an occasion. He said, 'our lives begin to end the day we become silent about things that matter.' And these things matter. Finally, he suggested that, 'There comes a time when people get tired of being pushed out of the glittering sunlight of life's July and left standing amid the piercing chill of an alpine November. In the end, you can kill the dreamer, but you can't kill the dream. And darkness cannot drive out darkness; only light can do that. Hate cannot drive out hate; only love can do that.

"Tonight, I am going to ask you to follow that sage advice and commit to nonviolent means of communication, negotiation, and problem solving. To commit to supporting all people to live in life's July, all being a part of the American dream, and let love be our driving force.

"I ask you: 1) to commit this night to nonviolent behavior; and 2) to resolve any differences you have with others from an open heart using peaceful means. Please take a minute to consider your willingness to such processes and whether these are important to you" Audri pauses to let the audience think about what she has asked of them.

"If you are willing to take on these two commitments this evening, please say, silently or aloud, I so commit." Audri pauses again as she hears a rumbling of 'I so commit' ring out among the crowd.

"Thank you, and thanks for your show of support for Tanika, Reggie, and change in our community and world."

Following a supportive applause, Audri introduces the Mayor, who seems a bit stunned as he approaches the microphone.

"If you had any questions about the future of our city and our nation, I think they may have been answered here tonight by Audri, her friends, the Washingtons, and the students and community members who just took the same commitment we did on this stage."

The mayor goes on to talk about changes the city council wants to make to improve this community for all members, including the reduction of violence between people. The other dignitaries make similar remarks about the importance of nonviolence and feeling of inclusion in the community, schools, the university, its football team, and all of its other programs.

The final applause is loud and long.

As Audri descends the platform, Tanika comes up to her and gives her a huge hug.

"You're such a great friend, Audri. Thanks!"

Mr. and Mrs. Washington are next to express their appreciation for initiating this event and supporting ongoing change to make this community a better place for everyone to live. Soph also gets in on the thanks as a part of the *Mousquetaires* who stick together.

When Audri steps back from her hug, a hand touches her arm. She turns to see Cheryl.

"Nice job, Audri. This was great of you to do. I wish I had the balls to talk like you did today."

"Thanks, Cheryl. I appreciate that and you coming to the vigil. By the way, I'm sorry to hear about the death of your grandmother. I'm really glad you got to spend so much time with her before she passed. I wish I could have known my grandmother like you did."

"Thanks. I'm going to miss her. But I'm glad, too, that I got to spend this time with her. Well, glad you organized this. I'd better go. We have some girls to trash tonight," Cheryl says with a smile.

As she leaves, Audri notices a small group mulling around. Then Santiago emerges from the crowd and walks her way. She smiles as he comes near.

"Great job, Audri. You and your friends have done a very supportive thing here for Tanika and her family, as well as the school and community. I didn't know you were so keen about talking in front of a large audience."

"Oh, I'm not generally. But this made me very upset. And I think I found some strength inside to make this all happen. Not sure where it came from though, or if I could call it up again when I want it," she laughs.

Santiago reaches out and gives her a hug, which speeds up her heart a bit. As Audri releases and steps back, her mom also approaches.

"Hey Audri, great job. Hi Santiago. How are you?"

"Doing well, Mrs. Giovanni. And it was great to see Audri up there tonight. Alex would have been proud of her."

"Yeah, I wish he could have made it back from California. But it's a long way. Great to see you again. I've missed seeing you since Alex went away to college. And you were great, Audri. Well done!"

"Thanks Mom." She gives her mom a hug just as Sarah comes up to congratulate her too.

"Sorry your dad couldn't make it. He tried to get off, but he had another person out sick."

"Yeah, that's OK. I know he has lots going on," responds Audri.

"Well, I have to get going," adds Santiago. "Have a great weekend, and I'll see you in school next week."

"Yeah, you too," responds Audri.

"Hey Mom. We're going to go get some yogurt and hang out a bit. See you later, OK?"

"Yeah, see you at home. Great job, kiddo!" her mom replies as she turns and walks towards her car.

Chapter 19

An Inflamed Schism

As Audri gets up on Sunday, she pulls on her jeans and a black t-shirt, then heads down to breakfast. She stops dead still at the top of the stairs as Bella and Rick's yelling rockets up from the kitchen. She can't make out the actual words, and she isn't sure she wants to. Yet, she's both frightened and curious sprinkled with concern.

Shit! What's going on this time? Is it worse than before?

She takes a few steps down, then stops as she spots Rick approaching the front door with suitcase in hand.

"I'll talk to you when you've become more reasonable," he shouts. He opens up the front door and slams it shut after him.

Audri notices her heart pound and lungs barely taking in air as she remains frozen in her tracks. Her hand goes up to her heart as she fears the worst. Her breathing becomes shallow, and she fixes her eyes on the front door.

Will he change his mind? Is he coming back in? Should I check on Mom, or leave her alone?

But silence prevails, and no door reopens. Apparently, there will be no apology in this moment.

She wants to know how her mom's doing, yet doesn't want to intrude too quickly. Her curiosity gets the best of her, and she continues down the stairs and into the kitchen.

Her mom's sitting at the table with unbrushed hair, her soft white robe, a tear tracked face, and a tissue in each hand. Audri takes a slow deep breath and focuses for a moment on expanding her heart.

"What's happening, Mom? You and Dad have another fight? I saw him leave," Audri asks in a tentative tone, not wanting the conversation to leave the kitchen while also not sounding too intense.

"Well … I guess… I guess,… you heard it too. Yeah,… he may be away for a while," responds Bella, grasping for words between sniffles. She pulls out another tissue and blows her nose.

"What's it about this time?" asks Audri with a compassionate look on her face and tears in her own eyes.

"Not much new. Just a rehash of the last few," Bella replies, twisting her hair with a finger.

Noticing the absence of a coffee cup in front of her mom, Audri asks, "Want some coffee? I think I'll make me some."

Audri tries to create something normal for them and takes another slow deep breath.

"Yeah, thanks. That'd be great," responds Bella as she stares at the empty chair across the table.

Audri goes to work with the coffee maker, allowing her a few minutes to consider how to approach her mom with such a delicate issue. She gets out some frozen mango, shredded coconut, spinach, and protein powder to make a smoothie. After blending ingredients with some water, she pours it into two glasses, fills two coffee cups now that it's finally ready. She puts a cup of coffee and a glass of smoothy in front of her mother.

"He'll be back when he cools off," suggests Audri as she grabs her smoothie and coffee, sitting down next to Bella at the table, looking at her plain face that looks rather striking, even in deep sadness.

"I . . . I . . . don't think so, not this time," sobs her mom, as tears begin to dilute her coffee. She picks up her cup in a routine manner and drinks the tear drenched jitter juice, recycling the tears and continuing to look straight ahead.

"You thought he was finished last time, Mom. Remember?" responds Audri, wanting to be encouraging.

Bella turns her head to look directly at her youngest daughter.

"The difference is, I may be finished this time. There's nothing more lonely than being alone in a relationship, and that's the way I'm feeling these days. He's more married to that restaurant than to me, and he seems to feel the same way about my work. I think we've jumped into our careers as our relationship dissolves, and, in retrospect, we both have had a sense of that without pushing for a change."

Bella turns to stare again at the empty chair, wiping away another tear.

"But you don't know that. He may be back. I just wish I hadn't been mean to him yesterday when he asked about the vigil. I was disappointed he didn't come, and it might've shown."

Bella lowers her cup after taking another sip of coffee and turns back to look intently into Audri's eyes. She reaches out and puts her hand on Audri's arm.

"I want you to listen to me very carefully, Audri. This has nothing to do with you. NOTHING to do with you, got it? He and I've been growing apart for years.

He loves you kids, and this separation is about my relationship with him. It has nothing to do with any of you. I want you to be clear about that."

"OK, I get it. I know Mom. But it's hard not to think about how I might've contributed."

"No! Don't even start down that road. This is just between your dad and me. We're becoming very different people. And it's hard to change a relationship without a partner's support."

"You haven't seemed happy with each other for some time."

"You're right, Audri. We tried to keep it just between us. But that's difficult to do with older kids around, especially ones who are very sharp."

"Makes me think about never getting married, let alone having any kids."

"Well, I'd suggest you wait until you know who you are and have a solid foundation from which to connect with a guy, assuming you are attracted more to men than women, like your sister. Of course either's OK. I just want you to be happy and in a healthy relationship."

Audri smiles at her mom. She knew Sarah was gay from a private conversation they had about a year ago, but she wasn't sure her mom knew.

"Is there anything you don't know, Mom?" chuckles Audri.

"Nope! Moms know everything. So don't bother trying to hide any of it," replies her mother with a hint of a smile.

"And you knew that I knew about Sarah being gay?"

"Oh yes. Sarah told me about your conversation. I thought it was great you learned from her and not someone else, especially in this small town. But don't get overly discouraged about marriage either. It's been an important relationship with your dad in many ways, including having you three. We just seem to be moving in very different directions, with more and more distance between us. And I think we got married so young that I didn't know what was most important to me."

"Well, I don't plan to marry any time soon, so no worries there," says Audri reassuringly.

"I'm glad for that! And no sex without protection either! We don't need any grandchildren right away! Do we need to go get you pills?"

"No, no, Mom. I promised you I'd be careful, and I am. I don't need any pills right now. There's no sex with anyone. Not yet, anyway," says Audri with another smile.

I don't want her to worry about that now. But it doesn't hurt to keep her on edge, either, thinks Audri.

Her smile gets a little brighter as she thinks about Santiago. "Besides, I have lots to practice from my sessions with Doc."

"I'm glad you're seeing him with this going on, too. I think he may be helpful if your dad and I don't stay together."

"You don't know that Mom. Dad could change his mind. He'll see what a terrific woman you are and come back."

"Who says I'll take him back?"

"Is he seeing someone else?"

"I don't know. But I'm not happy with the kind of person I am with him. He sure doesn't bring out the best of me, and right now I don't do that for him, either. And that's a primary way I look at the quality of relationships. It seems like we used to do that before. But not so much any more."

"It still could change. Wait and see."

"I appreciate your positive attitude, Audri. But I'm not holding my breath."

Bella continues to slowly consume her drinks, still apparently staring at the empty chair.

Audri glances away from her mom as she takes her last sip of her coffee, then the smoothie. She knows her mom may be right. This separation may be different. She sits in rare silence, aware that this may be the beginning of a divorce.

Audri notices that sinking feeling in her gut as the possibility appears to be more real. She thinks about calling Alex and Sarah to talk with them about it. She needs to talk with someone, and Tuesday feels like a long way off.

Audri stands and walks to the sink. "I'd better get some homework done."

She puts her dishes in the washer and walks back to her mom, leans over and gives her a hug.

"Love you Mom," she says, then leaves the kitchen.

"Love you too, dear"

She heads upstairs towards her bedroom. But her focus is more on her phone than books.

Along her way, Audri stops by Sarah's room. There's no response to the knock. She must be at the library studying already or maybe out on a run with Marsha.

She heads for her own bedroom to find her phone and open her Favorites, tapping Sarah's number. Again no response. She hangs up and hits Alex's number. Now that he is at UC Davis on a baseball scholarship, the two hour difference can be helpful at times. Fortunately for Audri, he picks up.

"Hey, what's up?"

"Mom and Dad. Big fight this time. Dad left, maybe permanently."

"Oh wow! When?"

"This morning. Dad left with a suitcase. And Mom seems sadder than their previous fights."

"Oh shit. He still seeing that waitress?"

"WHAT WAITRESS??"

"Oh hell. You didn't know, did you? Does Mom know?"

"No, I don't think so. She may wonder, or else she's just trying to be nice. Not sure which. She gave no indication of that when I talked with her a few minutes ago. But I think it would be helpful if you called. And don't say you know about the divorce. Just see how she's doing. I think she'd like to talk with you."

"OK, I'll call her now. Thanks for the heads up!"

"Yeah, sure. When you coming home next?"

"Hell, I just got here a few weeks ago. Not till Thanksgiving probably. I think I can fly out of Sacramento easily with only one stop. So then or at Christmas."

"Think you could come home for a long weekend before that? I think she could really use you around here right now."

"I'll see. Or maybe she could come out here for Parents Day weekend. I'll talk with her about it."

"Cool. Thanks Bro."

"Yeah. How's Sarah taking it?"

"I haven't talked with her yet. Not sure where she is this morning. Maybe on a run with Marsha. But I'll let you know, or she will."

"Great. I'll give Mom a call now."

"Perfect. Thanks."

Audri hangs up the phone. She still wants to talk with Sarah, but she figures she'll be here sometime today. She thinks about calling Tanika or Soph, but she isn't sure how she would want to talk about this with her friends. She'll think it through a little longer.

Chapter 20
Expanding Choices

As Audri takes her chair in Doc's office, once again she's full of competing emotions. There's still a glow from the vigil last Friday. Yet the jeans she is wearing feel tight, and her light blue shirt feels itchy. Her white sneakers are uncomfortable, and she reaches down to raise her blue and white striped socks that will not stay up.

And Mom and Dad! Overall, she feels frustrated, which lies somewhere between thrilled and shit.

"How are you today, Audri?"

"Great and messy."

"I love that you can hold such opposing feelings. Well done! You also gave a powerful speech last Friday evening," says Alberto. "You feel successful with the vigil and what you said?"

"Yeah, I think it went well. Tanika and her family were grateful."

"You don't sound pleased. Did something go wrong, or is it difficult for you to feel satisfied with such an event?" asks Alberto, cocking his head slightly to the right as he looks at Audri from what seems like a distant observation yet emotionally connected.

"No, I do feel terrific about that. But Mom and Dad had a big fight Sunday morning, and Dad left. Not sure how long. Mom thinks the separation may be permanent."

"Oh my. I'm so sorry to hear that. Such events are difficult for any young person. Sorry it also followed such a wonderful Friday evening. But that happens sometimes, two conflicting experiences that raise the question of which side you will focus on primarily."

"But they don't feel equal to me. Dad's leaving feels devastating, in contrast to some rally."

"Yeah, I get that. I didn't mean to suggest the two were equally important in that way. At the same time, you don't get to control your parent's relationship.

So part of the question is how much you will take on personally. In contrast, from my point of view, it was not just another rally. This was you finding your inner strength to address something you felt was wrong and encouraging parts of our whole community to bring about some change. It may not end up having an extensive impact. That depends on lots of others too. But such an event can have a long term change for you, learning to take initiative from your inner strength or essence. You're learning to ignore the lie that you are unlovable while also encouraging others to feel love and peace. That transformation may be more important in your personal life than any decision your parents make in theirs, even when the possible dissolution can hurt so badly in the moment."

Audri sits there, trying to allow Alberto's words about the vigil to permeate her whole body. She usually just lets positive comments slide off her skin and fall where they may. Today, she knows she wants to let them seep in and integrate with other information she's been learning in an attempt to have it take root in her new inner nursery. She wants these alluring ideas to invigorate this new part of herself.

At some level, she knows this is the only way to counter the lie she has been nourishing and support an alternative sense of who she is.

OK. Let's see if I can open my heart more and allow what he's saying to penetrate my protections. I so want to believe him. Funny. Before I wanted nothing to do with this old man, and now I want to hold on to his every word!

"Well done, Audri. I understand the struggle when a comment challenges a fundamental lie about yourself. To pause and allow that to enter is a wise and timely decision."

"How did you know what I was doing? I might have been resisting."

"We can lie with words. But energy illustrates what's happening with a person. I haven't shared this with you before now. But I can see what your energetic body is doing. That often gives me important information about what's occurring when you spend time processing. It takes some practice to understand it. But I can see the expansion going on as you sit with it in contrast to a resisting contraction."

"How do you do that? Have you always been able to see energy?"

"No, it developed slowly over time. But I kept opening to the possibility, to compliment what I was feeling energetically. The feeling happened early, and the seeing developed much later."

"Can you teach me to do that?" asks Audri as she leans forward in her chair.

"I am. If you don't see energy now, I don't know when or even if it will ever happen. But all you're doing will lead you in that direction as a possibility. Not everyone develops such skills. You may end up feeling energy more than seeing it."

Audri leans back in her chair, feeling a slight disappointment. Alberto continues.

"We don't all have the same skills, like in other parts of our lives. We seem to expand those aspects we need most for our own healing and supporting others in that process. It may come, and don't get discouraged if it isn't quick. Just explore and stay with it. But let's get back to what's going on in your life today."

Audri still shows some disappointment, wanting to feel special with the development of such skills quickly.

"I want to believe what you were saying about acting from my inner strength. But I don't always know how to access it. I don't know how to fix what's wrong with me."

Tears come to Audri's eyes as she feels into her plea.

I hate this feeling of damaged goods when I start to think of all the things wrong with me. I hate it! And I would love to be able to live without such a feeling about myself!

"Ah, another lie you've accepted and live with on a daily basis. As humans, there are ways to grow and change. There are aspects of our life we may want to improve. But the assumption we as children develop that there's something fundamentally wrong is a lie that's spread by ignorance and institutions wanting control and wealth. Parents, thinking it's for the good of children's development, often focus on what needs improvement to live successfully in this earthly realm. With a constant focus on amelioration, we typically come to believe that there must be something wrong with us, there must be some fundamental defect to change. The truth is, there is nothing inherently wrong with you. This is simply another extension of feeling unlovable."

"I guess so. But in some ways it feels irreparable, no matter how much I try," responds Audri with tears escaping once again.

"There is a significant difference between fixing and improving. Think back for a minute about the time you changed your interactions with Cheryl. You were feeling some jealousy, which you wanted to change. Jealousy is a natural response when you feel that you are not as good as Cheryl in some way. That is part of the lie. At the same time, you may want to improve you relationship with her, which you did to some extent. Because improving also is dependent on her participation. There may be aspects to enhance, ways to improve, something you want that's different than how you are. But that's a choice, not an intrinsic defect."

"It sure feels like part of me. It feels like a very real defect."

"It feels like a defect when we believe the lie. But what is the defect if we are love?"

"Well, maybe because we love too much? Or maybe we love so much we hold on when we need to let go?"

"I don't believe we can love too much. But we can need too much, or hold on from insecurity to someone we love. But that isn't about love. That's more about the lies we hold on to. That's about our insecurities, not our love."

"But this all still feels like it's part of me. Like I'm defective in some way."

"Beliefs and judgments are real, in part, because we define them that way. That doesn't mean that everything you come to believe is based on some objective reality. But we also can change our beliefs and reality over time as we've talked about. People have expressed all sorts of ideas that turn out not to be real, like the earth being flat or that people can't run a mile in less than four minutes. But we later changed the way we saw reality. We know, for example, that a table feels solid. But when we look deep into its structure, there is more space than structure in any object."

"So I just need to believe it and it'll come true?"

"Believing in the possibility is the first step. And it takes work too. For example, when I first talked about opening your heart more, did it happen instantly and automatically?"

"Well, no. I needed to practice, too.""And does it happen more easily now? Like a few minutes ago when you were wanting to allow my words to seep into your being, was it easier to open today?"

"Yeah. And sometimes it is harder than others."

How do I open my heart to Dad leaving, Mom's sadness? It just hurts right now. It feels awful!

"Please share with me a time that feels more challenging to open your heart?"

Audri stops to think for a moment, searching for the most difficult times to expand her heart opening.

"Well, when Dad walks out on Mom, or when I hear he may be having an affair."

"Yes, that would be a very difficult time, a real challenge for anyone. Opening your heart isn't an easy task, especially in times of strong emotional situations. Such sadness and grief often takes us to a contractive place energetically. At such times, expansion of the heart becomes more challenging. So what might you do to expand your heart when the more automatic response is to contract?"

Again, Audri stops to think through what he just asked. She goes inside to look at how she might do that.

What do I do? Relax? Cry? Breathe!

"I guess I would take a few deep breaths before trying to shift my heart."

"Excellent, Audri! Yes, it's critical to get the body to relax from contractions before trying to move it into expansion. And that's one useful way to move towards relaxation. Stop and take a few deep breaths. Stop and breathe."

"But it often seems like a challenge to do that when I'm so caught up in details."

"Yes, that's true too. It isn't an easy shift, just like other big changes or improvements. It takes practice. Like learning something new in tennis. Heart expansion, allowing lies to dissipate, and making choices from your essence rather than the distortions we believe about ourselves. It takes work, dedication, commitment, and practice. But with that, we can transform how we see ourselves and the world around us. We can learn to pay attention to our energy, where most of us don't bother. We can let go of lies and learn to come from our inner strength, our own essence."

"You make it sound so easy. It doesn't feel that easy most of the time."

"The more we work at it, the easier it gets. Any fundamental change is a challenge in the beginning. But with time, we give ourselves more choices and options in what's available to us."

"Yeah, I get that. But when my folks fight or separate, it's harder to remember such ideas."

"What's your desire for your parent's relationship," asks Alberto to Audri's surprise.

"I want them to be happy together."

"What if their happiness comes from separation more than togetherness?"

Audri stops for a moment, leans to one side of the chair, considering a different possibility.

"I'd want them to be happy most of all. But I figure that comes from being together."

"And what if it doesn't come from being married?"

After considering his question, Audri leans forward again and responds.

"Then I would just want them to be happy. I guess I can adjust to them living apart. At least I wouldn't have to listen to 'em fight."

"You also might learn from such circumstances that marriage doesn't inherently include fighting, as certain families have come to believe. For some people, they're most at ease and peaceful being single."

"I get that in my head. But I worry about them, too. I want to fix their relationship."

"Like you want to fix what's wrong with you?"

Audri leans back in her chair and chuckles. "Yeah, like that."

"And what if there's nothing wrong with them, except they may have grown apart with little incentive to grow together. Maybe they prefer the direction in which they're moving? Maybe the ways in which they are changing are important to them, but it pushes their spouse away, like the response your friends had to you."

"Then I can let them go their ways and love them both separately, I guess. But like other new skills, it'll take some practice," says Audri with a scant smile.

"That's exactly what I mean about you accessing your inner strength. You get into your heart, your head gets clear, and you let all these parts of you collaborate as you provide responses to what the world brings you. There still are options in what you choose to do, where you want to go, and how you want to live in this world. But such choices are from the clarity of the mind, the relaxation and pure awareness of the body, and the wisdom of the heart. When they work together in that fashion, without distortions, you are living from an open heart. You are accessing your essence. You are sharing your clear insights and wisdom with others."

"For the first time since we met, I feel like that's a real possibility for me. And it feels difficult at times when I'm in doubt, chaos, or falling into the endless dark hole."

"Yes, they all still exist, just as their contrasts exist when you fall into the black hole. Increasingly, however, as you stay with the practice, you'll experience more availability of choice as to which side you want to reside, knowing you can go with either. That's the huge difference from where you started, simply sliding into the darkness without any other option."

"And having another option feels great. I even begin to feel that with my barfing. I feel like I can see and increasingly make another choice when the urge comes."

"That's awesome. And practicing the choice, choosing something different from the wisdom of the heart, will make another option stronger, even if you don't feel that way every time. It's like we test ourselves. How badly do we want it? Are we truly committed to an alternative outcome?"

"But... ah... but.... sometimes another choice can feel so unavailable."

"Very true, Audri. Just remember, that's more perception than reality, even when it feels like no other option exists. It can feel like the world is against you, like you have no choices. That's your perception in the moment. And the more contracted you get, the less likely you'll see another option. So expand. Relax, open your heart, and breathe. Keep breathing slowly and deeply, then reach into the wisdom of the heart."

"Yeah, keep practicing. I don't become a tennis pro overnight," smiles Audri.

"Exactly. You're developing some strong tools, and it's important to keep using them. If you don't play tennis or baseball consistently, your skills atrophy a bit. Then you need to practice more to get back your timing, sometimes even your form."

"I wish it were easier to make these skills a central part of my life like you seem to have done," responds Audri with a slight watering of the eyes.

Alberto leans forward, looks at her with that smile, that caress without touch, holding her while also seemingly present in himself.

"I've been working at these changes since I was your age, and I still don't feel like it's always automatic. And I'm an old man," he says as he laughs. His eyes twinkle again as his grin seems to light them from somewhere deep inside.

"You don't seem that old to me any more, though I did wonder if you were some kind of pervert when I saw you at that first baseball game!" chuckles Audri. "Why is this old man hanging out at a young boy's baseball game all by himself, I wondered? Pervert was the only thing that came to me. And now it is the furthest thing from my mind."

"Yes, perception and judgment are powerful parts of our lives, aren't they?" Alberto smiles.

For a moment, Audri just looks at this man who seems to have gotten younger and more normal as she has spent intense time with him. "Judgment does seem central to our lives."

"The saddest part is that judgment separates us from others, when what we're wanting is connection. We think we're using it to understand others when what we are doing is distancing ourselves from them, usually for a sense of safety or self-reassurance."

"Huh. I never thought about it that way. I'll need to explore that a bit more. Not sure I believe that one."

"I'm glad. Don't take my word for it. Check it out for yourself."

"Oh, I will," laughs Audri. "Maybe you've created a monster, a therapeutic Frankenstein!"

"Exactly as I intended," Alberto laughed. "Questioning from your essence is to examine what others say and do, not just accepting them or following rules and examples other people establish. There can be great wisdom or wonderful nonsense in what others say and do, and our task is to sort out which we think it is. Because sometimes our wisdom is seen by others as nonsense, too."

Audri peers at Alberto and laughs again.

"Oh thanks, Doc. Now you're really messing with my mind and my reality, aren't you!"

"I just don't want you to be too complacent with an answer, whether from me or others. It's important that you're taking different perspectives into consideration, then making the decision for yourself. The tricky part is to consider something from your expansive heart rather than primarily from your contractive fears. And only you know when that's happening fully. Only you can feel that place and experience inner peace when it happens from the heart. I can guess from your energy and how you feel. But you're the real authority and the one it impacts most, either by contraction or expansion. The greatest impact is on yourself."

"In other words, what I do impacts me the most."

"Yes, exactly. All we say and do can impact others, but we are the common thread and greatest cumulative impact."

"Wow, no pressure there, eh, Doc?" chuckles Audri again.

"Yeah, no pressure. But it's wonderful that through all this, you also can laugh a bit at yourself too, not taking yourself and all you do too seriously. We certainly want to consider how our words and actions impact others, especially wanting to minimize our hurting of others. And we can't take responsibility for all their previous hurts. Just the ones we may add to the pile."

Breathing seems easier as Audri feels the chair supporting her relaxing body.

"I feel nervous about continuing all this. Yet I feel some hope too," remarks Audri, taking another deep breath.

"You're doing great, Audri. Don't worry about all the details. You won't get everything right immediately. Just hang in there with it and keep practicing. It isn't any different than developing other skills and habits. You have a fabulous week, and we'll meet at the same time next week."

"OK, Doc. See you next week." Audri gets up from her chair and heads for the door. Then she turns and says, "And thanks!"

Chapter 21

Joy and Disappointment

The next morning, Audri arises earlier than usual and decides to meditate. She finds her old pillow to sit on against the wall and sets her alarm for 20 minutes. She practices letting thoughts pass through or releasing them when she realizes they have 'captured' her. She breathes, then thinks about the vigil. As she realizes her focus, she lets go of that thought. Later, she begins to worry about a possibly missed assignment. Again, she breathes the thought away.

As she sits with her breath, her heart slowly opens, finding more space in her chest, allowing her shoulders to relax and lower. She feels her butt and whole body relax. She sinks deeper into the pillow. After the alarm sounds, she gets up slowly.

She notices how spacious she feels and more in her heart. Audri likes this feeling and the expansive state of her being. She remembers her session with Alberto and believes, at least for the moment, that such a response can happen when she relaxes and allows it to occur.

Then she moves towards the shower before starting her day, hoping to carry this feeling forward with her.

She arrives at school a little early to see how Tanika's student council meeting went. They planned to meet at their lockers, but she doesn't see her dear friend anywhere.

"They're running late," said a voice behind her.

Audri turns around and immediately smiles as Santiago stands near. She hasn't talked with him in a while, and his attention on her stimulates her heart.

"There's some issue about an upcoming dance that apparently is creating a bit of drama in the group."

"Oh, OK, thanks. I was wondering. I hope they solve it. I love to dance."

"But that isn't why I'm here. Just throwing that in as a little extra.""Oh? So why are you here?” asks Audri as her heart skips another beat, hoping against hope that it's not bad news!

“I was wondering if you'd like to go out this weekend? It would be enjoyable to spend some time with you and maybe talk a bit. And I'd like to treat you for all your work with the vigil.”

Audri's heart pounds as she attempts to display calmness over her body. She doesn't want to appear too easy or overly excited by the possibility. “Yeah, I think I could work that out. When?”

“How about Friday? Would that work into your busy schedule?” asks Santiago with a smile.

“Let me check my schedule.” Audri glances at her phone, then returns her gaze immediately back towards Santiago's lovely smile. “Ah, yeah. I think I can work that into my busy schedule.”

“Great. Dinner and a movie? Pick you up at 6:00?”

“Yeah. See you then.”

“Perfect.”

Santiago turns and heads for his class. Audri tries not to look at him too long. She also feels resistance to turning away. While she had a couple of dates last year, the guys were not nearly as super cool as Santiago. Then she starts to worry that he knows about her seeing his grandfather.

Would that interfere with him possibly liking me? Is he feeling sorry for me, being crazy and all? What is this all about really?

Audri's heart switches from excitement to panic in a flash. Finally, she takes a breath and turns to her locker so people won't see her staring at him. Then she turns and spots Tanika coming towards her. She smiles at her friend, assuming Tanika saw the end of the discussion with Santiago.

“Sorry I'm late. Big drama this morning about the dance next month. Wasn't that Santiago just talking with you?” she asks with a smile from ear to ear. “You gotta tell me all about it at lunch time! But we'd better hurry now.”

Over the next two days, Audri finds it hard to do anything except wonder about Santiago's intention. Yet she keeps returning to her breath, trying to assure herself with whatever it's about. She feels the anxiety in her stomach and trust in her chest, as if the two emotions are vying for her attention. As she feels the anxiety, she keeps shifting her attention to some reassurance of her ability to handle whatever happens, even if her courage doesn't last long.

On Friday evening, exactly at 6:00 pm, the doorbell rings.

Audri hesitates for a moment, not wanting Santiago to know she's been standing behind the door for the last five minutes. Her hand finally twists the handle and pulls it open.

"Hi there. Right on time. Impressive!"

That seems like a plus for me.

"Yeah, my mom is kind of a punctuality tzar," says Santiago with a chuckle. "Ready to go?"

"Actually, my mom wants to say hello first. She's not seen you in a while."

"Oh yeah, sure."

At that moment, Bella walks into the foyer, holding out her right hand. "Nice to see you, Santiago. It's been a while. Great to see you again. So where are you two headed?"

"Well, I thought we'd get dinner in Coralville, then see a movie at the theater there. That OK with you, Audri?" he asks as he turns her direction.

"Oh, great. Excellent idea not to go to your dad's place tonight. We talked earlier. He isn't in a good mood," laughs Bella. "Well, have a great time. And Audri, be home by midnight. OK?"

"Yeah, sure Mom. See ya later."

Santiago smiles at Bella as he follows Audri out and closes the door behind him.

"What movie would you like to see," asks Santiago as they head for his car.

Audri notices his older green Honda that appears freshly washed.

Plus two for a cleaned car.

"How about <u>Hell and High Water</u> at the Coral Ridge. Maybe eat at the Mellow Mushroom near there?"

"Yeah, that sounds fabulous."

Santiago opens the door for her as she peers into the tan interior that seems clean and tidy.

Plus three for opening the door for me and plus four for the clean interior.

Santiago walks around, gets into the driver's side, and they drive down Clark Street.

"You hear from Alex much? Ya miss him?"

Minus one for asking about Alex first, but plus five for asking about me. Maybe he's just nervous. Plus six if he is nervous!

"Yeah, we talk at least once a week. I think he likes it out there in California. Not as humid. But he misses the family some too, especially me!" Audri says with a laugh.

Keep breathing Audri! Don't let him know you're so nervous! Hope he can't hear my heart!

"Yeah, I think I'd like it there too. We used to live in SoCal when I was a kid, and I miss the weather and ocean."

They turn down North Dubuque Street for the interstate, the easiest way to the mall, with Audri's heart thumping.

"So how did you get to Iowa City? They punish you or something?"

They both laugh a bit at that. But no self-respecting high school teen can show appreciation for his or her home town.

"My grandpa got a job here at the university, and my mom was missing my Gpa and Nana. So Dad applied for a teaching job at City High in order to live close to them. Mom was very glad to have spent time here when my nana died a few years ago. And my dad has liked this place. But recently he's missing the ocean."

"You have any brothers or sisters?"

"Yeah, an older brother who's going to school and playing baseball at UC Berkeley."

"He like it there?"

"Yeah, he loves it. It's his second year there, and I'd like to go there too. We're pretty close. And it would be awesome to play on the same team as him again."

"So why there?"

Audri begins to relax more as they get into a typical conversation. She asks questions to keep the focus on him, which helps. The car scent of oranges or tangerines, one of them, feels familiar and relaxes her further.

And plus six for him wearing slacks and a neat blue shirt that goes with his dark hair. MMMM.

"He wanted to go back to California. It's a great school with a solid program, and part of the Pac 12. The great thing for me is he tells his coaches about my strengths. I'm hoping to get a scholarship there, too, if I'm lucky. It's a great school and close to the ocean. We'll see how this season goes."

"That's cool. I'd kind of like to move to California myself. I'm going to visit Alex next spring and see a home game. Davis isn't Berkeley, but it's still a strong school."

Audri continues to relax with more casual conversation, and it's comforting to know more about his family, which turns out to be Doc's family too.

Small town!

"You look a little like your grandpa," says Audri without thinking about what she's saying. It's just a thought in her head that slips out before she can catch it.

"You know my grandpa?"

"Ah . . . yeah . . . Ah . . . didn't he come to your games sometimes . . . last year? At least it looked like your grandpa," Audri remarks, trying to cover her unintended comment.

"Yeah, but how did you know he's my grandpa?"

"I think I saw you talk with him one time, and I just assumed you were related, given your similarity in looks."

Audri hopes she can cover herself.

Quick covers will be important if I ever do become a detective.

"Huh, I don't remember that, but I might have. But yeah, he comes to watch my concentration and give me hints. It's been a big help, and he's an important part of my life. You have other family here too?"

Audri feels the tension building in her chest by not being more honest with Santiago about her own connection to Alberto. She wants him to like her, and she also wants to tell the truth.

Maybe this is too early to tell him? Maybe he'll think I'm crazy or something? But if I'm not honest with him now, how will that look later? Then I can't ever tell him. And how will I explain knowing so much about Doc if I'm not honest now? Shit, I hate this! It feels awful! And what if he knows already? Then he'll know I don't tell the truth.

"I'm sorry. What did you ask?"

"I just asked if you had other family in town too?" Luckily for Audri, they are pulling off I-80, and Santiago seems a bit distracted with traffic and turns. This gives her time for some inner debate.

"Oh no. I don't have any other family near here. Just my sister and parents."

Santiago pulls into the lot to begin searching for parking. "There's an open space, over by that blue BMW."

"Huh, you know your cars. I'm impressed."

"Yeah, Alex and I used to talk about our favorite models. So I learned to distinguish different makes. The expensive ones anyway. Not like him, of course. But pretty well."

"Yeah, I like Alex. It was fun to come over to your place once in a while. He's a great guy and a strong player. But, to be honest, later I was hoping to see you too."

Plus seven, eight, nine, and ten! A winner!

As they come to a stop, Audri unbuckles her seat belt and begins to open her door. Suddenly Santiago is there to pull the door open. She hadn't even noticed him jump out of the car. "Wow, a real gentleman!"

"Yeah, another thing my mom strongly encourages me to do," laughs Santiago.

"I think I like your mom already," responds Audri with a smile. "So, you came over to my place hoping to see me? Why didn't you ever tell me?"

"Ah, I think that's what I'm doing," smiles Santiago.

"Well, yeah, but I mean earlier."

"You were cute and all, but I didn't know you very well. As I see you now, you're different than I imagined then. You seem more genuine than other girls, and honest."

Fuck! What am I going to do now? How will he see me as honest if I don't tell him about seeing his grandfather in counseling???

As they approach the front door, Santiago steps ahead to open it for Audri, then moves past her to talk to the woman at the desk. "Two for dinner, please."

"Yes, come right this way," says the older woman in a dark brown suit with smiley eyes. She shows them their table and hands them menus after sitting. Then she says, "Christina will be your server tonight. She'll be right with you."

Audri glances at her menu, still debating whether to tell him about her own connection with his grandfather.

"So, what're you going to have this evening?"

"Good evening folks. My name is Christina, and I'll be your server this evening. Can I get you anything to drink to start off your meal? .... Ah, excuse me, but are you Santiago from City High?" asks Christina while staring at him.

Audri feels a knot form in her stomach, wondering if she's hitting on Santiago.

"Ah, yeah. Do I know you?"

"No, but my brother knows you. You guys clobbered our West High team in the regionals. I was there. After the game, he told me you were a big reason for the win. He respects your talent."

"Oh, well, thanks. What's his name? What position does he play?"

"It's Todd, and he played second base. Fortunately, he graduated last year and won't have to lose to you again," she said with a smile. "Anyway, sorry to interrupt your conversation."

"No problem, Christina. I remember Todd. He's a very solid player. Wish 'em luck for me, please. Audri, you want something besides water to drink?" Santiago asks as he turns toward her.

"No, water's fine. Thanks."

"And I'll have the same, with no ice, please."

"OK, coming right up."

With that, Christina turns and leaves the table.

"What would you like to eat this evening?" asks Santiago.

"I'd like the enlightened spinach salad with balsamic vinaigrette dressing. What do you want to eat, baseball star?" asks Audri with a half smile.

"Is that it? I think I'll get the Greek salad and the holy shiitake pie. Want to split the pie?"

"Yeah, I'll have a piece."

Christina returns with their water, takes their order, then leaves without any apparent flirting, at least that Audri notices.

Finally, Audri decides it must be now.

"Santiago, I want to tell you how I really know your grandpa. I've been seeing him for counseling at his office downtown. I didn't want to tell you, afraid you'd think I was crazy. But I also want to be honest with you. And I was afraid you already might know that I was seeing him."

"Seriously? No, I had no idea. He never talks about his clients. But lots of people get help from him, including me," says Santiago with a chuckle.

"You? What help do you need?"

Wow! What a relief. At least he didn't know and feel sorry for me being crazy!

"He's helped me a lot with my concentration, especially for baseball. But at other times too, like studying. He helped me learn how to meditate and focus my attention so I'm not so easily distracted. It's really helped my studying and my game."

"That's awesome. And Alex used to talk about how well you focused. It sure seems to help. But I worried you would see me as crazy if you knew I was seeing him."

"Hell no. If you're crazy for getting help, we're all crazy! He and I talk quite a bit, and he's helped my mom and dad too, in informal ways. He'd never see them professionally. Unethical, I guess. But, you know, we talk often. He can have some useful insights. And he's helped both my brother and me with focusing and keeping our heads in the game. He's a great guy. I love him."

"I get it. I like him, too. And I've only seen him for a few months. But he's been very helpful to me as well. And you don't think I'm crazy?"

"Audri, people aren't crazy to get some help. Crazy is not getting help if they need some. Doing the same behavior over and over, expecting the outcome to be different without changing anything. That's crazy. If there's something he can help you with, you're wise to see him. As I said, he's helped me a lot."

"What a relief! I was worried about your reaction or what you'd say."

"I actually admire you. You did a fabulous job with the vigil, and it was great for the city to come together, supporting Tanika and her brother. We shouldn't ignore such assaults."

Audri feels the tension begin to dissolve in her whole body as liquid approaches her eyes. She holds it back, not wanting to be overwhelming or seem like a sissy. This is her best interaction with this guy, and she wants to keep it that way..

"Thanks, Santiago. I appreciate it."

Audri takes a couple of deep breaths to get rid of her tears.

Keep breathing, Audri. Open your heart.

Christina returns with the salads while another server brings the pie. She places extra plates on the table in front of them. "Anything else I can get you two?"

"I'm good. How 'bout you, Audri?"

"Yeah, this looks great. Thanks."

"Well, have a wonderful dinner. You're a cute couple," she says, looking directly at Audri, then turns and leaves.

"There's something I want to talk with you about, too," says Santiago just before taking a bite of his salad. "I think you're sweet, and I'd like to become better friends."

He takes a bite and chews, then continues.

"But I don't see myself getting romantically involved right now. I'm pretty busy with school, grades, and baseball so I can have a strong senior year. I'll need it if I'm going to get a good scholarship. But I'd like to get together sometimes over the year, if you're up for that. I'd like to get to know you better and be friends."

Minus five, maybe 10!

"Yeah, sure. That would be great. It would be fun to spend time with you too and get to know you better. Besides, I've a lot going on with school too, and tennis. Not sure I'll get a scholarship. But I want to have a strong last two years here."

Did I just lie to him? Should I tell him about the disappointment? I want him to like me more than friends! But I guess that's better than nothing!

Then Audri remembers her session three days ago and takes a deep breath.

Here's a fuckin' great time to practice!

Then she takes two more slow, deep breaths.

"Oh, I'm glad. Some girls want more than that. They want romance. But I don't want to get into that right now. There'll be plenty of time for that after high school, I figure. But I'd enjoy hanging out and doing some things with you over the year."

The rest of the evening passes like Audri's in a fog. She can see everything happening close up, but one can't get much of a distant view. She hears him talking about other ideas, and she responds. But nothing seems clear. And there's little color to the activities. A dull, grayness hangs over the evening.

The show is enjoyable, but Audri isn't totally present. She feels the disappointment in her heart, yet there is some joy being with Santiago. She wants more and is happy with some connection. It all just seems confusing to Audri. Exciting and bad. Happy and sad. Disappointment and joy. Will she ever move beyond conflicting emotions? It sure doesn't feel that way in the moment. She finds it challenging to move from the disappointment to the joy, even though she can feel both. The disappointment just feels too strong. Maybe tomorrow. Or maybe next week.

After the movie, Audri and Santiago talk about what they liked and how much fun it was. Finally, she feels like the joy is expanding. She's happy to be with him, getting to know him, having him enjoy being with her.

Why isn't that enough? Over time, it may be.

And tonight, she has difficulty being in the moment. Tonight, her future feels like it is falling in on her, holding her down and tight.

As the Honda pulls up to her house, she turns toward Santiago.

"I had a delightful time. Thanks for the celebration and our time together. It was fun."

"So you're not disappointed that we won't be more than friends this year?"

"Oh, more honesty, eh? OK. Well, to tell you the truth, there is a little disappointment. And, at the same time, I want to be friends. I'll deal with any disappointment. That's my stuff. And it won't interfere with our friendship. Thanks for being upfront about it. Better to know now than later. And I do want the friendship. OK?"

"You bet! I appreciate your honesty, and taking on your disappointment."

"I guess your grandpa, or what do you call him?"

"I call him Gpa."

"I guess your Gpa has had some positive impact on me. And I'm grateful for it."

"And my hunch was right. You are more honest and authentic than anyone our age I've met. Thanks for being you!"

"Well, I better get in. Want to do something next week? Or is that too much too soon?"

"No, next weekend would be great. I have more time now than I will next spring. So let's see what we feel like doing, and we can make plans later. OK?"

"Yeah, that feels great."

Santiago opens his door and comes around to open the car door for Audri. "I'm a gentleman for friends too," he says with a chuckle.

"Thanks, friend," says Audri with a smile. "See ya in school."

"Yeah. And here's my number. Text me when you feel like it, and I will too, if that's OK with you."

"Oh yeah. Very OK."

With that, Audri goes into the house and heads upstairs. She still feels some disappointment, yet the joy is increasing as she likes her new connection with this super cool guy. Her first inclination is to go into the bathroom. Instead, she stops, takes three deep breaths, and turns towards her bedroom.

Chapter 22

Sun's Shadows

On Sunday, Audri again feels the slowness of the morning. She begins with another meditation, as she did yesterday. This morning it goes better, events and images riding the breath to that world beyond thought. With her school work completed, this can be a relaxing day.

After a 20 minute meditation, Audri goes downstairs to see if anyone is around for breakfast. The kitchen is absent of humans, yet smells linger from her mom's late night pizza party with 'the girls.' She makes some coffee and finds some granola to go with her low-fat yogurt. As she sits down to eat breakfast, Bella comes into the room in her robe and jammies.

"Morning Mom. How are ya?"

"I'm a little groggy at the moment. Any extra coffee?"

"Yeah, I made plenty. Is Sarah around? I've not seen her in days."

"No, I don't think so. I think she slept over at Marsha's place last night. They had a party near there and were going to walk home, just in case they drank too much to drive."

"Guess she's hot for her."

"Yeah, I think they have a sweet connection. Say, how was your date with Santiago? I haven't seen you since you went out."

"It was enjoyable. He's courteous and sweet. But he wants to be friends. That can be the kiss of death for any potential relationship."

"Still, you also can have an intimate emotional connection without being physical. Besides, there's plenty of time for relationships after high school."

"You two been talking?" chuckles Audri. "That's what he said, too."

"No, just great minds think alike," laughs Bella. Then, with a more serious look, she asks, "Are you disappointed with the way he wants to define it?"

"Yeah, in a way. I really like him. And I told him I was seeing his Gpa for counseling, which was fine with him. He didn't even think I was crazy. It was awesome.""Gpa? What's that?"

"That's what he calls his grandfather."

"Dr. Salvador is Santiago's grandfather?"

"Oh yeah. I didn't tell you? We ended up discovering it during an early session. And Santiago says his Gpa has been helpful to him and his family. He just sort of normalized this whole counseling thing. I guess that's what happens when your grandfather's a shrink," chuckles Audri.

"So will you two still see each other or do things together?"

"Yeah, that's our plan. We may get together again next weekend. He has more time now before baseball starts. And that part feels enjoyable."

"Yeah, solid friends are important. And you don't seem to have many male friends. This could be a good thing for you."

"I feel a bit bummed, though. And I just have to deal with my disappointment. That feels easier some days than others."

"Yes, disappointment is a challenging one, especially when we want a different outcome than someone else. So, how's your heart today?"

Audri felt successful from the earlier meditation. But as she turns inward, she feels the pain and sorrow once again. She hopes it'll yet go away.

Would Doc invite me to dig into the sorrow and pain, in addition to the joy?

Even her butt on the chair feels harder as the pain seems to settle in for the winter.

"Not so great, actually. It feels like another way of saying that I'm not good enough," says Audri with tears forming in her eyes. "I just want to feel loved and happy, then this happens." Tears begin washing her cheeks.

Bella reaches across the table, grabs Audri's hand and gives it a squeeze. "I love you, dear!"

"I know, Mom. I love you, too! It's just hard when I feel rejected by someone I like." Audri squeezes her mom's hand back.

"Of course it's hard, sweetheart. That's always a challenge. Welcome to the adult world of pain!" responds Bella with a tearful smile.

"Being an adult isn't all it's cracked up to be," says Audri with her own smile of tears.

"No, it isn't in many ways." Bella gives Audri's hands another squeeze. "And yet it's wonderful too, with many opportunities and a life with exciting possibilities. But you've got to look on the bright side, too. Don't forget to appreciate what you have. You don't want to become angry and bitter. I try to focus on gratitude for everything I enjoy and can do. I've some great friends, as do you, my dear. And Santiago may be another one who could be a positive part of your life."

"True. It's both sad and happy, and sometimes the sadness just feels overwhelming when you want something else."

"Yes, believe me. I get it," responds Bella.

They both have another sip of coffee. Audri needs a moment to decide how to approach the unspeakable topic. Finally, she simply blurts it out.

"Speaking of relationships, how are you and Dad?"

"Yeah, I've been wanting to find a time to talk with you and Sarah. But you're never home at the same time, it seems. So I'll do it individually. Audri, your dad and I are getting a divorce. I don't think there's any sugar coating this, and it shouldn't come as a big surprise. Still, when it happens, I know it can hurt."

"I'm sorry for us all, Mom, but especially you. I know you loved him. What're you going to do?"

"I'm going to keep working. You, Sarah, and I are going to stay in the house for the next couple of years, and we'll see how things are then. One of us may buy the other out, or we may eventually sell the home. But we won't change anything before you leave for college, I promise you."

"Well, I'm glad of that. But what happened, Mom? Why couldn't you two work it out? You've fought before. Why this time?"

"You're probably going to hear it anyway, and I doubt your dad's going to say anything to you. But he's having another affair, and I won't live with it any more. I would rather live by myself than keep worrying or suspecting something may be going on. In the end, we weren't close. So there's also a part of me that understands why he'd want an intimate connection with someone else. I just wish he'd asked for a divorce, then found someone else. But men, like your dad, who need to be in a relationship, seem to want that guarantee first, then cut the other cord after."

"That asshole," grumbles Audri.

"No, don't go there Audri. He is your dad. While we can divorce, you two don't. You'll need to figure out your own relationship with him now. But I don't want you bad mouthing him, especially to take care of me. In time, I'll be fine. There's lots of sadness right now, and there's grieving of the loss. But that's my stuff. You need to focus on you and how you'll maintain your own relationship with him. OK?"

Audri can see the tears around her mother's eyes, and she feels her hands trembling, maybe from the deep sadness in her own chest. But she doesn't feel like crying any more. Not now. She's too sad about Santiago, as well as her mom, and angry at her dad. And maybe even angry at herself for not trying harder to help them work out this relationship.

I should have done more. I should have paid more attention to their separation instead of being so focused on me. I'm so selfish! And so pissed at Dad! I hope he's as miserable in his new relationship as we are at his leaving!

Audri gets up and goes over to her mom, holding out her arms and inviting a hug. Bella stands, and the two wrap arms around each other, melting into a broken-hearted embrace.

Audri feels her mom's heart pounding and her body melt into Audri's relaxation. There is a feeling of sadness that permeates their lives, a deep shadow blocking out any sunshine.

As they separate, tearful eyes peer at each other.

"Anything I can do to help you?" Audri asks.

"No. thanks dear. I just need some time to settle into this new reality. I knew this was a good possibility but didn't want to face it. At the same time, there's some relief that the decision has been made. I'll need some time to adjust and find my grounding again. I've a lot going on with work, and that'll help. It was part of the problem before, and now it's a useful distraction. But I won't be so distracted that you'll start getting away with murder, young lady," Bella says with a half smile.

Audri knows her mom is serious about her last statement.

At this point, she has too many other worries in her life, solid grades, maintaining her tennis ranking, having some fun with her friends, and developing this new friendship with Santiago. Besides, she doesn't want to give her mom any more problems. She wants to be a support. She'll leave any trouble up to one of her siblings, if either reacts to this. She's tired of being the troubled, 'crazy' child.

Bella sits back down to finish her coffee. Audri grabs the pot to warm up both cups.

"Thanks dear. So I want to ask about something else, unless you have any questions about your dad and me?"

"No, I think I'm good for now. But I reserve the right to revisit the issue in the future," says Audri with a laugh.

If not a detective, maybe a lawyer. I'm even starting to sound like one! Watch out, Sarah!

Audri chuckles to herself as she considers yet another possible career.

"How are things with Dr. Salvador? I don't want to pry too much. But in general, is it going well? Are you getting something out of it? Is it helpful?"

"Yes, yes, and yes," replies Audri again with a laugh. "Any more questions?"

Audri wonders if her smiles are as big as Doc's these days, hoping she's approaching his at least.

"OK, I can see I need to ask my questions differently," says Bella. "Would you mind sharing a bit of how the sessions are going? I'd really like to get a sense of whether he's helping, and if so, how. We haven't talked since our discussion about near-death experiences, probably three months ago."

"It's not at all what I expected. But I find it helpful. He's helping me slow down and pay attention to what's going on inside. He's also challenging some of the negative views I have of myself. I still have them, but they don't feel as overwhelming. I can stop and breathe when I start to get upset, allowing me to see issues from a larger point of view."

"That's great to hear. Anything else?"

"Well, he's taught me how to meditate, which helps my mind relax. That's also helped with the slowing down. And probably most importantly, he's been teaching me how to open my heart more. That helps me see and experience a different point of view. In fact, I shocked the hell out of Cheryl when I had a pleasant conversation with her a while ago. And understanding from Doc how we may be more alike than different made it possible. That all feels good to me."

"Oh, Audri. I'm glad for all of that," says her mom as she places one hand on her heart. "Can I ask about your throwing up? Is that still happening?"

"It was for a while, and I certainly feel challenged at times. We didn't focus primarily on that. But some of the issues we've been discussing help me not feel so out of control. I have more of a choice. But there's still that urge when I get stressed."

"When was the last time you threw up?"

"It's been about three weeks now. I can't say it won't happen again, but I certainly don't feel as much compulsion to do so. I feel like I have more space sometimes to make a choice. And I actually like that."

"Audri, I'm so happy about that! Is there anything you don't like about seeing him?"

Audri takes a final gulp of her coffee. "Yeah, one thing," she says as she holds up her index finger with one hand and lowers her cup with the other.

"What's that, if you don't mind me asking."

"Having to leave sometimes at the end of an hour. I often want to talk with him longer."

"Wow, that seems like a big change."

"Yeah," laughs Audri. "It shocks me too, Mom. It's been a real change from the first couple of sessions. But I had no idea how much this would end up meaning to me. I'm glad I'll have more time with him. I have more questions and his support feels important. Will I be able to continue with you and Dad divorcing?"

"Of course, Audri. I wouldn't change that. I don't think your dad has any idea of how useful this has been for you so far. Well, why would he? I didn't even know until today. But that's something he and I can talk about. And even if he wouldn't help financially, I'd make sure it happens. You can count on that. And for that, I'm grateful to have a solid job and my own income."

"Thanks Mom. Appreciate your support."

"Of course, honey. I've been worried because I essentially forced you to see him. So it's a relief that you've found it helpful."

"Well, no need to worry about that now."

"I'm glad."

"Yeah, it's a relief for me too, Mom."

The two talk some more about school and Bella's work. Then Bella notices it's time to get ready for an open house. She stands, kissing Audri on the top of her head as Bella leaves for her bedroom.

Audri puts their cups away and goes upstairs to her sanctuary.

Her sadness has decreased, and she's feeling lighter. She walks over to her window. The sun is partly shining, but her focus is on the shadows.

I love the sunshine, but today feels more overcast than sunny.

She looks out for a bit, then goes over to her desk. Given her mood full of mixed feelings, she writes the following poem:

Shadows

I wake to morning due,
peering out windows,
soaring with birds,
dancing with leaves,
rolling with ocean waves,
pale colors surrounding all.
As sun warms earth,
shadows give life contrast.
In the garden
shadows provide shade;
In my consciousness
they hide my secrets.
On the beach
umbrellas protect me;
hiding my shame
darkened vision makes me look good.
Show me the light
I say to others,
and in that brilliance,
I can hide many things.
But in total authenticity
luminescence shines from inside out,
and in that reversal
there's nothing to hide.[1]

Hum, I guess some of this stuff Doc has been talking about is seeping in. And I like what's happening, even with the shit flying around me. What a contrast to six months ago!

---

1. Shadows was previously published in Torrid Literature Journal under Audri's pen name.

Chapter 23
Finding Strength

While Audri's in school Monday morning, she receives a phone call from Dr. Salvador's assistant. Because Audri's in class and can't take the call, his assistant, Catherine, leaves a message.

Apparently Dr. Salvador is ill and won't be able to meet with Audri the next day. That's disappointing for Audri, who wants to talk about the impending divorce. While she's glad to have spent time yesterday talking with her mom, she's interested in Doc's perspective, as he's frequently helpful. She'll have to be patient, not her strongest asset, and wait for their appointment the following week.

This gives Audri the week to adjust to her new classes, focus on homework, plan some ideas for hanging out with Santiago this weekend, and practice with her potential new doubles partner. Sophie is doing well after her ACL surgery. But it looks like at least nine months before full recovery.

That means I'll need to get to know my new partner well for this year's season. And our potential first place ranking is even more in jeopardy. This could be a long fall semester. Luckily, we're juniors, finally, next to the top rung of the ladder, with two years of students below us. Yes!

Being a junior gives her some additional confidence in school. But this also is a key year for college prep. And Santiago could get a letter soon if he is offered a scholarship somewhere.

No, not much pressure this year! Ha!

There might be a party this weekend to ring in the new school year, or she and her friends could do something else.

She grins and says hello to Santiago as they pass in the hall on her way to lunch. He responds similarly, which gives her a little excitement and reminds her of Doc's embracing smile. It always helps when he shares that fabulous smile with her. During lunch, she receives a text from him:

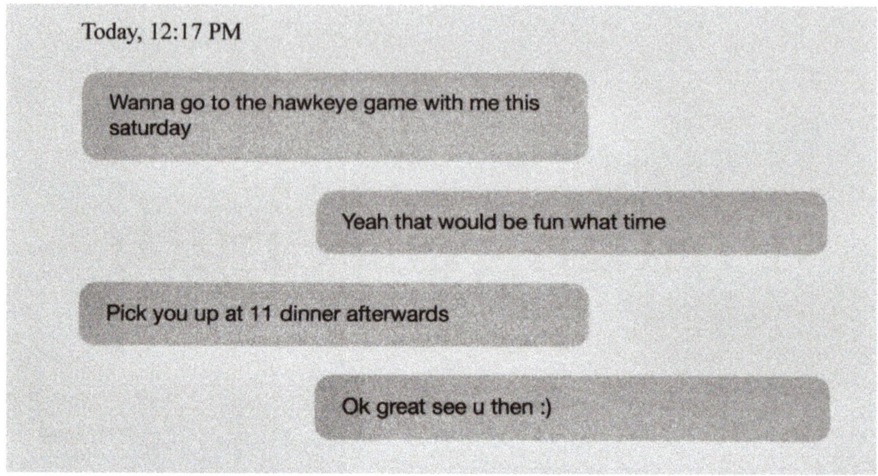

Yeah, that improves my week. Even if we aren't dating, it'll be enjoyable to hang out with him, see the big game against Iowa State, and maybe have some fun afterwards. Great to balance out some of the shit happening these days.

Now Audri can enjoy her salad a little more relaxed.

Tennis practice goes well during the week, and Tammy, her new partner, is a solid player. Still, she can't read her like she does Soph. But they may get it together before the season starts.

And homework is not overly difficult yet, so it doesn't overwhelm her. Mostly, Audri's now looking forward to Saturday and some time with Santiago.

The more recent *Trois de Mousquetaires* get together on Friday to eat dinner and watch a movie. While both are enjoyable, Audri's thoughts wander towards the following day's plans.

On Saturday, Audri gets dressed by 10:30, as she doesn't want to feel rushed. Both friends wished her a fabulous time the night before, and she's ready for that.

Santiago drives up just before 11:00 and is at the door right on time.

OK, great sign, thinks Audri.

She doesn't wait to open the door this time and heads out after locking it, as her mom is already at an appointment. Santiago again opens the car door for her, then gets in on his side as he drives off towards what will be crowded parking near Hawkeye stadium.

They find a spot relatively close given this late in the morning, with crowds of people already tail-gating. But they go straight for the stadium.

"You see many of the Hawks' games?" asks Santiago.

"No. I get to one or two a season. But with Alex gone and Sarah attending with friends in the student section, I probably will see even less over these two years. You?"

"No. Dad sometimes scores some seats, but he spends more time going to see the baseball team. And Mom likes to go to the women's basketball games, which are great. I sometimes go with her when Dad can't make it, especially with my brother gone."

They find their seats, which have a great view of the whole field, given how high they are. Still, it's fun just to be there.

They cheer loud and strong, but hardly come close to losing their voices, given that the Hawks trounce the Aggies.

But it's a tentative sign when Iowa beats their cross state rivals. If they win this in-state game, they sometimes have a mediocre remainder of the year. But this time, the team looks good, so the season may be a winning one.

After the game, as they head for the car, Santiago asks "Where'd you like to have dinner?"

"How about the Trumpet Blossom Cafe on Prentiss Street? I haven't eaten there in a while."

"Yeah, sounds great. They have some healthy options I enjoy."

He drives towards downtown slowly with all the traffic. They finally find a place nearby to park.

Dinner goes well, and Audri is enjoying her time with this new 'friend.' Yet, there's a tinge of disappointment in her heart about the friendship limit, especially when she so enjoys her time with him.

Still, some friendship time is much better than no time, that's for damn sure!

When they get back to Audri's place, she tries to focus on her gratitude for their time together rather than the part of her that feels disappointment. And she becomes aware of her pattern to turn enjoyable experiences into something negative or missing.

That's a familiar modification, for sure. Mom's right. Focus on the bright side.

By Tuesday, as Audri drives to her appointment, she feels like she has so much to talk about she isn't sure she'll be able to cover it all in an hour. Instead of the time being drawn out into a sense of eternity, it now seems too short for her. At this thought, she does some internal chuckling, with a slight laugh on her lips.

OK, now I'm beginning to feel like Mom, talking and laughing to myself out loud. Oh dear!

After entering Alberto's office, Audri flops into her regular chair. Alberto's face somehow seems older today. "Hey there, how are ya feeling this week?"

"Much better, thanks. I think I had the flu. But I'm feeling better these past few days." "Yeah? Did you have a fever and chills? That's what my sister had a couple of weeks ago." "I had some indigestion and the chills, but no fever. I also had no energy and some congestion. I wasn't able to breathe deeply. Just glad to be over it. And how have your last two weeks been?"

"Well, Doc . . . um, it looks like Mom and Dad . . . are going to get that divorce."

Audri's pauses as the words finish spilling from her mouth.

"Dad's moved out, and . . . and Mom's serious about it too."

Audri can feel her eyes water and her voice shake as she mentions the decision, even in a casual manner. She's surprised how suddenly and strongly the sadness resurfaces.

"I'm very sorry to hear that, Audri. It can be a tough time for everyone, especially the kids, who sometimes get overlooked when they act like they are doing so well. How are you really doing with your parent's decision?"

"I try to focus on the bright side, but there's a lot of sadness. Sometimes I laugh. Sometimes I cry. Sometimes it switches from one to another in a flash."

Audri's surprised at how emotional she feels. It creeps up on her at unexpected times.

"Yeah, it's typically a very emotional time for everyone. Can you allow yourself to feel both emotions fully? Or do you tend to shift or ignore one or the other?"

"It's mostly sadness these days, although I try to pull in the bright side, too. Worst of all, I feel alone. Mom and I had a great talk the other day. But I know she's more connected to Alex and Sarah's more connected to Dad. I just feel alone."

"And the black hole? Does it show up at times like these?"

"Oh yes. It comes back in force. I'm not feeling it strongly right now. But it's always near."

"And what do you do these days when it seeps in?""Cry, feel the pain, the aloneness."

Audri can feel the water intensely gathering around her eyes, then starts to seep out and down her cheeks. She grabs a tissue and wipes it away.

"Do you try to meditate and open your heart?"

"I haven't the past few days. Just feeling overwhelmed, I guess."

"Yeah, a very challenging time. And it's a period when a consistent practice becomes even more important. These are the circumstances where meditation can play a critical role in your life, especially the heart opening exercise. For, as we've discussed, we tend to close our hearts around such pain, and it can create a contractive energetic field with our whole body. The meditation will help you keep your heart open when your tendency and pattern, like most of us, is to close it under the circumstances."

"I guess that makes sense. But it's difficult to be motivated at times like these, especially when I feel so disconnected from everyone, even Tanika. I keep thinking that if I don't talk about it with anyone, it won't hurt so much."

"Yes, burying it is a common approach. But in the long run, that doesn't help. It just postpones dealing with it. Having a consistent practice can help with that tendency to close the heart. For right now, I suggest you just keep practicing, even if it doesn't feel successful. One never knows what can happen during such times of struggle."

"What do you mean, Doc? What can happen?"

"Audri, I want to share one of the core teachings that my Shaman taught me. I think you're ready for it now, and it might be timely under the circumstances."

"What teaching? I thought you had given me all the important stuff."

"I've given you most. But this one's more challenging for people to understand. At the same time, it can be one of the most essential, especially during times when people feel alone, isolated, or unsure of themselves."

"OK, Doc. Don't keep me in suspense. What is it?"

"The concept is what my Shaman called the 'first disconnect' in this earthly experience. Do you remember when we talked about different densities of energy?"

"Yeah, kind of. But I don't remember it all that well."

"That's alright. It's new to most people. Let me review them again briefly. And ask any questions if something doesn't make sense.

"The densest energies are the physical ones, like our bodies, physical pain, physical objects, objects in their physical form. The second layer is more subtle energetics like emotions, which are less dense, and where it can take a little work to get in touch with them. When they grow strong, they get amplified and easier to get our attention, like physical pain brings your attention to your body. But they still are less dense than feeling our face or a chair we're sitting in."

"Yeah, that makes sense so far."

"Well, the next or third level of subtle energetics are our thoughts and mental ideas. That's the world of making plans, creative designs, mental responses, and problem solving. And these are more subtle than both the physical and emotional levels. This still making sense?"

"Yeah, I get it. I'm pretty sure."

"Then we have the next or fourth layer, which some call more spiritual energetics and less noticeable for most people beyond infancy. They are the energetics of intuition and the heart meditation, energies that are quite subtle to notice and ignored by most people. Because they are so subtle, it is important to quiet our physical body, emotions, and mental thoughts in order to access them in their purest form. This is also the level of connection with our core or essence, as well as our connection to the divine. Still with me? Making sense to you?"

"It's newer, but I think I'm getting it."

"The first disconnection we experience as babies is from our higher source. Because the energetics are so subtle and people usually don't pay a lot of attention to this level, it's more challenging to reconnect. It's not because the source has gone away. But rather that we have lost our sense of connection to a greater source. This is where meditation and some type of altered state can be a useful place to rediscover it. It helps to get our thoughts and denser energetics out of our way.

And it's closer to the dreamlike state than the typical awake state."

"Ah, wow, this feels a bit confusing and overwhelming."

"Understandable. This is not something people talk about or focus their attention on much. What we usually focus on is the feeling of disconnect that babies feel from parents as they grow older and their mental capacity increases to realize they are separate human beings. But I believe that actually is the second disconnect. This separation gets amplified by the lack of a bond at our core, a relationship we feel with our own source. The second disconnect occurs at the emotional level, a denser level of energetics, more easily noticed. When we have lost that initial cosmic connection at our essence level, the sense of being all alone at the emotional level is amplified. Then these separation feelings rise up again at different times later in life, like what you experience with your parent's impending divorce. And from that double disconnect, lots of other fears get generated."

"OK, kind of interesting, but it's still hard to get my head around completely."

"Yeah, most people aren't aware of such an issue. But I think it's a critical piece to healing and healthy living. It's essential because we can repair and reconnect to that basic bond, whether or not we feel an emotional disconnect with parents. You're lucky that you have at least one parent who wants to be close, even if you feel like she cares more for your brother. That isn't always true. But as kids we certainly can perceive it that way."

"Yeah, perception, truth. They feel equivalent right now."

"I get it. They often do, at least until we check out perspectives honestly with a parent. But that's a later discussion. What I want to talk about with you right now is healing the first connection. I know it's a challenging idea. But I think it will make more sense from your experience than from a conceptual explanation."

"Yeah, maybe. I mean I kind of get it, but not really sure."

"That's where I think your exploration with it will make a big difference. I don't have a large number of cases to support this result. But what I do have is very consistent. Whenever someone has tried to heal this sense of disconnect, it's happened 100% of the time. So while it's a small number of cases, I strongly suggest you explore this and see if it works for you. This reconnection occurs frequently through the heart opening meditation, which is why I think that is such a core piece of an ongoing practice for you.""OK, you have my attention. What do I do?"

"The awareness and healing occurs typically when you're in a meditative or some kind of altered state, like when you first wake up in the morning and aren't quite fully awake. Do you ever spend time just as you wake up thinking about things in a different way?"

"Yeah, it's a good time to see things in a creative light. It's like thoughts and ideas are more airy or something."

"Yes, exactly. It's like you're in a half dreamy state. That's a great time to see things from a more expansive place, especially at a more subtle level. And in that place, as you're feeling the pain of being all alone, ask yourself the question: Is there a higher or divine connection that I might experience? Just sit with the question in that airy, rather dreamy space or during the heart opening meditation, where you allow your heart energy to expand, even to your core. That's another place to ask such a question."

"Is that the only way to ask that question?"

"No. You also could expand the loving heart energy to your abdomen area and ask it to heal your relationship to divine love and the cosmos. The feeling of love there and throughout your body or even beyond is what's important. Such love exists at that same subtle level."

"And do I get an answer to this question? What would an answer feel like?"

"I can't guarantee an insight or response. But don't expect the answer you typically would experience. It's more of a feeling than a hearing. I can tell you that I received one and everyone I know who has stayed with the practice has received an awareness of something greater than themselves, some link to a more expansive or divine love. And it feels like a relationship people have known before and forgotten. Their reports often are something like, oh yes, I remember this connection. This feels familiar. I know this love. Maybe it's not divine outside of ourselves, but at least it is a feeling of being more whole, something beyond our physical being. And the sadness and sense of being alone mostly or completely dissipates, at least while you are in touch with such a connection."

"When is this most likely to happen? Will I get a response soon?"

"Sorry, but I don't know enough about this reconnection process yet to understand any consistent timing. There seems to be no telling exactly how long it takes to experience an answer. My sense is that you will experience it sooner when you stay with the practice and question consistently. But even that I don't know for sure. This reattachment just seems to happen if you commit to the process. Given the speed of your changes, I can't imagine the process will take a long time. But I can't promise that."

"The way I feel right now, it would be worth the wait, no matter how long it takes. I just know I want to feel this bond. I'm sure willing to explore the possibility."

"I thought you might, which is why I bring it up. And I know from my own explorations and what I have seen in others that it's one of the greatest gifts I've experienced in this life. The biggest challenge is that such a connection is more subtle than most energies we experience, which means we need to pay close attention at that level."

"OK. I think I understand why we don't notice a response as easily. And I get why it would take some practice to get there. As people continue the process, does the connection get stronger?"

"Yes, certainly in my experience and from what others report too, the relationship gets stronger. Actually, the divine love is always present. It is our ability to become aware of it that changes. The reconnection is on our part, our awareness and experience of it. That's also why it's important to not just notice the feeling once, but to keep reconnecting. When we feel that black hole or the disconnect, this practice helps us access the reattachment when we need it most. It's important to be familiar with the subtle level and the cosmic link, so you know how to feel into the bond during more challenging times."

"OK, I'll do it. I really want to feel more connection. Especially when I begin to fall into the black hole."

"I love your audacity, Audri. I had a sense of that from our first couple of sessions."

"Ah, is that a compliment? I thought that meant kind of rude or disrespectful. Is that how you see me?"

"Audacity also means a willingness to take risks, be bold with something. There's always a part of you that seems to have the courage to stand up for something you believe in or try something new, even if it isn't the easiest thing to hear or for you to do. Such responses can often feel disrespectful to someone who may hold an opposing opinion or point of view. But more than that, you're willing to be bold in taking a chance with something very different that feels useful. That isn't the easiest thing for many people, and you seem to have a wisdom of when it's helpful for you and when it's not. Such wisdom is a key in distinguishing between risks that are simply rude and risks that are unknown in terms of outcome but feel right to you. Risks that help you heal and grow. That's how I see you."

"Seriously? Just because I am willing to try this connection thing?" "It isn't just this reconnection experience. Your strength, vulnerability, and openness to this whole process we've been exploring demonstrates your boldness. You don't just say you're interested. You work at it, giving yourself more choice in your life."

"And this reconnection will help me?" "I'm sure it will. And accessing the bond as you begin to fall into the black hole or feel it coming on will be the easiest time to have a choice, to choose connection over disconnection. Once you are deep into the black hole, it's more difficult to make a shift. And the practice will help you make that reconnection when you need it most."

"How often do I need to practice this so I can easily access it?"

"Daily is not too often. A heart opening meditation would be a great foundation for this practice and for your life. But I'd suggest that until you feel such a relationship, you practice every day if you can. The closer to that goal you can be, the faster a clear link should come to you. It would be a fabulous way to begin your day, if you can meditate or contemplate then. And don't get discouraged if it doesn't happen right away. Stay with it and trust the process."

"Will I recognize the link when it happens?"

"I'm sure you will. While the attachment is a subtle shift, it's also very noticeable once you become more familiar with the subtle energetics. The biggest challenge is to reacquaint yourself with this level of awareness and allow yourself to remain there for a while. It's having the courage to increase your vulnerability and allow yourself to remain at that level. You're already doing that with the heart meditation. That takes you to this level, and just paying attention there will help you be aware of these energetics. As you get more comfortable being in your heart, you'll gain ease in accessing more subtle information and bonds, like other skills we've discussed. With increasing experience, you'll be more familiar with this territory, allowing you to explore such questions and feel answers or changes when they occur. This link also will increase the inner strength you feel with your own essence. When you are aware at this level, it is easier to experience the love and wisdom you can access there."

"This idea sounds a little crazy, but no more than some of the other suggestions you've introduced to me." Again, Audri chuckles with her response. "And you haven't misled me yet. It feels like this exercise could be very valuable. Will it help shift the black hole and the lack of options I feel around that?"

"I think it will be an essential shift. Do you remember when we did the heart opening meditation here in the office after the interaction with Cheryl?"

"Yes, I do."

"When you go into that space, do you remember how you felt about Cheryl then?"

"Humm. As I recall, I didn't care about what was going on with her when I felt deeply into my open heart."

"Yes. And I suspect you will have a similar experience with the black hole as you are in a state of grace with the reconnection at the core. It's as if you shift your relationship to sadness and pain when you are feeling into your core of love. It shifts your view of everything around you. I think that's why people's lives change so drastically with a near-death experience when they realize we are love at the core."

"Wow! Yes. I do want this. I want that kind of connection in my life."

"And I hope with all my heart that you're successful and that it has a positive impact on your life. It certainly has had a strong effect on mine, especially when challenging times come along. And, as you're experiencing with your parent's divorce, challenging situations do come into our lives, often when we want them or expect them the least."

"Oh, thanks for your sunny outlook, Doc," says Audri with a hint of a smile on her face.

"Not fair to mislead you, my dear. I know it's not appealing news. But I'm just verbalizing what you already are experiencing. I also want you to know that I'll be here as much as I can for you as you go through this transition. And while it seems dark, there also can be gifts along the way. So don't forget to stay aware of those as you go through the impact of other people's decisions."

"Yeah, I see some gifts already. I'm glad not to worry about fights when I'm at home or arguing at the dinner table. And I think I'll get more one-on-one time with Mom, which would be wonderful. I'm just not sure how much I'll see Dad, especially if he is in a new relationship."

"Oh? He's involved with someone else, too?"

"Apparently. That's what Mom said, and Alex seemed to know it already. And he isn't even in town!"

"Yeah, and in that way, this is a small town too. It's not easy to hide secrets here."

"No, it's not. Luckily, I don't see her, unless I go to Dad's restaurant. So I probably won't go for a while!"

Audri and Alberto talk more about the divorce, decisions that seem to be happening, and how she is doing with it all. Yet Audri feels a curiosity and desire to explore this "reconnection" thing, and in some ways she feels finished with the session and ready to leave. She becomes aware that a part of her already is out the door, wanting to get home to her sanctuary where she can begin this new exploration.

As Audri is thinking about such things, Alberto changes the subject. "Well, OK, it feels like we may be about finished for today. Is that right, Audri? Or is there something else you want to talk about before ending the session?"

Audri again chuckles to herself that Alberto seems to track her so well. "Yeah, I think I'm finished. I want to go home and try this process you suggested."

"I can't think of a better reason to finish our session today. See you next Tuesday then? And you can report on your experience."

"Sounds great, Doc. Thanks for this!"

With that, Audri is up, walks over to give him a hug as he stands, then heads to the door.

She pulls the car keys out of her pocket as she approaches her car. On her way, trees seem greener than usual, like right after a strong rain. The yellow flowers appear brighter than she remembers upon her arrival, and people walking down the street seem somehow happier.

Is it them? Is it me? Is it Doc's influence on me? I don't know. But I like it!

She opens the door, gets in, and moves in the direction of home, enjoying the scenery along the way. Again, there is a hopeful feeling and gratitude for Alberto's suggestions. And she loves being able to drive herself to these appointments now.

Chapter 24

The Shock

Over the next four mornings, Audri is consistent with her heart meditation practice. She gets up earlier so she can spend at least 20 minutes sitting in contemplation. She also meditates a similar amount of time Tuesday and Thursday evenings before going to bed. She's feeling more comfortable with the exploration, and her ability to let go of thoughts is improving. Yet she doesn't sense an answer to her question regarding a possible link to divine love.

This morning, with no pressure to go anywhere early on a Saturday, she lies on her bed after her meditation, wondering about the question and when an answer might come. While it's challenging once again to have patience, she's also clear she wants to continue exploring this process. And she'd rather have it take time than to quit without a sense of reconnection.

She breathes deeply several times, hoping the increased oxygen with each inhale will provide some patience along with a relaxing feeling. While the slower breath and increase in oxygen help her to relax, it is the heart opening in addition to her relaxation that seems to enhance her patience.

As she lies on her bed paying attention to her slower heart rate and heart opening, her phone rings. Her body responds with excitement as she sees that Santiago's calling.

"Hey there. How ya doing this morning?"

"Hey, Audri. Hope I'm not calling too early, but I couldn't wait any longer. Gpa had a heart attack, and he's in the University Hospital."

"What? When?"

"He went in late last night. I haven't been there to see him yet. But I'm going over at 11:00 so Mom can take a break for lunch. Gpa also told Mom he wants to see you today. Want to go over to the hospital with me?"

Audri's chest feels frozen and stumbles trying to find words to say. Her breath suddenly is shallow and her brain feels scrambled, maybe from the speeding heart rate. Finally, she finds a few words to express.

"Ah . . . yes, yes . . . please. I can't believe . . what you're telling me. Yes. What happened? Is he alright? What time will you be here?"

"I'll fill you in when I get there. I have a couple of things to do before coming over. I'll swing by about 10:45, OK?"

"Yeah, great."

"Good. See you then."

Her phone goes silent, and Audri's still having a hard time finding thoughts with all the fuzziness in her head. She sits down on her bed to relax a minute and slow her breathing. A few more deep breaths allow her to begin to process what she needs to do to be ready.

She gets up, goes in to shower, then puts on a little makeup. After all, she's seeing Santiago too.

She finds some casual clothes that are comfortable as well as cute, puts them on, then tops it off with her favorite purple jacket. Her mind is getting organized, yet her breathing, she notices, is still shallow. She stands still to take three more deep breaths, then wonders what else she should do.

I can't believe Doc asked to see me! I wonder if I should take him something. Is there something that would cheer him up or be comforting? Would he want flowers? I don't know what to do.

At this point, Audri glances around her room, thinks for a minute, then goes over to her desk. She picks up her rose quartz shaped heart that she bought a couple of years ago at a street fair. She slips it into her jacket pocket along with some money.

I love this piece. And I think it might mean a lot to leave it with Doc, at least for now.

Audri goes downstairs and smells the coffee. She pours a cup, then gets some granola and skim milk so she isn't hungry at the hospital. She sits at the kitchen table, thinking about all the time she's spent with this old man over the past few months.

How could an old man have such an impact on me in this short time? He'll probably be just fine. But it scares me. He can't abandon me now!

As she finishes breakfast, a knock at the door brings her back to the moment. She takes a last sip of coffee, then puts her dishes in the sink. She walks to the front door and opens it. Once again, Santiago is standing in front of her.

"You ready?"

"Yeah, let's go."

With Santiago picking her up to go to the hospital, Audri becomes more aware of the potential tragedy facing them. Still, he opens her car door, even now when they're in a hurry. He then slips into the driver's side, and they hustle towards the hospital.

"So tell me what happened? When did he have the attack? Is he OK?" asks Audri as soon as Santiago climbs into his seat.

"It happened late last night. Gpa called Mom, who called 9-1-1. Then she rushed over to his place to meet the ambulance. Luckily, we live close."

"Yeah, that is lucky. Was he still having an attack?"

"Apparently, he was still pretty miserable. The medics arrived right after Mom. They identified the attack and rushed him to the hospital. Mom and Dad both went over for a while last night, and Mom stayed there. They didn't know much at the time, but now it looks like he'll need surgery for at least one blockage."

"Oh no! Really?"

"They seem to think he's in good health, although there is always a chance he may not survive. But he'll have a much better chance of living longer with surgery than without. So they're going to try, I guess. Don't know much more than that."

Audri sits still, trying to take it all in. It was just four days ago she was having a normal conversation with no indication of any problems other than Doc's bout with the flu. It's still hard for her to take it in and has trouble believing this is happening now.

A hospital tragedy faces her while driving with this dope of a guy. She takes a deep breath, then notices the rubbing of her thumb and forefinger again. Today, her habit seems to generate greater anxiety.

"I guess what he thought was the flu were symptoms of heart trouble. But no one realized it at the time."

"Yeah, we talked about the symptoms on Tuesday. But I don't know much about heart problems, either."

They sit in silence as they pass over the river and hurry towards the west side of campus.

"Do the Hawks have a home game today?" asks Audri.

She knows traffic is much worse around the hospital during game days, given its proximity to the football stadium.

"No, they're playing at Rutgers this week. So I think we'll easily find parking."

Santiago pulls into the Ramp 4 lot and finds an empty stall. Then they get out, Audri not waiting for him to open her door. They both are too focused on the potential tragedy.

They rush towards Colloton Pavilion and up the elevator to the ICU information desk for the room number. Then, as 'family,' they head to Alberto's room.

The old man smiles as Santiago and Audri enter. Santiago's mother turns to say hello and give her son an extended hug. Audri walks over when Alberto holds out his hand. She grabs it, and they give each other a squeeze. After letting go of his mom, Santiago walks around to the other side of the bed and gives his grandfather a hug.

"How ya feeling, Gpa?" asks Santiago.

"I'm doing well, right now. I guess the doctors want to operate first thing in the morning."

"Do they know how bad it is, what they're going to have to do?" inquires Santiago.

"It looks like I need a double valve replacement. Could be worse, I guess."

"It could be better too," replies Gabriela, Santiago's mom. "I've been trying to get you to eat better. But I also know it's been hard since Mom died."

Alberto responds with one of those loving smiles that Audri knows so well. But it also surprises her that he shares them with someone else, even if she is his daughter.

"Yeah, I've been a bit lazy since my fabulous chef retired."

Audri notices some wetness in Alberto's eyes. She never thought about him as a husband. She's still dealing with the fact that he has a daughter and grandson in his presence. She's used to having him to herself.

"Yeah, understandable. Speaking of cooking, I'm going to let these two young people visit with you while I go get some lunch. I'll see you in a little while."

Gabriela walks over to his bed, leans in for a hug, and kisses her father on the cheek. Then she leaves.

"So how are you two doing?" asks Alberto with a curious smile on his face and the penetrating look in his dark eyes.

His hair is messed up a bit, and Audri notices more bald on the top than she's been aware of in the past.

Never saw him from this angle, thinks Audri.

She's also able to read him better, which warms her heart. She's paid close attention over the past few months, as his reactions have been essential.

"We're spending some good time together and having fun," responds Santiago.

"Yeah, it's been enjoyable," adds Audri.

"Any big plans for this weekend?" asks Alberto

"No, not yet. But who knows. There's still time," says Santiago, making Audri's heart skip a beat.

"Well, no need to hang out here all weekend. You kids should have some fun."

"Yeah, maybe we will. But everyone's concerned about you. There're lots more weekends for all of us, including you, Doc," chimes in Audri.

Alberto chuckles and squeezes both their hands again.

"Yes, that's true. But I hate to see you waste one, too."

Then he turns to Santiago.

"Would you mind letting Audri and I talk for a few minutes alone? There are a few things I'd like to share with her in private, if you don't mind."

"Not at all, Gpa. I know you wanted to talk with her. Think I'll go get a drink with Mom."

"Thanks. We can talk after."

Santiago leans down and gives his grandfather a hug, then he also leaves the room.

"Why don't you come around and sit in this chair? It'll be more comfortable."

Audri walks to the other side of the bed and sits in the tan padded hospital chair that appears more inviting than it feels. But she also likes sensing something solid under her while they talk, as her legs suddenly don't feel as strong.

Audri pulls the quartz heart out of her pocket and holds it out towards Alberto.

"I wanted to leave this with you to help with your recovery. It'll also remind you of how much people care about you and your big heart."

"That's beautiful, Audri. Would you put it on the table there so I can see it? I appreciate your thoughtfulness."

"I appreciate all you do for me, too. So what did you want to talk about?"

"I just wanted to share a few thoughts with you before surgery tomorrow. I know there's a solid chance that I'll pull through all this, but there also is a possibility that I won't."

"Oh Doc. Don't talk like that. You're going to be fine."

Alberto smiles one of those loving responses. He takes Audri's hand, then continues.

"Yes, quite likely. But it doesn't hurt to say what's in my heart. And I don't want it to go unsaid."

Audri feels her heart drop, her hands begin to perspire, and her throat get a bit dry.

"Doc, you have to be OK. I still have a lot I want to talk about with you."

"Yes, there's more we could do. And, at the same time, you have come a long way in a short time. And I want to make sure you recognize that. It may be challenging for you to put all of the changes you've made into perspective, as this is the first time you've gone through such a process. But that isn't true for me. I've seen others take this path. But no one has done it as consistently and wholeheartedly as you have. And I think it's important to step back and recognize that in yourself."

Tears now come to Audri's eyes as the possibility of losing Alberto feels more imminent.

"Thanks Doc. That means a lot coming from you."

She takes a deep breath in an attempt to again stop the crying.

"There're also a couple of skills I want to emphasize, making sure you continue them. The two most essential ones to practice are the open heart meditation and the reattachment question that we talked about last Tuesday and you've been working on recently. The meditation can be useful, but the reconnection request to a universal love takes your meditations to another level, in my opinion."

"Oh, I'll keep at it, I promise. They feel essential to me, too. And I think I get why they're important, even if the reconnection hasn't actually shown up yet. At least I haven't noticed it."

"It will, I'm sure. Along with that, be sure to pay attention and honor your intuition and the subtle sources of information that come to you, especially during meditations, early in the morning, and when your heart feels wide open. Such sources can be very useful, especially when combined with the wisdom of the heart. And you are doing so well at that. Be sure to keep it up."

Tears slide down Audri's cheeks, betraying her stoic attempt. She reaches over and grabs a tissue, grateful the box is handy.

"Of course, Doc. I will."

"One more thing. You're doing well at stepping back and observing yourself and others, paying attention to what's going on beyond or underneath the obvious. That's a rare and amazing gift. It will be helpful too, especially as you become more attuned to feeling or even seeing energy. It'll help you pay attention to information in the energy field, even before you see it. That field holds lots of information when we allow ourselves to access it. And it's a place where people aren't dishonest like we are with words or even their insights. For we typically don't pay attention to our own fields."

"Wow, I guess we've done more than I realized in just a few months. Doc, I very much appreciate all your help and the skills you've shared with me. You've been great!"

"Well, it wouldn't go anywhere if you weren't open and ready for it. I'm grateful you're so willing to explore what I've suggested and ideas I've tossed your way. You're quite an amazing young woman. And I've never had another person who has taken in so much in such a short amount of time. Thanks for being you."

"Well, I couldn't have done it without you!"

"Thanks. You're very sweet. But you've been doing the work. And your willingness to try what may seem like crazy ideas is critical."

Alberto looks deeply into Audri's eyes again as he smiles at her once more.

"One more thing I want to say. Know it or not, Audri, you are a 'Cib.' You remember what that is?""A crazy person?" Audri says with a chuckle. " No, I remember. It's like a warrior or something?"

"Yes, a person that stands her ground as well as accesses or pays attention to information that others don't notice. It's like a combination of warrior and shaman. And that's you. Pay attention to that inner strength that's developing, and it'll be a wise guide for you throughout your life. You're a Cib, whether you practice it or not. But the more you practice, the more you'll be able to help those around you find their own inner strength and wisdom." Alberto squeezes Audri's hand once again. "The best gift you can give to yourself and those around you will be that heart wisdom, reconnection, and finding their own inner, loving strength."

"And are there others, too, Doc? Other Cibs?" she asks.

"Oh yes. There are. But they, too, must find their inner strength. They, too, must live by their heart wisdom. Otherwise, it doesn't matter whether they are or not. The Cib only manifests when they do the hard work first."

Audri reaches over with her other hand to squeeze his with both of hers. Then she leans in and kisses his hand.

"I am so grateful for you, Doc. I really am!" Audri says, her voice choking up as the words exit her mouth.

"I know, Audri. I'm so happy we've been able to do this exploration over the past few months. And I hope there will be lots more time for additional discussions. But I also wanted to share these thoughts and make sure they don't go unsaid."

"Yeah, well, I'll see you next Tuesday. Or maybe the following Tuesday. I'll give your body a few days to recover. But then we have to get back to work!" says Audri with a big smile.

Alberto laughs out loud.

"OK, then. That's a deal. Oh, sorry, but one more thing. While you are learning that you are more than your body, it's still an important part of this earthly experience. So please, take good care of yours. And making yourself throw up when you're not sick is not a useful way to do that. There are plenty of ways we're hard on ourselves. Please continue to work on avoiding that one any time you can."

Audri looks deeply into Alberto's eyes, feeling the intense caring he's expressing through all this.

"Ya know, I'm still just starting this class. This isn't my final exam!" says Audri with another smile.

"Yeah, OK. I'll save the exam for a few more months. I guess I'm giving you the study guide to be ready for it," laughs Alberto.

At this point, Santiago and Gabriela step into the doorway. "It's sounding like you two are winding down. Do you need any more time?" asks Gabriela.

Alberto glances at Audri. "You good? You feel finished? I think I am.""Oh yeah. I don't need any more homework, and the study guide feels plenty long," responds Audri with another smile and pressing her hand against his.

She stands so a family member can have the chair and walks to the foot of the bed.

"Thanks for giving us the time," she says to Santiago and his mom. "It was great to have."

For the first time, Audri notices the picture of dolphins swimming in the ocean above Alberto's bed. Somehow the blue waves remind Audri of her father's eyes and triggers a little sadness in not seeing him much these days. His absence makes her connection to Doc even more important in this moment.

"You're very welcome. Glad you could come," responds Gabriela.

Audri notices her similar smile to Alberto and Santiago. But then again, they're all family.

Audri hangs out with the three of them while they talk about more ordinary stuff. Gabriela talks about the cafeteria food, which was better than she expected. Alberto asks Santiago about this week in school and whether he has received a letter about baseball scholarships. It's fun to eavesdrop on a family discussion, as she isn't familiar with this side of Doc's life.

The casual conversation also provides a great distraction from the tension of the impending surgery for all of them. After a while, Alberto asks to talk with Santiago alone.

Gabriela is going to run a couple of errands and agrees to drop Audri downtown. She and Tanika have plans to hang out this afternoon, and this feels like an appropriate time to leave.

After Gabriela gives her father a hug and kiss, Audri walks over and gives his hand a squeeze, thinking a hug may be too intimate in front of his family. But Alberto holds out his arms, and Audri gratefully leans over for a loving embrace.

"See you soon," says Audri as she stands back up.

Audri walks with Gabriela down the hallway towards the exit.

"Your father sure has been a help to me," says Audri as they get into the elevator.

"I'm glad to hear that. So nice to meet you. Dad mentioned a young woman that he's immensely enjoyed working with recently. But I had no idea who you were or that you were the one Santiago has talked about seeing, too. This is a small town in many ways, isn't it?" continues Gabriela with an Alberto chuckle.

"Yes, it is," says Audri with her own laugh.

They chat about the town and school as they walk towards her car.

They talk a bit more about life and the community, then drive in silence. Soon, they're downtown before Audri really notices.

Typically the silence would make Audri nervous. But she's been busy paying attention to Gabriela's energy, wanting to know more about her and what she's like.

Then Audri surprises herself, amazed that she's able to do what Alberto has been discussing with her for some time. She also feels pleased that her skills continue to expand as she pays attention to the subtle aspects, as Alberto suggested. While the skill may not be greatly honed, she knows she's getting the basics, anyway.

"Thanks for the ride. I appreciate it," says Audri as she climbs out of the car. "You're welcome, Audri. So nice to meet you."

"Great to meet you, too, Mrs. Garcia."

Audri finds Tanika soon after, and they walk over to the Heirloom Salad Company for lunch. She brings Tanika up to date about Alberto's attack, but doesn't share much detail regarding their private conversation. She's still processing that part of it and isn't ready to share it with anyone.

The two girls talk about school, friends, walk around the downtown area, then go back to Audri's place.

Audri's happy to be hanging out with Tanika as a distraction from the surgery. But all afternoon and evening, her thoughts drift back to the risky procedure. They watch a movie that night after Bella fixes a delicious salmon Caesar dinner. Then Tanika returns to her home.

Audri goes to bed early but has trouble going to sleep. She just wants to get the call from Santiago telling her everything went well with the surgery. He promised to call, and that'll be a relief when the good news finally comes.

After Audri wakes the next morning, she sits for another 20 minute meditation. As her heart opens, she tries sending loving and healing energy to Doc, who would be deep in surgery by now. She feels the energy, focuses on expanding her energy, and sits in this pleasant sensation the extends to much of her body.

The meditation feels moderately successful. Still, she wants to experience the reconnection that eludes her so far. With a touch of disappointment on her right side that exists without permeating her energy field, Audri puts on old clothes. Then she and her phone go down for breakfast, with thoughts floating Alberto's way.

Audri makes coffee and breakfast, then slowly eats and remains at the table. Finally, as her stomach feels full of knots, the phone rings, startling her. She can see it's from Santiago.

"How is he? Everything go well?" asks Audri, half holding her breath.

There was silence on the other end. Finally, Santiago speaks.

"No, ... No, Audri.... Gpa died this morning.... I'm sorry.... I know you liked him . . . very much, and he cared tremendously about you. I'm glad we had a chance to visit with him yesterday."

Audri hears Santiago's choked up voice transition to crying over the phone. This is the first time she's heard him cry, and she begins to sob too.

Audri notices all the energy plummet from her body and she sits. She doesn't know what to say. Finally, she responds.

"I'm sorry for your loss too, Santiago! ....Very sorry! ....For all of us!"

"Thanks Audri..... I'll talk with you more later. I'll let you know about the funeral…. But I'd better go now."

"OK. Thanks for letting me know."

Audri hangs up the phone and feels more alone than she did when her father left, for now both men seem to have disappeared from her life.

This is shit! Totally unfair! How could he just die? He was so full of life. And I should have talked with Santiago more. He must be feeling it worse. Fuck! Shit! I hate this!

As Audri is sitting with her heartache, Bella walks into the kitchen.

"Good morning, dear. How are you?" says Bella with a slow, sleepy voice, wearing her nightgown and robe.

"Not great, Mom. Dr. Salvador died this morning."

"Oh Audri, I'm so sorry! Did Santiago call you to let you know?""Yeah, just a few minutes ago."

Bella walks over, pulls Audri lovingly up by her arms, then draws her into a nurturing embrace. She holds her daughter there, knowing he was becoming an important support for her. She kisses her on the cheek and slowly releases her.

"How are you doing, my dear?"

"I hurt. …And this is shit. Sorry, but it is!"

"Yes it is! And I'm so sorry for your sessions to end this way. It seemed like he was really helpful to you. Anything I can do to support you right now?"

"No…. I don't know what anyway. But thanks for asking. And thanks for being here with me. I think I just want to sit with this for a while."

"OK. But if you think of anything, I'll be around, except for a showing at 1:00 pm today."

"Thanks Mom. Love you!"

"Love you too, my dear Audri."

Audri puts her dishes in the dishwasher. She goes over to her mom, who's sitting at the table, drinking her coffee. She gives her mom's shoulders a squeeze, then goes up to her room.

As she flops onto her bed, she feels into the words Alberto shared with her yesterday and the support he has given her.

This isn't how he'd want me to react, she realizes. *He would want me to pay attention to the hurt while also being grateful for the gifts we shared. He really trusted me, and now it's time to trust myself more, partly in his honor. I'll call Santiago back later. Right now, I just want to feel the deep grief for losing a dear friend and cherish all the gifts he shared with me!*

Though they did not know each other for a long period of time, some connections intensify with the intimacy and authenticity that happens when people open their hearts to each other and truly interact in a genuine manner.

Chapter 25

Missing and Remembering

Lying on her bed, Audri keeps reviewing the shocking news and how this man, whom she didn't even want to meet or spend more than a few minutes with months ago, has made a huge impact on her.

She contemplates what Alberto shared with her, information that feels like has shifted from ideas to wisdom. She thinks about what he said about judgments separating us further rather than bringing us closer together. In fact, her own judgments of him had done just that. And no matter what she said or did, it seems he accepted her while challenging some of her views and behaviors.

But he always felt supportive of her as a person. Now, rather than relief for the sessions being over, she's feeling deep sadness for losing an influential support in her life.

What will I do without him? Do I have the strength to continue down this road by myself?

As she feels into her grief, her phone rings.

"Hey, Tanika," says Audri.

"How did the surgery go," asks Tanika, knowing how worried Audri was yesterday.

Audri can't respond immediately. Finally, after another breath, she finds a few words.

"He died this morning."

"Oh my God! I can't believe it. I'm so sorry, for you and Santiago. What a shocker! You doing OK? Want me to come over? What can I do?"Audri pauses, considering what it is she wants.

Company? Be alone?

She isn't sure what she desires most. Then she gets clear.

"Yeah, it'd be great if you'd come over. I don't think I want to be alone this morning."

"I'll be there in 20. I ran this morning and stink. I have to shower first. You wouldn't want to smell my current scent when we hug."

After hanging up the phone, Audri considers calling Santiago back. Then she thinks better of it. He'll be focused on his family, and she doesn't want to interrupt that.

She's just feeling the loss and not sure how to fill herself up or create a distraction.

Then, as she feels deeper into the situation, she pulls out her pillow and sits it on the floor for a heart opening meditation. She sets her alarm for 15 minutes, as it will take Tanika at least that long to get here.

She closes her eyes and begins taking some deep breaths, feeling into her connection with Alberto. A peaceful feeling comes over her body. Alberto didn't work with her to create distractions. He didn't spend the last few months on this earth so she could avoid her feelings. And at some level, she feels like he's at peace. She remembers their discussion of near-death experiences, with people going through it reporting that at their core, they are love.

Can I feel such love now? Can I find such a feeling? Is there something more than my mind and this body? Will you somehow still help me, Alberto?

Suddenly, Audri begins to feel an immense love fill her core that slowly extends outward. As she explores this sensation, she begins to detect a connection to something greater than her own being, greater than any sadness, any disconnect that she's been experiencing. Here, in this ordinary bedroom, her sanctuary, a place of anger, distress, laughter, distraction, work, and sadness, Audri also feels a wholeness like never before. It's a sense of cosmic love without it being focused on anyone.

This change in sensation happens so suddenly, she begins to question her experience.

What's happening? Is this real? Am I finally feeling what Doc talked about with me?

As she moves into mental examination, the connection begins to fade. She goes back to her breath, letting thoughts and questions float away.

Taking two more deep breaths, the connection increases again.

Yes, it's back, and stronger.

Her legs feel relaxed, her eyes remain closed, her shoulders lower to a more comfortable position, and her heart expands. Here it is. In the midst of all this turmoil, with her brain somewhat scrambled, her heart opens to an experience she wants and thought might not happen for a long time.

Beyond the immense sadness, here is an amazing love, a feeling that Audri experiences as overwhelming, like nothing she has encountered before. Here is a loss and a gift in the same moment. Yet she can feel them both, some sadness in her gut, the connection to love in the center of her chest. Here they are, both happening simultaneously.

And as Alberto suggested, it comes at a completely unexpected time. If she couldn't have a physical connection with him, at least she can feel the connection to herself and beyond. And she just sits with it, paying attention to her breath and her bond with a core love, her loss and sadness dissipating, experiencing an overwhelming love through her entire being. Finally, Audri feels whole. And she sits. Just sits in the joy and gratitude of the greatest gift she remembers.

Thank you, Doc!

As her alarm sounds, Tanika opens her bedroom door. She kneels downs and wraps her strong arms around Audri's relaxed body.

"How you doin', girl? Your mom let me in." Tanika settles more comfortably on the floor with her back against the wall, her hands still holding one of Audri's.

Audri stares deeply into Tanika's eyes and begins to cry. "I'm feeling better. I just had an amazing experience that will be difficult to describe, and I don't want to try right now. Just know that there's both sadness and joy, and both are OK. For now."

And I'll never forget his smile and those eyes, looking deep inside of me!

"I'm so sorry. Losing him right now? That really sucks!"

Audri feels the loss reawakening again.

"It's ironic in some ways. I didn't think I would like this old man, who turned out to be an awesome support. And the gifts he gave me are amazing. I get that now. And in this moment, I'm filled with gratitude. I know the sadness and loss will return at the same time, for missing a dear man. It's wonderful and it's fucked too."

"I get the fucked part. I know you grew to like him. I'm just a little surprised that you can feel gratitude in this moment as well. I'd like to know more about the gifts he has shared with you, when you're up to talking about them."

Both girls shift their weight and turn towards each other, able to look face to face more easily.

"Yeah, I will later. Right now, I suddenly feel like crying," replies Audri with tears beginning to stream down her face, as the sadness comes back in force.

Tanika leans over again and takes her in her arms. She kisses her on the head and holds her tight.

"So... glad ... to have such a fabulous friend. You're ... dope to the max!" whispers Audri. "And ... I don't know what I'm going to do. Doc's perspective ... he's become very important in my life."

Tanika lets Audri go and straightens up, looking her in the eyes again

"Is there someone else who could support you, someone who's like Doc?"

"I ... I seriously doubt it. And I don't want to talk with anyone else. I want to talk with Doc. And he certainly didn't mention anyone yesterday when we talked about what we've been doing in counseling."

"You two talked about your counseling sessions yesterday?"

"Yeah.... He asked for me to come see him. So I went over with Santiago." "And what did you talk about?"

"He emphasized what he thinks are the important skills for me to focus on, to keep in mind." "It almost sounds like he had a premonition he might die."

"Yeah, it looks more like that now. Although we talked about seeing each other again."

"So what are you going to do?" "I don't know. I'm not sure I can remember and hold on to all the skills he's taught me. I just feel lots of doubt rising up with his loss."

Doc, what should I do? What can I do?

Tanika reaches out and takes Audri's hand.

"But did he think you could do it?"

"That's the way it seemed when we talked yesterday. That's what it felt like to me anyhow."

"So maybe he's right. Maybe he saw something you're not seeing."

"Yeah, maybe," Audri says with a tear and a pause. "But I don't feel very strong right now, ... not without him."

Tanika leans over to wipe a tear falling down Audri's cheek with her thumb, then sits up again.

"That isn't what I see, Audri. You've changed in the past few months. For you to stand and lead a verbal commitment in front of the vigil crowd, to make the shift with Cheryl, to let Angelina drift from our group without any hurt or anger, it's clear to me that you've changed. And maybe he saw what you're not seeing. Maybe he trusted what you've been doing more than you do. Because he knew how important these skills are and how hard you've been working. I don't know. It just seems like there's more to the shifts I've been seeing than you give yourself credit for."

Audri pauses for a moment, looking deeply into Tanika's eyes. "You really think so?"

"Yeah, I really do!" says Tanika, with a squeeze of Audri's hand.

"Then what would you suggest? I can't just keep going like nothing's happened, nothing's changed."

Tanika pauses, taking a breath, apparently to consider Audri's comment.

"No, but I suggest you keep going with what you've been doing. Maybe it would be useful to write all this down. Start writing about the skills he's taught you."

Audri lets go of Tanika's hand as both girls shift their backs to the wall again, allowing the solid sanctuary structure to support them both.

"Yeah, that might be helpful. It may assist me to remember it longer."

"Or better yet, teach them to Soph and me."

"What? I'm not ready to teach anything to anyone."

"Mom always says that one of the best ways to learn something is to teach it. I'd actually enjoy learning what you've been practicing, and I'll bet Soph would appreciate it too."

Audri shuts her eyes and takes a couple of deep breaths, wanting to allow Tanika's words to permeate her being. She checks in with her heart, which feels less open as the grief rises.

"But I don't know this stuff well enough. I can't teach it."

"Well, teach us what you can. Then maybe we could all explore it together. It doesn't have to be formal teaching. Just share his ideas, roughly in the order he shared them with you maybe. Then we could talk about them and see where it goes. Even if Soph isn't interested, I am for sure.

"Oh, I don't know. I don't think I can."

Instead of allowing Tanika's words and confidence to seep into her, Audri's doubts double down and spread like a virus to every part of her brain.

"Well, sharing them with us might help strengthen them in you, too. It could be a win-win for us all. And if you stumble a bit, who cares. It's not like we'll pass out some teaching evaluation at the end."

A big smile comes over Tanika's beautiful face and her eyes sparkle even more.

"You're a great friend. Love you."

"Love you too, Audri! And glad to have this friendship. I'm excited that you'll help us learn some of what you got from Doc," responds Tanika, wanting to convince her friend to make such a choice.

Audri pauses for a moment.

What do I do? Can I really teach this? Instead of confidence, I feel full of uncertainty. That's about all I could share right now.

"OK, let me think about it before we talk with Soph.""No! Don't just think about it. Start planning out how you want to present these ideas. You wouldn't keep such gifts from your best friends, would you?"

Again, a smile appears, that kind of smile that Audri never could refuse. Suddenly, it also looks a bit like Alberto's loving smile, which makes her feel like he's near. That comforts Audri in this moment, allowing some of the sadness and doubt to dissipate. That Alberto smile also feels like support for what Tanika's saying about sharing his ideas with her two best friends.

Well, maybe I can. Maybe Alberto's confidence will help me. He was fairly persuasive. Maybe if I keep practicing every day, I'll find a way to do this. Maybe I can call on that 'Cib' in me to make this happen. Maybe he was right. Maybe if I show up for myself and Tanika, just maybe I can do this. Oh Alberto! Please help me again now!

"OK. Let me start writing some of this down," responds Audri. "Then we can plan one day a week when we meet to talk about these ideas and practice the exercises he gave me. This will help me remember things he shared and maybe strengthen these remarkable skills.""Awesome! And with Soph's ACL surgery, what else has she got to do? How about Tuesdays?" suggests Tanika with another Alberto smile.

"Yeah, Tuesdays would be great," says Audri as she leans over to give Tanika a side hug. "You're always such a great support to me."

She lets her dear friend go, straightens up, then looks deeply into her eyes again. She knows her friend is being very serious.

"Yeah, I've got your back, your front, your side. I've got your whole self. It's a lot like you've got for me. Ever since fifth grade, when you slapped that kid for calling me a name."

"Yeah, ever since fifth grade, when you covered for me with the phone."

"OK, how about some coffee and chocolate? It's one of my favorite pairings! And I think we deserve such a breakfast today," suggests Tanika as she stands, then extends a helping hand to Audri, wanting to physically support her friend too.

"For breakfast?" asks Audri in shock, aware of her automatic body response to such an idea.

"Sure! Why not? It's been one hell of a weekend, and the combination seems perfect! Don't we deserve such a combination this morning?"

Audri contemplates the possibility for a moment, then responds.

"You mean like Audri pairs with Tanika?" Audri laughs at her own comment. "You're on. Mom just got some fresh beans, and she bought some new dark chocolate that you're going to love! I tasted it the other day. And I'm sure she won't mind us eating some. Maybe she'll even join us."

As Audri gets to her feet, she grabs the other *Mousquetaire*'s arm, and the two of them head for the coffee maker in the 'pairing' room, full of sadness for the loss of Alberto, deep gratitude for each other, and excited about the possibility of sharing gifts given by the old man.

End of Book One